EMMETT SWAN

Eden's Shadow

River
Path
Press

First published by River Path Press 2020

First edition

ISBN: 978-1-7336403-5-0

This book was professionally typeset on Reedsy.
Find out more at reedsy.com

Contents

Chapter 1

I awoke. Or rather, I emerged from my previous state. Heavy, thick, and dark. No dreaming. Only barely being.

I tried to open my eyes, but congealed sleep residue had sealed them shut. I picked at them until I could force them open, letting in a harsh wash of light. I cautiously squinted at my surroundings.

I seemed to be in a small log cabin. There was an unlit hearth on the far side of the room, and in the middle, a rough table made of split logs. The scent of stale wood smoke hung in the air. The floor was hard-packed dirt.

I was lying naked on a bed of sorts, but it was a crude thing. There was no mattress. Just a hard wooden plank packed with dried grass and covered with a piece of animal hide that stuck to my sweaty skin. Confused, I lay there and listened intently, but only heard the steady gurgling of flowing water from somewhere outside.

I had no idea where I was or why I was put here. I had no memory of the cabin, nor much of anything else. My thoughts were sluggish. Foggy. I had difficulty recalling who I was or where I was from. But I knew the knowledge was somewhere in there, deep within the fog, so I focused my thoughts. I needed to pierce the mental gloom and remember. Who am

1

I? Why was I here?

Slowly, my efforts paid off. Bits and pieces of memory trickled into my muddled brain. I have a son, Alex. And a wife. Her name is Pam. I have a house in the suburbs of Indianapolis, and my son and wife live with me. An image of the house came into my mind. I thought about my bedroom. I could see Pam lying in our bed, with the lamp burning and a book in her hand. Yes, I have a wife and a son. *But, where are they?*

More memories came tumbling in and I began to regain a fuller sense of who I was. I remembered my name—Charles Beck. And my job—sales manager for Ricoh International. Other aspects of my life began to resolve in my mind.

Though much started coming back, I still could not remember the cabin. Or why I was lying in it. And there was something else lurking in the fog, something troubling. Something I wasn't sure I wanted to remember. And then, with abrupt clarity, it came to me.

Strange events had happened in the world. All communications had gone down—cell phones, internet, even network broadcasts. And then there was that sound. A strange, piercing, unpleasant sound that came from everywhere and nowhere at once. For two days it had sounded every twenty seconds—a series of sharp noises, each one like the clack of billiard balls colliding. And always in the same pattern. Eight clacks, then a second's pause, then eight more.

I didn't know what it was. And without communications, there was no news. No explanation. Where did it come from? The sky, perhaps? But the strange, sharp noises followed everyone everywhere and their loudness never diminished. And it put everyone on edge. Eight clacks, pause, then eight more.

We couldn't work, so everyone went home. My wife and my son greeted me at the door. They were freaked out. Hell, the whole neighborhood was.

In the two days that followed, everyone stayed home, waiting on news. But there was no communication of any kind. And the weird sound continued unabated. I remembered standing on the front porch of my home. People were milling around the neighborhood, talking nervously and glancing up at the sky with anxious grimaces whenever the clacking repeated. I found my neighbors' worried prattling pointless and did not join in their conversation. I just stood on my porch and watched.

Like everyone else, I had not slept since the clacking noises started. They pierced into one's mind and would not let one rest. So desperately did I crave sleep, that even standing up, I would immediately begin to drift off during the pause—the sweet twenty seconds of silence between each sequence of clacks—only to be awakened abruptly by another round of the penetrating noise. It had reached the point where each clack seemed to resonate within my nervous system. It had become disruptive, even painful.

But then, without fanfare, the noise stopped.

After a quick glance around them, the neighbors who had been standing in their front yards just lay down right where they stood. I watched them with amazement, but also felt overwhelmed with the need to sleep. So much so that I lay down on my porch, resting my head upon the wooden boards. I knew what I was doing was odd, but couldn't stop myself.

Now, lying quietly on this rustic bed in an unfamiliar cabin, I reviewed these memories urgently in my mind and became sure that lying down on my porch was the very last thing I recalled doing.

Despite a sense of foreboding, I had to get up and figure out what was going on. I felt physically weak, but pushed myself up into a seated position. The exertion caused my head to start throbbing, so I hesitated a moment, sitting on the edge of the bed. I made a move to stand, but was unstable. I grasped the log headboard as my head swam. I wanted to lie down again, but I couldn't. I had to find my son and my wife.

Hanging on the corner of the bed frame were two pieces of stiff buckskin. As I looked closer at them, I realized one was a pair of trousers with a thong belt and the other was a buckskin shirt. They smelled funny, but as I was naked and saw nothing else in the cabin to wear I put them on. I found a pair of leather moccasins on the dirt floor next to the bed. I had no idea who they belonged to, but they fit my feet pretty well.

Now attired in these strange clothes, I took a step toward the table and grasped its edge. I stood there for a while, just getting used to standing up.

I tried once again to piece things together. *Where am I? How did I get here?* Maybe I had been put into this cabin for a good reason. Maybe my family was nearby and they would explain everything. But the fact that this was a log cabin and not, say, a hospital room was unsettling. Something wasn't right, and I had to get out there and find out what.

I took a wobbly step toward the solitary window, and leaned on the sill. The daylight was painfully bright, so I shielded my eyes with my hand and squinted.

About ten feet away stood another cabin, and a few more beyond that. I saw grass and woods, and a small creek just a few steps away. I didn't recognize anything, but saw nothing obviously threatening.

I felt a tingling sensation in my limbs as the circulation to them increased. I began wiggling them back and forth, vigorously and rubbing my arms and shoulders as if to warm them up. My joints were stiff, but my legs were feeling stronger by the second. I tried to stand again, and seemed more stable. I paced back and forth a few times within the small space and managed to remain upright. Encouraged, I eyed the door.

I had no clear idea what I would find outside it, but I didn't have a good feeling about it. I thought it best to be as mobile as possible, so I stretched and began doing jumping jacks. It was slow and painful at first, but soon my limbs felt warm and my motions became more assured. And while I exercised, my mind continued to race.

Perhaps I was silly to be concerned. In a few minutes, Pam or a doctor would walk through the door and explain everything. Maybe I had an accident and was suffering from some kind of amnesia.

But then I remembered that sound. That God-awful noise. I had lain down on the porch and fallen asleep. How did all of that connect to my current predicament?

Suddenly, my bladder screamed for release. I scanned the interior of the cabin, but saw nothing I could pee in. I could let it go in the corner. But what if I was worrying about nothing? Wouldn't I feel foolish? It was time to step outside.

I lifted the wooden plank that held the door closed and stepped out quickly. Despite the pressure in my bladder, I took a moment to survey my surroundings. A warm sun shone. There was a light, fresh breeze and the sound of birds and insects surrounded me. There were cabins on both sides of the little creek, and beyond them was a larger building, roughly fifty yards away. Two crop fields were some ways distant. The place seemed like some kind of rustic agricultural compound, but I saw no one tending the fields. In fact, no one was visible anywhere.

The edge of a thick wood was around a hundred feet away. I considered making for it before relieving myself, but I was reluctant to cross the open space until I knew more about where I was. So I leaned on the side of my cabin and let it flow.

And boy, did it flow. I couldn't remember ever having peed so much. I had just finished and was tying up my thong belt when I sensed movement behind me. Startled, I turned quickly to see a woman, her buckskin trousers at her ankles, squatting down and urinating by the cabin next to mine.

"God," she said, looking up at me without a hint of embarrassment. "I've never had to pee so bad in my life!"

She was stocky and about sixty years of age, with grayish-black hair. She stood up, used the rawhide thong to cinch her waist, and smiled at me.

"Hi," she said. "I'm Missy."

"Charles," I replied. "Where are we? What is this place?"

The woman looked around. "I don't really know. A bunch of cabins in the woods. It looks like some kind of camp."

"How did you get here?"

Missy shrugged. "I woke up here. Don't remember coming to this place."

Voices echoed a few cabins down.

We walked toward the source and found two men, standing by one of the other cabins and dressed in the same rough garments Missy and I were wearing. They were looking around, as puzzled as we were.

"Does anyone know where we are?" I asked.

"No idea," one of the men said. "We just woke up here."

More doors opened and more people, looking lost and confused, exited the other cabins. Most of them paused to urinate near their cabins and walked toward us. "What is this place?" asked a striking young lady with long, blond hair. The only responses were more shrugs and shaking heads.

I scanned the surrounding woods, which were mostly oak and maple hardwood with a scattering of pine trees. It seemed typical of most of the woodlands across the eastern United States.

More bewildered people joined us. Another young lady with shoulder-length brown hair. An older Hispanic gentleman. A wiry fellow of about thirty, with runaway freckles. A dark, dangerous-looking man, with close-set eyes. And a handful more. Sixteen of us in all. We were evenly divided according to gender, we all wore buckskin clothes, and our ages ranged from young adult to late middle age.

We looked at each other with puzzled expressions and more questions followed. We were all from the United States, though one woman had recently emigrated from Slovakia. Otherwise, there seemed to be nothing in common to connect our group, except that each of us, no matter where we lived, remembered the strange, clacking sounds. And the last thing each of us remembered was lying down to sleep immediately after noises had stopped.

Until we woke up here.

Chapter 2

As we stood around looking at each other and gazing about the compound, several of our party called out. Only their own voices echoed back from the trees.

"Let's spread out and look around," said a man named Cook. He was blond, with intelligent eyes and a noticeable gap between his front teeth. I liked him immediately. "See if we can find anybody who knows what the hell is going on."

"Right," I said. "We'll meet back here and share what we find."

Everyone agreed, and we went wandering off in random directions. I headed toward the large building I spotted earlier.

As I walked, I counted sixteen cabins. One, apparently, for each of us. The creek flowed between them, eight cabins on either side, before meandering toward a river just visible downstream.

The large building was also made of logs, and was about three times the size of our cabins. It was rectangular in form and contained a single door and several windows. Attached to its side was a lean-to roof covering a fire pit and a long, banquet table built of split logs mounted on a trestle. There were a few work tables, and several clay cooking and eating implements stacked by the pit.

The door was open, so I went inside. I found several half-log benches along the wall, some rough tables, and a raised platform—perhaps a podium. The building was some kind of meeting hall. But there was nobody inside.

I went around to the back of the building and followed a faint trail to the nearby river, perhaps thirty yards away. The bank at its far side was heavily wooded, and I saw no structures of any kind.

I walked along the bank of the river a short distance, forcing my way through the thick rushes. But the going was tough, so I headed back in the general direction of the cabins. Not far from the river, I came across one of the agricultural fields. Whatever the grain was, it seemed to be flourishing. I plucked a stalk and rubbed it between my fingers.

"Red durum," said a voice. I looked up to see Missy, also studying a stalk in her hand. "A kind of wheat. Of course, that's corn over there," she added, pointing to a second field bordering the one in which we stood.

"Hmm," I said. "See anybody?"

"Nope," she said, and walked past me toward the river.

Other than the members of our little group, there was no one to be seen. No nurses, no farmers, no Pam or Alex anxiously awaiting my recovery. No one.

I headed back to the cabins, where several of the others were already waiting. The walk had cleared the last of the fog from my brain, but the questions remained. *What the hell is this? And where is my family?*

"Anybody home?" Cook asked as I strode up.

"I didn't see anyone."

"Nobody saw anyone," added the striking blond named

Rebecca.

"There are animals in that building over yonder," said a young woman named Christie, pointing to a building upstream of the cabins. She seemed to be in her mid-thirties, with layered auburn hair and high cheek bones. "Chickens and pigs."

"Well, somebody must care for them," said Eileen, a middle-aged woman with bob haircut and a double chin.

"I guess," I said. "But right now the place looks fucking deserted."

"I found an orchard," said a red-haired woman as she approached. "And a garden. It's well-tended, too."

I was surprised I hadn't noticed her before. She was about my age, and had soft, honey-colored eyes with shoulder-length hair and an ample bosom.

She looked at me and smiled. "Cindy Nelson," she said, extending her hand. I wasn't sure why she chose me for a personal introduction, but I was pleased that she did.

I held her hand and smiled back, oddly at a loss for words. "Charles Beck," I mumbled, and turned to the group.

"There's a cornfield over there," said a tall fellow with a jutting jaw, who was named Harvey.

"And a wheat field too, or so I've been told by Missy," I said. "There's a river just beyond the big building."

The wiry man, whose name was Dillon, pointed to a small outlying building. "That building houses a workshop. It has a forge in it, and tools."

"And those little structures on the top of that hill seem to be storage containers." This from a diminutive, pale young man named Michael. "Some of them are filled with grain."

We all looked around, silent.

"What the fuck is this?" blurted a black man named Trey. He was solid-built with copper eyes.

None of it made sense. Sixteen of us waking up in cabins in the middle of nowhere, and not another person to be found. It was confusing and creepy.

My mind kept returning to those strange clacking noises.

"Look," I said, glancing over their faces. "I hate to bring this up, but, well, could there be a connection between those weird noises we heard before going to sleep and us being here?"

"What do you mean?" asked Eileen, her eyes darting left and right.

"Somebody had to have put us here," said Missy.

I nodded. "Yep."

"This might be some kind of convalescence center," suggested Cindy. "Perhaps we needed healing."

Missy chuckled and shook her head. "Pretty luxurious accommodations for convalescing."

"If this is a convalescence center, then where are the nurses and aides?" Dillon asked.

I liked the idea of it. That the noises had made us ill somehow, so people looking out for our welfare had gathered us together and placed us in this camp, where they would care for us. But where were they now?

"Let's just keep looking," I said. "There's got to be somebody."

"Look, you don't need to say that." This came from the dangerous-looking man with close-set eyes. He had pronounced jowls and a barrel chest. His name was Samuel.

"What do you mean?" I asked, puzzled by his response.

"Well, it's obvious. We need to look around. You don't need to tell us that."

I wasn't sure what the man was about, but I had no interest in arguing, I just wanted to figure this out and get the fuck out. I opened my hands wide. "Okay," I said. "I wasn't trying to boss anybody around."

"Kinda sounded like it." But he added nothing more and turned and wandered off. I ignored the odd confrontation. We were all stressed and confused.

We spent the rest of the day combing the entire area around our cabins, and found no one. But several facts became evident. For one, the camp appeared to be a fruitful but rustic agricultural community. Its primitive nature reminded me of the communities of colonial America. The garden, half an acre in extent, was full of plants—tomatoes, cucumbers, carrots, and squash. Nearby, an elegant grove of apple and plum trees flourished near the river. Just outside our community, surrounded by thick woods, were the wheat and corn fields, replete with crops.

Several small auxiliary buildings, including the workshop, were scattered around a clear area near the meeting hall. Along with the forge, the workshop contained an anvil, bellows, and an array of wrought-iron implements. Most were for agricultural use, such as hoes, plows, and a large scythe, but the purposes of some of the others were obscure. These tools were neatly arranged along the interior wall of the shop. In the corner sat a pile of used and mangled tool heads, and other bits and pieces of iron.

The pigs and chickens were housed in a small enclosure upstream of the cabins. The tenants seemed to come and go as they wished, scratching the soil or, in the case of the pigs, rooting in the nearby woods.

The creek that ran between our cabins began its life as

a spring gurgling up from the ground another fifty feet upstream from the animal pen. A small building had been constructed on the site, creating a cool interior environment. Several hams hung from the ceiling beams, their green coats of mold shimmering. A nearby building of similar size smelled strongly of smoke—obviously a smokehouse for curing meat.

A few trails wound through the community, connecting the fields, cabins, and river, yet we found no roads or trails leading out of the camp. All we saw beyond the boundaries of our immediate area were a river, dense woods, a range of low-lying hills to the south, and distant mountains to the north-east. There was no visible sign of human presence beyond the boundaries of our village.

As twilight approached, we gathered around the outdoor cooking/eating area under the lean-to attached to the side of the meeting hall. Most of us sat around the banquet table, large enough for everyone to find a seat without cramping his neighbors. The day's explorations and the anxiety of uncertainty had left me tired and hungry. As we sat there, we were quiet. But I, for one, was glad to have the company of others as I tried to process what was happening.

A small stack of wood and a handful of wood shavings had been left next to the fire pit. But we found no lighters or matches, so Trey attempted to start a fire with two sticks. His efforts lacked conviction, and nothing came of it. After a while, he gave up.

"Sorry," he said. "I'm not sure what I'm doing."

Cindy and Missy had gathered tomatoes and cucumbers from the garden, and apples and plums from the orchard. "Well, let's just pass these around," said Cindy. "They'll do for our supper."

"The plums aren't fully ripe," added Missy.

They had gathered enough for everyone to have at least one of each.

"This has to be the best cucumber I have ever eaten," said Amber. She was about Rebecca's age—early twenties—but didn't possess her striking beauty or grace of movement. She seemed self-conscious, constantly adjusting the curls of her shoulder-length sandy-brown hair.

"All of it is delicious," said Trey, chomping away on an apple. "But it's because we're so hungry."

"I guess," replied Amber. "I wonder how long we were asleep."

No one answered. No one knew.

"May I ask where this water came from?" asked Rebecca, frowning as she peered into her cup.

"I fetched it from the creek," said Missy.

"But shouldn't we boil it first? Can you drink water out of a creek like that?"

"I think it's okay," said Cindy. "The spring is right there."

Rebecca wrinkled up her nose in obvious disgust. "But not downstream of the pigs, I hope."

"For Christ's sake, don't drink it if you don't want it," replied Missy.

Rebecca glared at the older woman, then sighed, and slowly put the cup to her lips.

Chapter 3

We had just finished our light dinner when Cook stood up, looked us over, and propped his foot up on the end brace of the table. "All right, guys," he said. "We've got a pretty good idea of our situation, although we have no idea why we're here. The question is, what do we do about it?"

"I have something to say," said a woman named Veronica. She had dark-hair and olive skin and had, until now, been quiet. "I remember raking the leaves in my yard the day before those noises came. But now, this is summer. Late summer, maybe, with the crops so ripe, but it's definitely not fall."

Everyone mulled it over. "You know, you're right," said Cindy. "We had plans to attend the North Carolina State football game next weekend."

"North Carolina State!" said Trey. "You're a Wolfpack fan?"

"No way," replied Cindy. "We're Tar Heels. We were road tripping to Raleigh for the game."

"Veronica's right," I said, redirecting the conversation. "So either we were all moved somewhere with a different seasonal progression, or we've been asleep for months."

"Or possibly longer," added Cook in a somber tone.

Again we were silent, blinking and looking around. My stomach churned. If we had been asleep just a short while, it seemed likely that our families and the rest of our lives were still intact. It was a matter of getting back to them. But if we had been out for a year, or maybe more, then where were our families and loved ones? Why hadn't they looked for us? Were Alex and Pam safe somewhere? Just what in the hell was going on?

I heard broken sobs and saw tears streaming down Eileen's round face. "Where are my children?" she asked. Nobody knew what to say.

A long, plaintive howl broke the silence, and a chill went down my spine.

"What was that?" asked Amber, sliding closer to Harvey, who was sitting on the bench next to her.

"Sounded like a wolf," I said.

"A wolf? I doubt it," said Samuel. "A coyote. Or someone's dog."

"Charles is right," said Dillon. "Wolves sound different. Their howl is deeper."

Samuel snorted, but we all stared into the woods opposite the creek. In the twilight we could see few details. And then, a minute later, we heard shuffling in the woods on the opposite side, toward the wheat field. Then a low huffing sound.

"What's that?" Rebecca's eyes were wide with concern.

"That breathing? It could be a bear," suggested Dillon.

"A fucking bear?" asked Rebecca.

"I think you're right," said Cook, who was still standing and looking hard into the woods.

"What should we do?" asked Christie.

"He's probably checking the place out," said Dillon. "I wouldn't think he would attack a group of us."

"I have a proposal," I said. "It's been a long day. Why don't we all retreat to the safety of our cabins and continue our search tomorrow?"

Amber pressed more closely to Harvey and smiled sheepishly. "Anybody care to walk me to my cabin?"

Harvey shrugged. "I guess," he said, looking nervously around the table. "Sure."

"Let's all go as a group," I suggested.

The cabins weren't far from where we sat. We all briskly paced to the cabin area and then, everyone looking around with intent stares, we made for our cabins and closed the doors without incident.

As I lay on my wooden plank bed, the warmth of the night making my skin sweaty and sticky, my mind raced. I listened to the sounds of the forest and could just make out sobbing from one of the other cabins.

I tried to figure out a scenario that made sense.

It seemed reasonable to suppose that our predicament had something to do with the strange events that had occurred the day I had fallen asleep on the front porch—the failure of communications, the annoying sound. But what, exactly, the nature of that connection might be, I couldn't say. No television broadcasts, no internet, no cell phones, nothing! I had no idea how global the phenomenon was. And if it was global, who could cause a communications blackout on that large of a scale? My worried neighbors, in the hours before they lay down in their yards to sleep, had offered several theories. Maybe Russians. Maybe terrorists. One guy was sure it was aliens.

I thought about this strange day and wondered. Could someone from another planet have put us here?

I shook my head in disbelief, sat up on the edge of the hard wooden bed, and rubbed my face with my hands. *You're losing it, Charles.* It was the uncertainty of our situation that was so taxing. We knew nothing other than we were alone.

I considered the possibility that the caretakers of our little community had been forced to leave. Some emergency in a nearby town or the like. Yet we had all awoken on the same day. At the same time. That would be quite a coincidence.

The more I thought about it, the more implausible every scenario seemed. My body suddenly felt tired. It seemed strange that I would feel weak and tired after so much sleep. I slumped back down onto my bunk, trying to think. But I was exhausted. Soon I gave up and closed my eyes, hoping next day would bring answers.

Chapter 4

The next morning, a cacophony of chirping birds outside my window woke me. I opened my eyes in the dim light to see I was still in the little cabin. As I sat up and looked around, my sense of foreboding returned.

Though fearful as to what was outside, I felt thick and grimy and really wanted to clean up a little. And after a night's rest, I felt better equipped to deal with whatever the day may bring. I decided an early dip in the river would be refreshing so I donned my buckskin trousers, shirt, and moccasins, and poked my head out the door of the cabin. I saw no wolves or bears, so I stepped out into the cool morning and followed the trail I knew would take me to the little beach on the river.

I kept studying the woods as I made my way down the path. It was early, and the forest was still shrouded in shadow. The trees still held wisps of mist entangled in their branches. But I felt safe in the gaining daylight, so kept going.

I saw no one else along the way, but when I made it to the bank of the calm river, I saw the woman named Cindy already in the water. She had piled her buckskin garments on the bank.

I was unsure what I should do. I didn't want to disturb her morning swim, but as she was nude in the water, I didn't want to stand there like a pervert watching her. I opted to let her decide.

"Good morning," I said.

She jerked her head toward me as she dipped low in the water. "Oh!"

"Sorry. I didn't mean to startle you."

She watched me for a moment, and then nodded. "It's okay. I'm just a little on edge out here. Wherever *this* is." She frowned briefly and then beamed a smile at me. "Charles. Right? The water is wonderful. I just wish I had a bar of soap."

"It looks inviting. Will you be in there for a while?"

"Nope. I was about to leave, so it's all yours."

Without warning, she began to stand up in the waist-deep water, so I turned my head. I heard her footsteps on the sand behind and heard her lay down on the beach. When I turned, she was lying back on her elbows on the small area of beach, still nude.

"Sorry," she said. "I just want to dry off a bit before I put those gross buckskins back on."

She was beautifully proportioned so I could not help surveying her before prying my eyes away. "No problem," I said, looking around at the trees.

"I'm embarrassing you, aren't I?"

"Nah," I said and gazed toward the river as casually as I could. "We're all adults here."

"That's right," she said. But after a moment she grabbed her clothes and put them on.

"You have a beautiful body," I offered.

"Thanks, I guess. I was two weeks out from breast reduction surgery. What a relief that would have been."

"I'm sorry to hear that," I said, still undecided whether I

should undress in front of her. "They are very attractive."

"Yeah, you guys are all alike—it's all about how big the boobs are. But trust me, these aren't fun to carry around, especially in the middle of the summer."

Now dressed, she sat back down on the sand. "Charles, what the fuck is going on?"

"Don't know. Not yet. But we will figure it all out."

She watched me fidget with the rawhide thong that held up my trousers. "I'll look away. Until you get in the water."

"Thanks," I replied. She turned, and I disrobed and entered the cool water. It was clear, and the bottom was loose sand. And like she had said, the water was wonderful.

Cindy turned back. "Where're you from, Charles? Or should I call you Chuck?"

"Please don't. Or Charlie, either. Just Charles."

"You got it."

"I'm from Indianapolis. I live there with my wife, Pam, and son, Alex."

"First marriage?"

The question surprised me. "Um, no. As a matter of fact, it's my second. Alex is from my first."

"I see."

"What about you? Where're you from?"

"Winston-Salem. I'm married, with two kids getting close to college age."

"What do you do in Winston-Salem?"

"I'm a nurse. Emergency room, mostly."

"That's noble. I manage a staff of copier salesmen. For Ricoh."

"I see." Cindy closed her eyes and tilted her head back. "You know, it's kind of nice out here this morning. I just wish I

21

knew why we were here."

I looked around at the mist still hanging above the rushes along the far bank. A sliver of sun accented the sky with a streak of saffron, and cast a golden light across the surface of the quiet river. Birds were chirping in the nearby branches. She had a point.

"Yeah, not too bad," I said. "But you're right about that bar of soap. I could use a good lather."

I reached down and scooped up a handful of sand from the river bottom and rubbed it into my skin. Sand may not lather much, but at least its coarseness would exfoliate my skin.

"Well," said Cindy, "I'd better hit the garden for our breakfast."

"Sounds good. I'll see you in a few."

Cindy walked off. After a few more minutes of rubbing sand into my skin, I sat on the bank to drip dry before putting on my buckskin garments. It was cool, but the morning breeze began drying my skin. As I sat there in the quiet, I surveyed the lifting fog and wondered where my wife could be.

Back at the cabins, some of the others had awakened and were standing around the big banquet table in the outdoor kitchen. They were a raggedy group, with their primitive leather outfits, tousled hair, and worried faces.

"I don't know about you guys, but I'm starving," I said as I walked up. "Shall we take advantage of the hospitality of whoever put us here and make breakfast?"

"Sounds good," said Missy. "Why don't you whip it up for us?"

I shrugged. "Cindy is already getting stuff from the garden, but I wouldn't mind something more substantial. Maybe some eggs from the chicken coop?"

"Sounds great, boss man," said Samuel, sitting at the table. "Do you know how to start a fire?"

"No, not really," I said. "Not without matches, anyway. How about you, Samuel? Can you start a fire?"

"It was your suggestion," he replied curtly.

"Let me try," said Cook, walking up. "I'm handy at these kinds of things."

"Absolutely." I gestured toward the cold fire pit. "But… why didn't you try last night?

Cook shrugged. "It was dark and would have needed to gather a few things. Besides, I haven't done this in a while." He looked around him. "Does anyone have a piece of rawhide about three feet long? I need a sturdy stick, about two or three feet. A flat rock—like those by the river bank. These shavings, and I need a split log—not too big."

We helped him gather what he needed. Christie went to the river for the flat rock. Samuel retrieved an iron-bladed ax from the workshop and split a log. Cook found a sturdy stick in the nearby forest. All we needed was a piece of rawhide.

"As long as I don't have to stand up, you can use my belt." I took a seat at the table, pulled off the leather thong that held my trousers in place, and handed it to Cook.

"I'll do my best not to break it," he said, winking. "But no promises."

He bent the stick and attached the rawhide thong to its two ends, creating a bow. He then used the ax blade to carve out a niche in the split log. "The flat rock, please."

Christie handed it to him. Cook looked over its surface and found a slight depression near its center. "This will do nicely," he said. "Oh, and I need one more stick—dry. About two feet."

All of us had been watching Cook with interest. Amber

jumped up and ran into the woods.

"Will this do?" she asked, returning moments later.

"Perfect." He took the stick. "And now the magic happens." Clearly, Cook was enjoying his performance.

He placed one end of the stick into the carved notch he had made in the split log, looped the taut string from the bow around the stick, and held it in place with the flat rock pressing down from above. He piled the shavings near the notch in the half-log. Then, by sliding the bow back and forth, the stick began to spin rapidly. At first, the stick kept slipping out of position, but after a few minutes, Cook got the hang of it. The bow spun the stick back and forth, back and forth. It wasn't long before I spotted smoke coming from the pile of shavings. I heard a "wow" from the gathered onlookers.

Cook bent over the pile, cupped his hands on either side of his small pile, and blew gently. A tiny little flame poked its head above the pile, and Christie clapped with joy, like a child, amid a low round of scattered applause. Cook added more shavings as the fire grew. Next he added small twigs, then bigger branches. As the fire matured, he stood and swept his arms in a grand gesture. "Voila!"

"Impressive," I said.

"All right," said Cindy, putting her hands on her hips. "And now we all know how to do it ourselves."

Cook nonchalantly brushed the dirt off his hands. "Well, it does take a bit of practice."

I smiled at him. "I can see you might be a handy fellow around here. Now for breakfast." My eyes found Christie.

"I'll grab eggs," she offered.

"We'll need fat," said Eileen, looking thoughtfully at the kitchen area. "Unless we boil them."

"I'll get bacon," said Samuel. "I saw some hanging in the springhouse. It'll make grease when we fry it up."

Soon we were all sitting around the table eating a crude but satisfying breakfast: bacon and eggs served on rustic clay dishes. More tomatoes and cucumbers. And water served in clay cups.

The hearty breakfast roused everyone's spirits. Missy, who was sitting next to me, elbowed me in the shoulder. "So go fetch us some coffee," she said with a wink.

"Yeah, coffee would be nice. But I'm reasonably clean and well-fed, so I'm good for the day."

"Rumor has it you're a salesman."

"Sales manager, actually. I work for Ricoh International, selling printers and copiers. Not much difference between them these days."

"I'm retired," she replied. "I actually—"

She suddenly slapped her neck. She opened her hand and showed me her palm with a splat of red blood in the center. "These damned mosquitoes are obnoxious," she said. "Anyway, as I was saying, I got a big inheritance and quit my job working with a landscape designer. Now I got to figure out how to not wither away and die."

"That sounds grim," I said.

"Well, I don't have a disease or anything—at least not one that anyone has mentioned. It's just that when you retire, you have to fill in the void. So now, I exercise to stay in shape and spend lots of time in my garden."

"It's true," I said. "Our identity is often wrapped up in our work. I suppose it's natural."

"So," began Missy, looking around at the woods, "will the animals in the forest stay in the forest during the day?"

I shrugged. "I hope so. And now that we have the gift of fire, we can keep them away at night, too."

I was eager to get out and resume exploring our surroundings, but the others seemed to find a refuge from our pressing concerns by socially connecting. We all sat around the table for some time and engaged in small talk. Gradually, we left the table and wandered around the encampment. Some took dips in the river. Others fanned out in several directions, taking forays into the woods. There were no trails to follow, so I worried about someone getting lost. As it turned out, no one went too far. Last night's creepy howls and mysterious noises kept everyone near at hand, in spite of our desire to find some sign of civilization.

Missy joined me, and we tried walking upstream along the river bank, keeping the river in sight, but the vegetation along the bank was thick and difficult to traverse, and the day was getting hot. After an hour of pushing aside rushes and laurel and sweating in the thick heat, we gave up on the effort.

We were returning along the bank and had reached the little beach when we spotted Trey and Cook waist-deep in the river water. They had balled up their buckskins and had tied them to their heads with leather thongs.

"Checking out the other side?" I asked.

"We might as well see what's over there," Cook said.

At the deepest point, the water came up only to their chests, so their buckskins stayed dry. We watched them climb up the far bank, dress, and wander into the woods.

"Anything?" I yelled, after several minutes.

"Nothing," Trey called back. "No trails. Nothing."

After a minute, they returned to the bank.

"There's nothing. We're going further downstream," Cook

called out.

They pushed through the rushes for about a hundred yards—no easy task. They then turned back into the woods and were soon out of sight.

After about fifteen minutes, Cook emerged again. "We found a salt lick," he called out.

"A what?"

"A salt lick. You know, a place where animals come to lick the rocks for minerals. Good for hunting."

I guessed it made sense to consider these things. There was no telling how long we would be stuck here, and we might need to fend for ourselves if our food ran out.

"Anything else?"

"Lots of deer sign. No "people" sign."

My hopes sank. Were there no other people anywhere? My thoughts ran to Alex and Pam. *Where in the hell could they be? What the fuck is going on?*

It was our second day since waking up in this bizarre situation. Though we kept looking, we found no sign of anyone besides us sixteen strangers, huddled in the wilderness.

Chapter 5

During the next several days, we wandered further and further into the surrounding woods, but there were no roads, trails or any sign of people other than ourselves. We were alone. Abandoned. Afraid.

Oppressive heat, bugs, and uncertainty followed us around everywhere we went. Most of us wandered aimlessly, or resting in the shade, hardly moving. Everyone complained about the lack of electrical lights, running water, or, could you imagine, air conditioning. I felt grubby in my buckskins and longed to bathe with soap or brush my teeth. On the fifth day, I felt something crawling in my hair and, after digging around for some minutes, extracted a little insect.

"That's a louse," said Missy, looking at it with some concern. "Where there's one, there are many. It won't be long before we are all lousy."

"The whole fucking situation is lousy," I said, in a pale attempt at humor, though there was really nothing humorous about our experience. I was becoming more anxious by the day and, still, nothing was making sense. I had no idea where Pam and Alex were, who put us here, or why no one came for us. I thought about the strange noises and the communications breakdown and wondered.

How could it be that I fall asleep on my front porch one day, and wake up in a rustic log cabin community in the middle of unknown wilderness with no sign of civilization? It didn't seem possible, yet it had happened. And I had no idea how or why.

Were my wife and child in a similar community somewhere? Were they even alive? If they were dead, then how did they die, and when? What happened to their bodies? Did they suffer?

I felt utterly helpless. I could be confident in many circumstances, but this? No modern technology or communication of any kind? No weapons, medical supplies, real clothing or vehicles? Nothing we knew or were used to? What were we supposed to do?

It became part of our regular pattern to gather at the outdoor kitchen and prepare dinner as the light faded. Frumpy Eileen, who had been devoted to her extended family, had the most experience cooking for a large group, and led our food preparation efforts. Cook had broken off a few chunks of the salt-laden mineral from the salt lick to season our food, although it was a stretch to call the product salt. It contained salt, sure. But there was plenty of other stuff mixed with it. But if animals ate it, I figured it wouldn't hurt us.

So far, we had relied on the hams and bacon in the springhouse, the eggs from the henhouse, apples and plums from the orchard, and garden vegetables for our meals. But as I reflected on the possibility that we could be here for a while, I thought about all the game in the surrounding woods and even the grain stored in the little silos. We may ultimately need to tap into these sources of food.

On our fifth evening, we sat quietly around the banquet

table. The heat had been oppressive all day. None of us had any energy, except to snap irritably at others over tiny transgressions. Amazingly, none of us had gotten permanently lost wondering in the woods without trails to guide us. Despite frequent dips in the river, we all stank. I itched all over and swatted away insects constantly to prevent the itching from getting worse.

I looked around at the pitiful group. Eileen's eyes were red from crying. So were Sasha's, a petite woman with an East European accent. Everyone was unhappy. Everyone was afraid. I worried that if we didn't change things, we would just sink into a melancholic morass.

I had been sizing up the other potential leaders in the group, and no one seemed to be stepping up to the plate. But something needed to be done. Someone had to take charge. Looking around one last time at our ill-fated group, I figured that someone would have to be me.

"Excuse me, everyone," I said, "but if you don't mind, there are a couple of things I think we should discuss."

The unhappy faces all turned toward me.

"Oh, God, here he goes again," said Samuel, rolling his eyes and crossing his arms.

I glared at Samuel. "What?"

"Let the guy talk, for Christ's sake, unless you were about to take the floor," said Cook, scowling at Samuel.

"Fuck you," returned Samuel, now staring at Cook.

"I agree," added Missy. "We could use a little leadership right now."

"Whatever," said Samuel, shaking his head. "But I don't like my leader to be self-appointed."

"Don't worry about him," said Cook, giving me his attention.

"Just say what's on your mind, Charles. We want to hear it."

I took a breath. "Okay. Here's the way I see it. No one has come for us, and there are no signs of other people. Who knows what the fuck is going on, but it seems if somebody knew we were here, they would have at least checked in with us by now. Right? So we should consider the possibility we will be here a while."

"But even if we have been forgotten about, why should we stay?" Trey asked. "Let's get the hell out of here and find our families!"

"Okay," I said. "I want to find my family as much as anyone. But how do we go about it? Nobody has found any roads or even trails. We can try going downriver, but we don't have a boat. We could build one, I guess—or several, since there are sixteen of us—but that would take time, and even then, we don't know what's downriver."

"He's right," said Dillon, rubbing his pointy chin. "If we didn't find a settlement or something, how would we survive? We know there are bears and wolves in these woods. Who knows what else?"

I looked around the group, trying to read faces. "It seems reasonable to believe that, eventually, whoever left us here will return. Instead of all of us trying to pack up and leave, I recommend we begin to explore our extended surroundings systematically, while using this camp as our base. Perhaps take short forays down and upriver. Take journeys of several days through the woods. Then we can head out later with a much better idea of our options."

Cook nodded. "Makes sense."

"All I am saying is that we may be here awhile. So we need to find out who knows what about this stuff. Like farming, or pigs, or working iron."

"I can tend a garden," said Cindy, raising her hand.

"Me, too," said Missy.

"Anybody hunt? Or fish?"

"I hunt," said Dillon. "Quite a lot, actually, and I know about woodcraft. Not too much about farming stuff, though."

"Can you get game for our dinner table?"

"Well, weapons are the problem, but we could fashion bows and arrows if we could get arrowheads. Maybe we can forge them in the workshop. And we can set up a trap line to catch smaller game, like rabbits."

"Sounds promising. We could use the scrap iron stacked in the forge for the arrowheads. Does anyone know anything about working with iron?"

"I'm interested in it," said Samuel, joining in the spirit of the discussion and seeming to soften a bit. "I could learn it."

"Yeah. That sounds good. There's a lot we must learn. Okay, Samuel, you're our workshop guy. Does anyone know about crops? Or how to slaughter pigs? How about making bread, or whatever, out of grain?"

"I'm afraid we're mostly city folks," said Christie, munching on a cucumber.

"Well, it doesn't matter. We're talking primitive technology, right? We can figure it out. Our ancestors did. We don't have to reinvent the wheel, just duplicate what we know they did. I think it'll be best if we assign everyone an area to focus on and try to figure things out."

"Might be a good idea," said Cindy. "It'll keep us occupied, at least. What do you have in mind?"

"Well, we have sixteen people to feed, so our most pressing need will be food. There's some already at hand here, like fruit and smoked pork. But we need to tap into other resources, like the wild game and, I guess, the grain."

"What do we do with the wheat?" Ramiro asked. "Can we eat it like it is?"

"I think we can. But if we grind it somehow, we can make flour. And then we can make bread with it."

"But you need to leaven it," said Missy. "Where do we get yeast?"

"Tortillas are unleavened," offered Dillon.

"Yeah, we can make tortillas. So what else? There should be plenty of fish in the river."

"How can we fish?" Samuel asked. "We don't have fishing lines."

"We can use spears," suggested Cook. "Friends of mine used to spear fish all the time. It's more challenging than with a rod and line. You need a long, sharp tip, attach it to a spear, and act like a blue heron."

"A what?" I asked.

"You know, a blue heron. He stands in shallow water and uses his beak as a spear."

"Yeah, why not? What've we got to lose?" I asked. "But I bet it'll take lots of practice."

"I used to gig frogs as a boy," said Ramiro. "I can the spear the fish. And we might fashion fish traps."

"Fish traps?" Dillon asked. "Interesting. I've never tried that."

"All right, who wants responsibility for the animals?" I said. "The chickens and pigs have to be fed and cared for."

"I don't know much about them," said Christie. "But I like animals. I'll do it."

"Okay, good. I think we should assign regular people to run

the kitchen for food preparation. And some people need to make bows and arrows and practice with them. They'll be our hunters—Dillon, you're an obvious choice. And someone should be a full-time explorer. Their job will be to explore in all directions from here to see if we can find anyone or even a road. Heck, even a trail would be nice."

Cook stood up. "Maybe we should climb up that range of hills we seen to the south," he said. "They would give us a good look around."

"But that's a several mile hike across what I presume is wooded terrain," I replied. "An all-day venture, or maybe two."

Cook shrugged. "Yeah, I'd be willing to do it. I used to spend a lot of time in the woods. Usually hiking or backpacking on the weekends, so I'm good at finding my way around."

"Okay then, I designate you our official scout."

"I hate to mention this," said Rebecca as she stroked her blond curls. "But we're getting nasty. Does anybody know how to make soap? And what are we going to do for clothes around here? I can't take these slimy, hot buckskins much longer."

"Wouldn't toilet paper be nice?" asked Missy.

"Um, I'll be needing tampons soon," added Amber.

"It's like we are living as pioneers," observed Veronica. "Except we don't know anything." We all looked at her. She was usually quiet, so it surprised us when she spoke.

"Didn't pioneers use soap?" asked Rebecca.

"You can make it," said Dillon. "You need animal tallow and lye."

"That sounds gross," Rebecca returned.

"Not as gross as you'll smell," rebutted Amber.

"At least I'll still look good," replied Rebecca. "Some of us... well, I'm not so sure..."

"Fuck you, bitch. Besides, if you had a mirror, you wouldn't be so conceited."

"Now, now, children, please behave," said Cindy.

Amber and Rebecca were of similar age, and both seemed awkward in this environment. They were used to cell phones, fashionable clothes. But Amber, stocky with a broad nose, seemed painfully aware she lacked Rebecca's advantages.

"Rebecca, I make you responsible for figuring out how to make soap," I said.

"Um, okay," she replied, shrugging her shoulders.

"Let's just hope we get out of here before too long," offered Trey. "I mean, how long can we go without brushing our teeth?"

"Until they fall out," was Missy's sassy reply.

"I don't understand this! Any of this!" blurted out Eileen. "Why are we here? Why doesn't someone come for us? And why are you all acting like this is our new home? I don't want to live here!"

"All this just blows." Amber's eyes welled up with tears. "I want to go home." I was amazed at how fast her emotions switched from anger to sadness.

"Amber, will you learn how to make pottery?" I asked, trying to divert her attention. I worried about our morale, and I needed to keep us all up and going. "We'll need more plates and pots. And some of the mud along the river bank looks like clay."

"I... I can try, I guess," she said, her lower lip trembling as she studied the ground.

"Good," I said. "I believe we will be rescued soon or find a way home, but just in case, we need to do this stuff. So please, everyone, focus on the tasks at hand and we'll figure it all out."

There was, in fact, a lot to figure out. We needed torches and candles. And if we were stuck here for the long haul, there were other important questions. What should we do with all that grain? Could we make cloth? And what about medicines? What were we going to do when someone got hurt or sick? That could get real bad real quick. And we needed something to repel the damned bugs!

In the days that followed, everyone seemed more encouraged and engaged since we began the distribution of responsibilities. I was encouraged, too. Regardless of how long it would take for individuals to master their areas, it would keep everyone occupied for now. And if they were occupied, then their minds were diverted from the bigger questions concerning our situation, such as why we were here, and where everyone else might be. I felt relieved that I had been more or less accepted as the leader and solved at least some of our immediate concerns. Even Samuel had gotten off my ass.

But I suspected that, eventually, the weight of our situation would bear down upon us like a sack of rocks. People could become unhinged due to the unusual stress of this situation. If it got bad, and anyone freaked out, then our survival could be at risk. We needed to become a village.

I had no clue if that were possible.

Chapter 6

The sweltering days continued one after another. My growing beard itched constantly, and everyone's hair had become matted and unruly. Our daily miseries and the lack of customary hygiene continued to sap our morale. Yet these negatives were balanced by the significant progress everyone made in their areas of specialization. These victories, though small, were meaningful.

Our meals had gotten better, thanks to Eileen's skills. And Amber was making progress at crafting tableware and pottery. I was glad to see it, since I considered her one of the more fragile members of our group.

Samuel was a big surprise. Despite his combative tendencies, he seemed to have a knack for making things in the workshop. It didn't take long for him to fire up the forge and create acceptable arrowheads out of the scrap metal stacked in the shop. Fortunately, they were straightforward to make—just pointy slivers of metal with a stem to allow them to be tied to the arrow's shaft.

I designated myself as a hunter to help Dillon. Our first task was to construct suitable bows and arrows. We spent several days searching the woods for strong and supple limbs to use as bows, but we had no cured wood to use. Bows made from green wood worked for a while, but, as we found out during our target practice, they would soon lose their ability to maintain tension and had to be frequently replaced. We cut down small, straight saplings to use for arrow shafts and stacked them in the sun to dry. Rawhide was an acceptable material for the bow strings, but it was less than ideal for attaching the iron arrowheads to the shafts.

"We need tendons," said Dillon, testing our latest attempt and finding it lacking. "Animal tendons."

"Well, before we actually kill anything with these, our only option is pig tendons," I said.

"Yep," said Dillon. "They should work."

I sighed, laid down my unfinished arrow, and went to find Christie. It was her responsibility to feed and care for our pigs and chickens. And like most of us, she had no experience. Fortunately, these animals mostly fended for themselves, roaming around the nearby woods. And Christie was competent and smart, so I was confident she would figure it out. I found her standing near the pens, casting out handfuls of grain for the chickens.

"Are they eating it?" I asked as I approached.

"Yeah, they eat it," she replied. "I see them eating all kinds of stuff. They even peck at the leftovers we dump out for the pigs."

"Speaking of the pigs, I'm afraid it's time we butcher one. Dillon needs its tendons for our arrow heads, and it would be nice to eat meat that isn't salted, don't you agree?"

She contemplated a nearby pig. "Okay, so... what?"

I sensed she was uncomfortable with the idea. But it was the job she had volunteered for, so she needed to master it if we were to get meat from our stock. I didn't want to be a dick about it, but our circumstances dictated that we all needed to do things we didn't really want to do.

"Christie, I don't know what to tell you. You're in charge of the animals. It is your responsibility to choose a pig, kill it, and cut it up."

"Just like that?"

"Yep. Just like that."

I handed her a blade Samuel had made from an old farm implement. She looked at it and then at me.

"No one else here knows how to butcher a pig either," I said in response to her unvoiced question. "It's a part of your assigned area. If you feel like it's too much for you to handle, we can change assignments. Would you rather make pottery or something?"

She sighed again. "No, I don't want to make pottery. I'll just figure it out."

"Take your time. And get someone to help you. Come find me by the river when you're done." It would be challenging enough for her, so I didn't want her to think I was looking over her should and judging her work.

An hour later, I was with Dillon on the river bank. We were setting out a couple of vine snares near the edge of the water, where we had seen snowy egrets stalking the shallows. We had just baited the snares with small bits of fish when a God-awful screeching reached our ears. My eyes opened wide in horror. It was an unnatural sound, full of terror.

"What in the hell is that?" I asked Dillon.

"That, my good sir, is the sound of a pig losing its life."

The screeching was penetrating and unnerving, and continued for a good five minutes before it stopped. I was tempted to see how she was handling it, but my days as a sales manager had taught me that it was important to give people room to figure things out on their own.

Dillon and I knelt down in the rushes, waiting and watching, but the egrets, scared off when we placed the snares, seemed to have no interest in returning. Finally, I couldn't stand it anymore.

"I'll see how she's doing," I said.

I followed the trail back and saw a crowd gathered near the animal pens. As I got closer, I saw Christie in their midst, covered in gore. Trey was standing with her, only slightly less covered in red.

"I did it," she said, her voice shaky. "I killed the son of a bitch." Despite her hard words, I saw the tracks of tears on her blood-splattered face.

Nearby was a freshly-dug pit, several feet deep, with a bloody spear lying beside it. The spear had Samuel's blade tied to it. The pit, only a couple of feet wide, still contained a pool of blood. Pieces of meat and gore lay about the ground.

"What happened?" I asked.

"I helped her dig that hole," said Trey. "We pushed the pig in there and, before it could get out, she, well, she jabbed it with that spear."

"I killed the son of a bitch," repeated Christie.

"God," I said, looking around at the bloody scene. "What a mess!"

"I don't know how to cut this thing up," said Christie. "But I'm cutting anyway. It's my job."

"I'm trying to help her," added Trey.

"Holy cow!" said Dillon, walking up and seeing the scene for the first time. He looked at Christie and then at the chunks of gory pig parts lying around her.

"That's not the way you do it," he said. "Tie a loop around its back legs and pull it up on a branch, and then whack it hard on its skull with some kind of club."

Christie bit her lower lip and nodded. "Okay. Probably better than my way."

"Yes, but then you cut a slit in its throat and let it bleed out before you cut it up."

Christie glared at me, pointing to the bloody mess on her buckskins. "Why the fuck didn't you tell me earlier? Look at me!"

"I didn't know," I said. I looked at Dillon with a questioning face. "I thought you didn't know about farm stuff."

"I don't, but that's how you do deer. I assume the same for pigs."

Christie stood up, threw her arms in the air. "I can't believe this!"

"Christie…" I began.

"Never mind Charles. I'll be fucking all right." She began walking toward the river. "But I'm going to get cleaned up."

I nodded and surveyed the carnage. "Well, let's get those tendons."

The tendons were long, white pieces of tough tissue. We used them to tie several arrowheads to their shafts and set them out to dry. They were pliable and wet, so I was a little skeptical about the results of our effort, but when we returned to them the next day, the formerly flexible tendons had hardened, squeezing each arrowhead tightly onto the shaft. I tested one arrowhead, and it was snug.

The next day, we got lucky and caught an egret. We failed to coax him into our snare, but we propped up a heavy log near the bank and waited for the tall, slim bird to step under it, feeding on our bait. Watching from nearby, we pulled the vine rope attached to the log and it grazed the bird as it attempted its escape, just enough to stun it. We ran over, and Dillon throttled it.

Now we had feathers for fletching our arrows. We split them in half and used three halves per shaft, exposing an inch of the central stem on the front and rear of the feather to provide a means of attaching them to the shaft. We couldn't make many arrows, but we had enough to get started. Now, if we took a deer, we would have more tendons and rawhide, and perhaps shoot more birds for their feathers. Then we could make as many as we needed.

But we were far from dangerous. Although we now had functioning bows and arrows, and the desire to use them for hunting, our skills were lacking—especially mine. So we began our mornings practicing our technique at a makeshift practice range. Using vines, we attached several pieces of wood to tree limbs and let them swing back and forth, attempting to shoot them with our arrows. Practicing with our new weapons became part of our daily routine.

In the days that followed, we would wait until the late afternoon and make our way across the river to the salt lick and climb up in a nearby tree. A steady flow of deer and smaller animals came by in the evenings in quest of the salt, and we often took a shot. Unfortunately, we took down no deer, and we lost several of our precious arrows. But the important thing was that we were determined to get better.

"We'll get there," Dillon kept saying. "We just need to keep practicing."

Dillon and I made a good team. He was a naturally reserved fellow and sometimes it was hard to get him talking, but he knew a lot about animals and the woods. He was a great asset for our group. And he seemed like a good guy, patient and supportive of my rookie efforts. I hoped his support and confidence would pay off.

Chapter 7

More days passed. We came to know each other's personal details pretty thoroughly, so small talk around the dinner table began to stall. It was Ramiro who suggested telling stories to the group. We couldn't watch TV or read, so it was at least a form of entertainment. And Ramiro's stories about his life in southwestern Texas, spoken in his deep but soft voice, were always engaging. And Sasha, who spoke little otherwise, relayed to the group what she could remember of the eastern European myths she grew up hearing. To me, her face had a cat-like appearance, and it was entertaining to see her eyes sparkle and her facial expressions mimic those of her characters as she told the tales in her accented English.

Our small successes countering our boredom were offset by the all-pervasive uncertainty hanging over us. Cook went off to the southern hills to see what he could see from their tops, and the hope of what he might find temporarily buoyed morale. There was a chance he would bring back encouraging news. Anything to give us a spark.

He spent three entire days on his journey away from the camp. Once he reached the range, he had climbed the tallest hill he saw and shinnied up a tree. But the news reported was not good. He saw nothing except woods and more woods.

No structures, no smoke plumes—just wild forest.

The news hit us hard. We seemed to have been dropped down in a vast expanse of unbroken wilderness. Were we in some remote corner of the world? If so, then why would someone go through all the trouble of sticking us here? The other, more troubling possibility made even less sense. That something had happened to world we had once known and, for some reason, we were chosen to be among the survivors. If that scenario were the correct one, I would never see my family again.

Sometimes, in the woods by myself, sitting quietly waiting for a deer, I'd close my eyes and remember when Alex was young. The expression in his eyes when he was curious. The huge smile that took up half his chubby face. God, he was such a cute little kid! The way he ran to me when he was scared. Holding his body close to mine so that I could hear his little heart race.

"It's okay, little man, Daddy's got you. Shh, shh." I could almost feel his tiny ear on my lips as I whispered.

But I tried not to not let my mind wander in that direction too often. Thoughts of my lost family always got me down. The challenge was to keep everyone alive and together. If nobody did anything stupid, we'd be okay. Just keep focused and do what we can here and now for our group. I'd worry about Alex and Pam when I knew more about them. It made no sense to worry myself sick about their welfare, knowing absolutely nothing about their circumstances.

If we were placed in a remote corner of the world, where could we possibly be? There were large tracts of wild lands in Alaska and perhaps some areas out west, but the vegetation didn't fit. Of course, there were vast unoccupied areas in

Siberia too, which supported the communist conspiracy explanation of our circumstances that some of us advocated. But I didn't know much about the vegetation of Siberian forests. In fact, the hardwood forests that surrounded us were not much different from those with which I grew up in Indiana. It seemed a little hotter than back home. If I had to guess, I'd say we were in Kentucky or Tennessee. But I wasn't sure.

Wherever we were, the news that there were no villages or towns to be seen anywhere was demoralizing. And, as I had feared would happen, the emotional stability of our group threatened to unravel.

The day after Cook's return, I took my regular morning dip in the river and went to retrieve Dillon from his cabin. He and I headed over to our practice range near the river and shot arrows at the various targets we had set about. After a while, I picked up one of the oft-used arrows and noticed its metal point had broken off.

"Our arrows are taking a beating," I said.

"Yeah," said Dillon, studying his arrows. "These weren't designed for target practice. It strains them every time we pull them out of the wood."

"At least I don't have that problem as often as you."

I sniffed the air and detected no smell of wood smoke. "I wonder if breakfast is ready. I'm getting pretty hungry."

"I don't smell anything cooking," replied Dillon.

"Hi, guys," said a friendly voice. We turned to see Cindy walking up. "Getting any better?"

"Well, we can hit our target at least fifty percent of the time," said Dillon.

"Yes," I added, "if we stand close enough to it. I doubt our prey will cooperate, though."

"That's encouraging," she said. Then her smile disappeared and she looked down at the ground. "I thought I would tell you, Charles, since you seem to be our de facto leader...when I brought vegetables and fruit to the kitchen just now, there was no one there cooking anything. No one has even started the fire."

"What!" I exclaimed. "You're kidding me."

"Great," said Dillon.

"Goddammit," I said, throwing my bow to the ground. "Here Dillon and I get up every morning at the crack of dawn, trying to learn how to bring in game, you're up collecting food from the garden, and Eileen and Harvey can't get out of bed. We've got to be a team."

I stomped off in the direction of the cabins. As I walked, I began practicing what I was going to say. I had to keep them up, moving, doing their thing, making their contribution or we wouldn't survive. *Not one of us can make it out here alone! We all have to pull together! We can't slack off or give up!*

Cindy followed behind as I headed toward Eileen's cabin.

"We've all got to do our part," I muttered, more to myself than Cindy.

"I know that," said Cindy, hurrying to keep up with my agitated pace.

"And it's not like they have to do everything. We bring the food, Sasha and Amber clean up, Veronica brings the firewood, and Eileen and Harvey cook the food."

"But look," said Cindy, "don't be too hard on them. Eileen is pretty upset. She misses her family."

I stopped and turned toward her.

"Of course she's upset!" I said loudly. "We all are. I think about Alex every single minute of every day. I don't know where he is or if he's even alive. But I'll never find out if we all die because some of us aren't doing their job."

I turned to continue my march toward Eileen's cabin, but realized I had just vented my angst on Cindy. I stopped and looked at my feet.

"I'm sorry for yelling at you, Cindy. This isn't your fault."

"It's okay," she said. "But try to calm down before talking to Eileen. It might help."

I nodded. When I reached the door of Eileen's cabin, I took a few slow breaths before knocking. "Hello. Eileen? What's going on? Everyone is expecting breakfast."

There was no reply.

"Eileen!"

Still hearing nothing, I walked around to the window of the cabin and pulled the wooden shutters open. Eileen was lying on her bed. I could see her body was convulsing.

"Eileen. What's wrong?"

"Go away!" she cried. "Leave me alone."

"C'mon, Eileen. We need you. You are a part of this."

"I can't help it," she replied, her voice broken with sobs. "I can't. We're alone and abandoned in this fucking place, and there is no one anywhere. Who knows where my children are? Probably dead. I don't care about breakfast."

I looked at Cindy. "She's very upset."

"Plus, I need my meds," added Eileen. "I need my fucking meds."

"What meds?" I asked. "Are you sick?"

"My anti-depressants! I take anti-depressants—or I did, until this happened."

Cindy tapped my arm. "I'll get the fire going. You check on

48

Harvey."

I turned back toward Eileen. "It's okay. Just take the morning off. We'll get breakfast."

She said nothing.

I trod across the small footbridge over the creek, walked up to Harvey's cabin, and knocked.

"Who is it?" a voice said.

"Harvey. What's going on, man? You and Eileen are supposed to be making breakfast."

"She doesn't want to do it."

"So she told us. But why are you still here?"

"I don't want to do it, either. Not by myself. I just..."

"May I come in?"

Harvey opened the door and sat back down on the bed. He was shirtless and there were dark circles under his eyes. I noticed scratches and blood-red patches on his torso. Harvey was tall and thin, with a prominent, jutting jaw which made his head seem too large, especially without a shirt on. Somehow, he always kept his hair neatly brushed, despite our living conditions.

"Are you okay?" I asked searching his eyes.

He shrugged. "I'm not sick or anything," he said. "I just don't feel like doing it today."

I sat down on a chair and rubbed my forehead. I felt tense, angry, and hot. I needed to calm down before I spoke. You can't will someone to feel better about their situation. I'd supposed depression would eventually start to settle in, but didn't know when. Guess it was today.

"Look," I said, "this life is hard, but we've got to eat. We've all got to do our part until we find our way out of here."

"Or until they come get us," said Harvey. He sighed lay back on his bed. "Where in the fuck can we be? Cook climbed those hills, but found nothing. No people. No buildings. No roads. Where could we be that's like that? Even in national parks, you can see signs of other people."

"I don't know," I replied. "There are large areas of uninhabited land in various places."

"Where? Fucking Alaska? A bit too warm, isn't it?"

I shrugged my shoulders. "I don't know where we are."

"I want to show you something." He pulled up his pants leg and revealed large clusters of bleeding weals and red bites covering his entire lower leg. "And this is only one leg!"

Then he jumped up and pointed to his torso. "Look at this! And this!" he demanded and turned. His back was also covered in angry-looking marks. A number of spots were bleeding.

"Goddammit, man! What've you been doing?" I asked incredulously.

"I've been rubbing up against the wall all night because I can't sleep for all the fucking itching. We're doomed! We're stuck here until we die!" He turned to face the wall so I wouldn't see him cry. His shoulders shook a couple of times, and he put his hand to his face. I thought about giving him a hug but wasn't sure if I should. So I put a hand on his shoulder instead.

"Harvey, I understand what you are feeling. I'm covered in bites, too! Everyone is. It sucks. But we have got to do our jobs, or we're in danger."

Harvey said nothing for a moment. "I know," he said finally, looking at the floor. He looked miserable.

"Sorry. I'm fine." His voice became choked. "Go on. I'll be out in a minute to start the fire." He sniffed.

I kneaded my forehead. "No. Just hang loose this morning. We'll get breakfast."

Harvey nodded. "Thanks."

I made my way to the outdoor kitchen. Dillon and Cindy had already gotten the fire going. A few others were standing around.

"Harvey's not feeling well," I said. "He's covered with bites."

"I know how he feels," said Trey. He pulled up his shirt and revealed an array of red marks covering his muscular chest.

"Yeah, they got me, too," said Christie, pulling the waist of her trousers down to reveal her upper hip. It looked like one continuous, swollen bite. "I hardly slept last night."

"I read the Native Americans used to coat their skin with bear fat to keep away insects," said Dillon.

"That sounds gross," said Amber.

"Well, kill us a bear and I'll cut it up and get you some fat," said Christie. "Or bring it here alive, and I'll kill it.." It wasn't hard to see her first butchering job had left her shaken.

"Fat might help," said Missy, who had just walked up. "But it would better to mix in herbal additives. The extracts of some plants repel mosquitoes. But I bet no one here knows which ones to use."

"I remember something," said Christie. "I read... what was it... St. John's wort?"

"No, that's a sleep aid," said Dillon. "I think."

I counted heads and noticed that five of our group were not with us. "Where are the others? Is Michael making cereal?"

"I don't think so," said Missy. "He's still in his cabin."

"Dammit!" I cried, slumping down on the bench. "Why are people doing this? If we fall apart, we're doomed."

"Not everyone is as strong as you," said Christie.

"It's okay," said Cindy, putting her hand on my arm. "It's just hard. They just need time."

I shook my head. "It's hard on all of us. We are all tired and uncertain. We all have bug bites and smell like crap. We all miss our families and our homes. But if we want to see them again, we've got to survive. And that means everyone doing their part."

"Yes. But taking time off doesn't mean they're giving up," said Cindy.

"But it's a matter of principle. What if it becomes a common trend?"

"Don't be such a hard-ass," said Missy.

Veronica stood up. "We won't see them again," she said in her quiet, nervous voice. "Our families. Never again."

Everybody looked at Veronica. It was almost comical how that happened every time she spoke. But what she said often resonated with everyone.

"Don't say that, Veronica," said Missy, gently taking her hand.

"They put us here," she continued. "And here we are, on our own."

"What?" I said. "Who put us here?"

Veronica looked beyond me, into the distance. "Whoever it was that made the noises."

I remembered the clacking noise in the sky and the total loss of communication. And the deep sleep we all took. My stomach tightened.

Chapter 8

Over the next several weeks, people took days off more and more frequently. But I was pleased that others willingly stood in for them. And usually, the person that took the day off would return to their chores the next day. There was no real alternative—sitting in the cabin during the heat of the day was not pleasant. And everyone understood the importance of working together.

But our efforts had become mechanical. There was little conversation or laughter, even when we all gathered around the outdoor banquet table and told stories. Harvey, who was constantly whistling a tune to counter our music-less existence, lost his lilt. We became almost zombie-like as we struggled through each day. The nights were miserable as we sweated on our uncomfortable beds and scratched at the lice that lived in the straw. The hot days were an endless chain of chores and exhaustion.

Despite my constant worry of total collapse, there was a surprising level of cohesion and camaraderie. Even with low spirits, somehow we carried on. If not for ourselves, then for our brothers and sisters in this imposed family.

Rescue aside, I had no idea how to change our march toward despair. For my part, I convinced myself that a hot shower with soap and shampoo would do wonders to lift my spirits. Perhaps it was true. Most of us took a morning dip every day, but the sand at the bottom of the river never completely scraped away body grease. The coarse rubbing did, however, offer gratification for our assortment of insect bites.

Despite having spent several weeks with it, I was still very aware of the beard growth on my face. It felt unnatural and, in the heat and sweat, uncomfortable. I couldn't imagine Samuel being able to forge a blade sharp enough to shave with, so I accepted that I would have it until we got out of here. But I did wonder what I looked like.

We had no mirrors laying around, so I filled a clay pot with water and sat it out in the sun. I was standing over it trying to see my reflection when Michael walked up.

He snorted a chuckle. "Don't worry, dude. You're looking good."

I looked up at him rather sheepishly. "Just curious what I looked like these days. Remember when we could walk into a bathroom and see our face?"

"Oh God, there are some many things I miss," Michael replied, his face brightening with the memories. "Hot showers, clean sheets, rock and roll. And I had so many friends on Facebook. I mean, you guys are cool and all…"

Michael had struck me as introvert lacking in confidence, so it was easy for me to imagine most of his relationships being through the computer. He was short and thin, and I wondered if he were gay. It would have worked out if he was, since Harvey wasn't shy about sharing his sexual preference. But there didn't seem to be anything going between them.

"I'm sure your friends back home weren't as old as us," I said.

Michael shrugged. "Some were, I guess. This guy that played Fortnite with us was in his seventies."

"Fortnite?"

"It's an online video game."

"Any girlfriends back home?" I ventured.

"I know you all think I'm gay, but I'm not. I just...I don't know. I like women, but I don't really understand them yet."

"Ha! Good luck with that! But seriously, just ask me if you want to know anything."

"Well, I'm not that impressed by your knowledge so far. Keep taking your time and Samuel will beat you to it."

"Beat me to what?"

Michael's eyes opened wide and he looked down at his feet. "Sorry, nothing. Better go. Gotta help Harvey clean out the storage bins."

Michael quickly walked off, and I gazed after him, having no clue what he was talking about.

The next morning I came across Amber squatting by a clay embankment near the river. She was scooping up handfuls of clay and forming cups, some of which were scattered around her. She was also stark naked.

Our buckskins quickly became sweaty and filthy. We tried rinsing them out frequently, but they became slimy when wet.And since we had no other options, we had to wear them that way. Apparently Amber felt differently.

"Um, hi Amber."

She looked up at me and smiled, but continued her work. She made no mention of her lack of apparel.

"Your buckskins must be drying." I said.

"Yeah, sorry. They get so gross when they're wet. I'd rather just not wear them."

Amber's brazen attitude concerned me. As the days passed, we would be tested to keep our individual dignity intact. Our rugged lifestyle in the wild boosted my libido, and I figured the same applied to the other men in the group. So far, we had all been respectful of the women. The uncertainly of our situation and our immediate focus on survival no doubt helped with that, since we were all distracted. That would change. Isolation in the forest and long stretches of boredom could tempt some of us to cross a line. I didn't want that to happen.

I sat down on the river bank next to her. "Amber, what I am about to say may sound mean, but it's for your own good. Please wear your clothes even when they are wet."

Amber flung down a glob of sticky clay onto a pile she was forming, rinsed her hand in the river water, and turned her attention to me.

"Why? Do you think I'm gross?"

"I don't think you're gross. You are an attractive young woman. But that is exactly the problem. We are on the edge of survival here. We want everyone to keep treating everyone else with respect. If you walk around like this, you make it more difficult for us men to, you know, behave."

Amber bit her lower lip. "Let me get this right. You want me to keep wearing those nasty wet buckskins so that one of you dudes don't get so horny that you try to force yourself on me. Is that right?"

I shrugged. "Yeah, something like that. All of us have gone without for a long time, so it gets harder to be a gentleman."

Amber shook her head slowly and scooped out more clay. "Okay, I'll put them on. But you should speak for yourself."

"Thank you," I said, but then frowned. "What do you mean

I should speak for myself?"

"Are you clueless, Charles? Cook has been banging Christie and Dillon has been doing Sasha. Trey is getting pretty cozy with Rebecca, and I've got my eye on someone."

This was news to me. I knew special connections were developing between some members of our group, but did they really get that far that fast? As I thought it over, I could see it wouldn't be difficult to find the opportunity. We each had our own cabin, and the compound got pitch dark at night, except for a few feet around the kitchen fire. Not much stealth required.

"I didn't know," I admitted. "Maybe I *am* clueless."

"Well, you had better get in on the action. Everybody knows Cindy is your girl. But don't wait all day."

"What? What do you mean Cindy is my girl? Why do you say that?"

Amber smirked. "Don't be silly, Charles." She stood up and put her hands on her hips. She apparently possessed not one modicum of modesty. "Well, I'd better put on my nasty buckskins. See ya, Charles."

My exchange with Amber left me wondering how qualified I was to be a leader of our group. And was there a connection with Michael's comment yesterday about not understanding women? *God, what I am doing in charge?*

And now I had to worry about someone getting pregnant, along with everything else. So far, no one had gotten really sick—just headaches and nausea. But it was a matter of time before somebody came down with something serious or was badly injured. And with no medicine and no real knowledge of herbal remedies, it was a disaster waiting to happen. Moreover, we were using up our food supplies at an unsustainable pace, and though Dillon and I spent every day attempting to shoot game with our arrows, our success rate was poor. The problem was that our handmade bows generated relatively low arrow velocity.

I was ready to acknowledge there were bright spots and isolated successes. Ramiro, our calming story-teller, often perched on rocks jutting out into the river. It gave me pleasure to watch him staring at the water with a spear in his steady hand, only to unleash it in an instant of fierce motion. And it was not unusual for him to hit his target. We all looked forward to having fresh fish with our meals.

And because our diet was so lean and we worked nonstop, we'd all trimmed down considerably and had become super fit. Perhaps that was why we had kept illness at bay so far.

Christie insisted on keeping her animal responsibilities, even butchering the hogs. But I assigned Sasha to help and hopefully give Christie a little emotional support. The two of them still had no idea what they were doing, but they followed Dillon's suggestions and on their next attempt clubbed a pig while it hung from its hind feet. And since they bled it before cutting it up into pieces, the whole affair was less messy.

"Nice work, Christie," I said, surveying her stack of relatively blood-free pig parts. "A big improvement."

Christie was rinsing her hands in a clay vessel. "Yeah. A little knowledge can go a long way."

"Sorry if you thought I was hard on you last time. I just—"

"Don't worry about it Charles," said Christie, cutting me off. "I know what you're trying to do. It's a hard life we are living, and we have got to push our personal envelopes. Else we won't make it."

"Yeah, that's kinda what—"

"But you were still a dick about it. I wanted to do my job, but I take care of the animals because I like them. You could have given the butchering to somebody else."

"I can see that now. Do you want me to assign that job to someone else?"

"Nah. I'm okay now. But still…"

"Um, do you mind cutting off all the fat and piling it up? We are going to make soap with it."

Christie threw her hands in the air. "I just cleaned up, but okay. I gotta do my job."

I helped Christie gather all the pig fat, dumped it into a clay vessel, and took it to Rebecca. She looked at the pile of white goop with a disgusted expression.

"Have you heard of rendering fat?" I asked.

"Nope."

"You just cook it for a long time, and the tallow will separate out. It will be reasonably clean, and you can use it for soap and candles. You can use deer fat, too."

"Really?" she said, suddenly interested.

"But to make soap, you have to mix in lye. I know how you can make lye, but I don't know anything about how much to use. You will have to figure that out yourself."

I described to her a demonstration I had observed during a Saturday visit to a reconstructed colonial village, where an old bearded gentleman had poured water over oak ashes. What leached through he called lye. I suggested she make a large vessel out of clay with holes in the bottom, put oak ashes in the vessel, and pour water over it. She would then mix the liquid that leached out with the tallow and form little squares from the mixture.

"And voila, you have soap," I said. "Hopefully."

I put Amber to work with Rebecca. To my relief, they managed to put their cattiness aside and worked hard over the next few days, breaking out in insult-laced tirades only occasionally. They fashioned a vessel out of clay and rendered the fat, which was softer than I had expected.

"That's just lard," said Missy, rubbing it between her fingers. "That's what you get from pigs. You can get tallow from deer fat. It has a different consistency."

"How do you know that?" I asked.

Missy shrugged. "I read it somewhere."

"Well, can we make soap with lard?" asked Rebecca.

"I can't say," replied Missy.

Rebecca mixed the lye with the lard, and the final product wasn't pleasant. It didn't lather like normal soap. But it did cleanse. In fact, Rebecca had to be careful not to add too much lye, or it would clean too well, irritating one's skin.

Veronica was responsible for the constant chore of collecting firewood, which she did well. I worried about her wandering in the nearby woods, but we hadn't heard the howling of wolves for a while, and she seemed able to take care of herself. I insisted that she take a spear with her, so she tied a strap to it and slung it over her shoulder, enabling her to keep her hands free for picking up and holding bundles of wood.

While we all appreciated our fires, Veronica's most significant find in the forest was a beehive. Wandering the woods, she had noticed bees, especially in the area behind the orchard. She took it upon herself to follow them and discovered the hive in a hollowed-out tree trunk. After numerous stings, we used a smoky fire at the base of the tree to calm the bees enough to cut out several sizable combs. We were keen to not destroy the hive, so we left plenty of it intact, but having honey in our lives, not to mention beeswax for candles, made a significant impact in our dull lives. It not only improved our diet but, somehow, even our moods. Everyone seemed more hopeful and happy since finding the honey. It was our one real sweet spot of the day, and quite the treasure, given we hadn't had coffee, tea, sugar, spices, real salt, or pepper in weeks. No milk or cream, no butter, or cheese. How we had taken so many things for granted before our time in the wild!

However, we did have an ample supply of wheat and corn, which grew in the adjacent fields and were stored in the small storage silos. We weren't sure of the best way to use the wheat, and tried several approaches. Sasha found a large, flat stone near the river bank and set it in the work area, between the storage bins and the meeting house. The stone had a shallow dip in its center, and if one placed a handful of grain kernels on it, and rubbed them with another stone, it broke the grain hulls open. Once we removed most of the chaff, the grain could then be cooked in water to make a kind of gruel. As a breakfast, it was filling, though tasteless. Our recently-acquired stash of honey brightened it up, but we had to be very conservative with its use. There wasn't much to go around.

If we continued to grind the grains even after the kernels had broken open and chaff removed, we would make flour. It was a time-consuming and labor-intensive task, and bits of stone often made their way into the flour, but we used it in an assortment of ways. Eileen would mix water and lard with the flour to make a kind of hard biscuit. Sasha experimented with tortillas, which she toasted on a hot rock. These options were sometimes acceptable, but we all craved decent bread.

But without yeast to leaven the dough, we knew of no way to make it.

Our little successes were gratifying. Everything we ate or used, we had taken directly from nature and fashioned ourselves. I sensed our confidence growing, counterbalancing, to a degree, our sagging morale.

When we gathered and talked among ourselves about things we missed about our past lives, I noticed the tone of our discussion went in one of two directions. Either we reminisced pleasantly about the way things were and wished we hadn't taken them for granted, or we became angry and resentful about our predicament.

Personally, I preferred anger over nostalgia, but tried to keep it on the down low; there was no need to bring down the others. I felt responsible for these people. I was getting to know each person individually, and we were a good group, on the whole. We'd become a family, and I was its father, for lack of a better term.

But the responsibility was a burden. It was stressful always worrying about our little family, to keep up with so many people. I knew winter and disease were coming, and I didn't like the thought of these people suffering. I would rather be hurt than let one of them get hurt. Well, maybe not Samuel, but most of the group. They were a good bunch. If we kept it together, we just might make it—though what "make it" meant was not entirely clear, other than just staying alive.

Was what we had at this moment all we would ever have? Had our normal, modern lives just disappeared? Were large, successful, cities just gone? Millions and millions of people—*poof*? Surely, they were somewhere. Beyond the horizon, maybe. Or beyond the next river bend. Otherwise, who would be capable of such a monumental feat? Capable of eliminating whole nations, and wiping them off the face of the Earth? That would be impossible, right? I looked to the skies and pondered.

I was not a particularly religious person, but some members of our community wondered if we were suffering from God's wrath. That a vengeful God was exercising his judgment by destroying civilization. But then why were we selected to survive? Or me in particular? I wasn't all that good. Or maybe this was hell, and that was why we were placed here. Had we died and now had to serve our time? I was starting to sound crazy, even to myself.

Ponder later, Charles. Back to surviving another day.

One evening, after I had discussed our situation with Cook for several hours, I asked everyone to hang around the kitchen area after our dinner so I could make a few announcements. We sat around the fire and listened to the sounds of the forest, which were no longer as threatening as when we first arrived. The meal, fried catfish with tomatoes and hard biscuits, went down pleasantly, and there was a slight coolness to the air. I felt a comfortable sense of camaraderie as we sat there waiting.

I was about to speak when Christie broke the silence. As she stood up, it dawned on me how much thinner she was now, especially her face. She looked wholesome and youthful. Looking around and smiling, she said, "As difficult as our situation can be, there are moments that aren't so bad. Moments like this, hanging out with you guys. It's…different."

"It's different all right," said Amber. "I stink to high heaven, and I itch in places I'd be embarrassed to mention."

"I'll attest to that," sniffed Rebecca, who was sitting next to

Amber.

"Rebecca, be nice," said Christie, glowering at the younger woman.

"I see what Christie is saying," said Samuel. "It's strange how God works sometimes. I've felt things here that I wouldn't have thought mattered before. Like the satisfaction of figuring out how to live on our own, to do the work and to sit here with others who did the work with you. To be under the stars in the fresh air while the fire crackles. It's just different."

Samuel had always struck me as an aggressive bully with little subtlety, so it was a surprise to hear these words coming from him. Maybe he wasn't such a bad guy after all. Who knew what his life was like before? Maybe he was just misunderstood and stressed because of our situation. It wouldn't hurt to try to lighten up on him. Heck, maybe he could show me how he forged arrowheads. I needed to remember to try to engage him, make him feel wanted and needed.

"Well," I said, ready to shift the tone of the conversation. "I didn't ask you to meet with me so we can wax poetic."

"Yeah, that's not what you're about," said Samuel. "So what's on your mind, copier salesman?"

I didn't remember telling Samuel what I used to do for a living, but I figured people talk. It was then that I realized he was sitting next to Cindy. In fact, as I thought about it, he often managed to find a seat next to Cindy. I remembered Michael's vague comment and wondered.

I focused on what I had to say. It was important, and it had to be said in the right way.

"I've been thinking. We all wonder if our presence here has

something to do with the strange events that occurred just before we all went into our coma, or whatever you want to call it. Maybe I'm crazy, but did beings from… somewhere else put us here? And these beings then did something with the towns and their people."

"What do you mean "beings from somewhere else?" asked Harvey.

"I think we all know what I mean. Aliens."

"Aliens!" scoffed Sam. "What a joke. God's vengeance is more like it."

"Our situation is hard to explain," said Christie. "But I'm not sure we should suppose little green men are behind it all."

"Yeah, that's pretty far out there," added Missy.

"You could be right," I replied. "Maybe we were overrun by forces from Russia and we were interred here. Or some terrorist psycho kidnapped all of us and stuck us here just for his amusement. But do these options make more sense?" I waited, letting it lie. If someone had a better conjecture, I wanted to hear it.

"Nothing make sense," offered Eileen.

"So perhaps we shouldn't assume anything until we know more," said Christie.

"Okay," I said, "let's not assume anything. But we have to allow the possibility that there *isn't* anyone else."

"Please don't say that!" gasped Eileen.

"Look, I don't know that for sure. I may be wrong. But what I am saying is that for whatever reason, we have to allow that possibility. And that we were placed here by… whoever. And that… well…" My words suddenly started sounding like they were coming from somewhere else, and I was hearing them for the first time. I felt weak, sick.

I forced myself to stand up. What came out was a hoarse whisper that seared my throat with every word. "We have to accept the possibility that there is nowhere else to go. That there are no towns and no authorities who will come to our rescue. That all we have is what lies before us."

Eileen began sobbing. She crossed her arms on the table and lay her head down.

"Of course, it's possible," said Missy.

"But there's no need to upset everybody," added Samuel. He was pacing and rubbing his neck. "Surely there's another explanation and someone will come for us soon." I couldn't tell from his tone if he really believed it. I suspected he didn't.

I caught Dillon's gaze. He was a young man, with tears in his eyes. He reminded me of an innocent, scared little boy. He was our best hunter, but he counted on me. I couldn't let him down. I felt more gazes upon me. I found Cook's eyes. I believed he looked up to me too, and he didn't need anything to sap his confidence.

"Charles, what is all this leading to?" asked Christie as she placed a hand on Eileen's shoulders in an effort to console the distraught mother.

I gathered my thoughts. What did I want to say? What did they need to consider? And how would we get through whatever this was? *Focus, Charles. Stand up and get yourself together for them. This is now, and this is real life.*

I stood up. I felt stronger. I took a deep breath, and my voice once again sounded normal.

"My point is that the way we live now is not sustainable. If we are to be prepared to live through the winter and next year, and the year after that, we have to learn to make warm clothes. We have to set aside some of the grain to use for planting next year's harvest and collect seeds from the garden plants for next year. We have to be careful about slaughtering our animals, to make sure there are enough to breed. We need to assume food will be scarce in the cold months. What I am saying is, we need to proceed as if we will be here indefinitely and start planning ahead, not just living for the moment."

"I don't know why you like this place so much," said Michael, wiping his face hard and slinging tears and snot onto the ground. "Well, I'm not giving up! There's no way we'll find out who's around unless we keep looking for them. And I mean further than Cook can hike in a few days. Right, Trey?"

"Yeah," said Trey, scratching at his clay dish. "Michael and I have been talking, and we believe we should build rafts. We could use them to explore downriver."

"I mean, why stay here?" asked Michael.

"Okay," I said. "That does sound good. Let's get the hell out of here and use the river as our escape. But maybe we can prepare for winter while we work on our escape. How 'bout that? You two can be in charge of building rafts. Fell some logs and figure out some way to lash them together. And maybe some pine pitch to seal it."

"Yeah, we'll do it," said Trey. "If someone is out there, we'll find them. And you all can get us prepared just in case."

This was a good sign. Interest, optimism, initiative. There were a few things to point out, though. "Keep something in mind. We know we can survive here. But if we go downstream, we have to be careful how far we go. We would have to camp every night, and the further downstream we go, the harder it would be to return if we find no one."

"Even if aliens killed everybody, there's got to be at least abandoned towns," said Trey.

"Well, unless we were moved to some remote location," I observed. "And remember, we don't know how long we were asleep. It could have been years. Who knows what's left?"

"But why would someone do that?" Eileen asked, her voice pleading. "What would be the point?"

"I don't know what the point would be," I replied. "I just know that it's possible that there is nothing left."

Cook stood, and I looked at him with interest. If Cook spoke up, what he said was worth listening to.

"Has anybody read *Undaunted Courage*?" he asked. "The book about the Lewis and Clark expedition?"

"I read it," said Dillon.

"They began their journey going *up* the Missouri river, not downstream. They used rafts and long poles to push themselves against the current. I propose we do the same thing. We go upstream. It would be hard work and our progress would be slow, but the benefit is that if we run out of food or our strength gives out, we can use the current to take us back here."

"Right. That makes sense," I said thoughtfully. I was starting to feel a plan coming together. *Attack this problem from both angles. Prepare and search.*

Cook turned to Trey. "So you guys making the rafts should keep that in mind. Keep them light. Don't worry about a cabin or gunnels or anything fancy. Just enough logs attached to one another to keep someone afloat."

"Okay," said Trey.

"What's a gunnel?" asked Michael.

"Gunnels are the sides of the boat that stick up above the deck," said Cook.

"We should absolutely do this," I said. "It would be great to get the hell out of here. But it changes nothing. It may or may not work, but we can't assume it will. Winter is coming, so we must be prepared."

"Okay, big boy," said Missy, smiling at me. "That means you and Dillon have to get better at killing Bambi. We need more buckskins to make warm clothes."

"Yep," said Dillon.

"Plus we could use the smokehouse to preserve the deer meat," I said. "These woods are full of food. We need to harvest it and put up as much as we can. This winter will test us. As miserable as we have been, this has been the easy season. The true hard times are a-coming."

Dillon slapped hard at his neck. "Well, at least colder weather will get rid of these damn mosquitoes."

"Ooh," said Amber, "imagine sleeping with a crisp chill in the air. Doesn't that sound wonderful?"

* * *

Early the next morning, I forsook target practice and took a walk upriver through the woods, just far enough from the river bank to avoid the thick growth that clogged it. I hoped to surprise a deer in the early morning light. I spotted several possibilities, but stalking a deer was a different proposition from hunting while sitting on a tree limb near our salt lick. The challenge was to get close enough for any of them to be a reasonable target.

I thought about the evening before. I don't know where all my emotion had come from, but it was almost scary it was so physical. I'd never felt anything like it. But I think it helped matters, in a way. Others seemed to come to my aid for a change and helped prop me up for a time. I had been both physically and emotionally drained, but now, after a night's sleep, my head felt clearer and I felt more confident about whatever our future held.

It wasn't my lucky morning, not getting off a single shot. On my walk back to my cabin, I spotted Missy in the garden. She was on her hands and knees, pulling out weeds by hand.

"Did you lose your contact lens?" I asked.

Missy shaded her eyes and looked up at me. "Smart-ass," she replied. "Why don't you get down here and help?"

I laid my bow and quiver on the ground and knelt beside her, half-heartedly pulling at a few weeds.

"Some of these are hard to pull out," I said, in mock exasperation.

"Wimp. Use your muscles."

"Whew! I need a break." I looked around the garden. The carrots and cucumbers were looking full. The tomatoes were down to green fruits, and not too many of them. "The garden looks great," I added. "You and Cindy do a good job caring for it."

"We do our best," she said. She didn't pause in her weed-pulling.

"Have the two of you come up with a plan for storing seeds for next year?"

Missy shrugged. "We'll figure it out, don't worry."

"It's kind of important," I added.

Missy stopped her weeding and looked at me sympathetically. "Do you ever stop worrying?"

"Sorry," I said. "I can't help it. Alex calls me an old lady. That's my son."

"I know Alex is your son. You've mentioned him a time or two."

I nodded. "He's quite a character. Spends hours on his

Xbox, yet still makes good grades. He's gonna be a good one."
I looked up at the sky. *If he still exists,* I thought to myself.
Okay, Charles. Don't think about it.

"We gotta believe our families will be fine," said Missy.
"I have two grandchildren in Des Moines and another in
Springfield. All young."

"We gotta believe," I repeated, standing up. I shook it off
and smiled at her. "Well, I'd better carry these deer carcasses
back to the village."

"Yeah," she said, smiling at my joke. "They look pretty
heavy."

"I'll see you at breakfast. Should be ready soon."

"Well, we can all hope," replied Missy. "Unless folks are
taking the day off again."

As I strode toward our cluster of cabins, I spotted Cindy
and Samuel sitting on the river bank, engaged in animated
conversation. I felt a heavy stab in my stomach, but I wasn't
sure why. They were having a normal conversation, though
Cindy seemed to be really interested. She glanced up at me
as I walked by and briefly waved, but immediately resumed
her conversation. I didn't like that.

Later that afternoon, I spotted her walking by herself in the
direction of the garden. I ran up to her to join her.

"Hey," I said, somewhat awkwardly. "Where're you headed?"

"Headed to the garden. That's where I work, you know."

"Gotta pull those weeds, huh?"

"Yep, weeds. So...did you want something?"

I shrugged. "Not, not really. Well, maybe. I'm trying to
figure Samuel out. He is such an ass sometimes. But you two
seem to get along pretty well. What do you think about him?"

She smiled at me, but in a way I couldn't quite make out.

"Samuel is complicated. Multiple layers, you know? Some good things, some things not so good."

She abruptly stopped walking and turned toward me, holding her gaze on my eyes. "And I think he has a thing for me." She didn't add anything else, but just stood there, watching.

"Well, that's nice. I guess. What about you? Do you have a thing for him?"

"That's a rather personal question, isn't it Charles? Why do you ask?"

I opened my hands. "Just curious." I felt nervous and uncertain, though I wasn't sure why. "Sorry. I'll let you get to your work."

Cindy let out a sigh. "You do that Charles." She turned and resumed her path to the garden.

Chapter 9

A few days later, several of us were by the river bank examining Trey and Michael's progress with the raft. They had hacked out several logs a few inches in diameter and had lashed them together with layer upon layer of pliable vines.

I tested the rigidity of the raft, and it seemed good. But I worried about how well the vines would hold out after hours in the water, constantly being worked back and forth. Trey and Michael had decided there was no point in making pine pitch, since there was nothing to seal with a log raft.

Dillon stood beside me, looking the rafts over.

"I wonder if there are any patches of big bamboo along the river?" he asked. "They would make a lighter raft."

"Bamboo? Would that hold our weight?"

"You would have to use two layers, but yeah. Bamboo rafts work well."

"Well, you got a log raft for now," said Trey, somewhat peeved. "If you wanted a bamboo raft, that information would have been useful a few days back."

I pursed my lips and looked at Dillon. "You know, Dillon. You have lots of valuable information. But you kinda keep it bottled up sometimes."

Dillon shrugged. "Sorry. It didn't occur to me."

"Anyway, this one will work well. Good work, guys."

Dillon and I left the two of them working on the raft—they still needed to find and cut suitable steering poles—and headed back to the cabin area and our daily chores. We had just passed the meeting house when Christie screamed. She and Rebecca came running toward me, their eyes wide.

"A bear!" cried Rebecca. "There's a bear!"

They stopped and pointed behind them. I saw the black beast in our open work area, about fifty yards away.

"Shit!" I said, watching it closely. "At least it's not chasing you."

"I killed a pig this morning, and hung it up to bleed," said Christie. "It's eating it."

Ever since my speech about thinking long-term, Christie had become careful not to over-harvest our swine. Fresh pork was a rare treat. Everybody preferred it to the salted version, or even fresh rabbit or deer. I wasn't happy about our dinner being snatched away from us.

"What do you think?" I asked Dillon. "Should we let it take our pig and hope it will go away when it's had his fill?"

He shook his head. "Not a good idea. It seems to have lost its fear of humans. More than losing the meat, we have to worry about the bear seeing our camp as a viable food source. If it surprises one of us at night, it would get ugly."

Several of the others heard the commotion and gathered around us. We stood watching the bear consume the pig.

"Dillon's right," I said. "Everybody go grab a spear, bow and arrow, or something to use as a weapon. We have to take action."

"What!" said Samuel. "You want to get somebody killed? Leave it alone and eventually it'll wander off."

Damn. I wished that guy would just cooperate without questioning everything for once.

"No, Samuel," I said. "In fact, I'm trying to prevent someone from getting killed later. Just trust me and go grab spears."

"They're stacked behind the workshop," replied Samuel. "Do you expect me to just walk by the bear to get them?"

"We have to find whatever we can. A bow and arrow. A stick. Whatever. And fast."

Samuel shook his head with an air of skepticism and ambled off. So did the others. I dashed inside my cabin and retrieved my newly-strung bow and several arrows and stepped back outside.

Though the bear was still engaged in its dinner, it would occasionally pause to watch what we were doing. But it did not advance.

The others soon returned.

"Look, everybody, Dillon is right. We must discourage wild animals from coming around here, or they will become a danger. So we've got to scare this guy off."

"Phew," said Missy. "For a moment there I thought you wanted us to attack it."

"No, no. We can't risk engaging a full-grown bear, certainly not here with everyone around. And with these pitiful weapons. If we wound it, which is the most likely scenario, it may attack."

"What do you propose?" asked Cook. He was holding a sturdy stick in one hand and an iron blade in the other.

"Let's spread out into a semi-circle and approach the bear as a group. Everybody yell and make a lot of racket. If it sees all of us approaching, that should scare it off."

"If you say so, boss," said Samuel.

"It should work," said Dillon. "There are enough of us to discourage him from fighting back. But don't run once we have the bear's attention. If you do, it might trigger its predator instinct, and it'll chase you."

"Its predator instinct? Nice," said Harvey.

"I can't do this," said Rebecca. "I'm scared."

"I'm scared, too," said Amber.

"We need you," I said. "We need both of you. Only if we have enough people can we ensure the bear will run and everyone will be safe."

"You can do it, Rebecca," said Christie. "We'll all be together."

Rebecca exhaled. "Okay."

"And you, Amber?" I asked.

She lowered her head and gave a brief nod. Once Rebecca had committed, Amber had to follow suit.

"Okay, let's spread out."

We fanned out into a semi-circle formation and walked toward the work area, where the bear was still eating.

"All right, everybody start yelling and hitting things and moving your arms."

We started our racket and slowly approached the bear. It stopped what it was doing and stared at us.

We came closer. I heard the bear making huffing sounds. It looked toward the woods. I thought our plan was working and that it was preparing to dart into the brush, but then it turned back and huffed more.

"Keep coming!" I yelled. "Slowly but surely."

We were now about thirty yards away and still approaching. We were moving slowly, but I had no problem with that. No need to rush things.

Suddenly, the bear stood up on its hind legs and raised its

front paws, growling at us. Its lips curled as he growled. Red blood covered his face.

"That's a big bear," Dillon whispered.

"Oh, God!" Amber cried. She backed away.

"Don't run," I called to her.

Amber was trembling and her eyes were wide. I feared she would bolt at any moment.

"You big baby," yelled Rebecca.

At Rebecca's chiding, Amber's demeanor changed. She scowled at Rebecca. "Screw you, bitch," she replied. Then her voice took on a different tone, and she started hurling curses and nonsensical expletives toward the bear. "I hate your stupid woods you stupid son-of-a-bitch. Take it! You can have it! Go back to it!" Then she threw the stick she was holding toward the bear. It sailed just over its head and to its left. The bear flinched away and huffed some more.

"Oh shit!" said Dillon. "Don't piss it off!"

"I'm pissed off, stupid fucker! Go! Get out!" she screamed at the bear again, her voice increasing in volume and force. She picked up a handful of small stones and threw them. "You can have that stupid fucking pig too, but you can't have us. We're humans and we rule!" She was screeching now and almost sobbing.

Following her lead, we all got louder and louder.

"Yeah!" I cried, feeling swept away with energy, fear, and adrenalin. "Louder, Amber!" And Amber kept yelling all kinds of things. She was yelling about Rebecca, about the bear, about the bugs, the heat, the fear, the confusion, all of it. Others started yelling obscenities at the bear, too, as we closed in, as loud and ferocious and angry as we could sound.

We were now about twenty yards away. The bear lowered

itself to all fours, huffed again, and charged.

We froze, staring in horror. Had we, at that moment, broken and run, the outcome could have been different. As it was, before we had the chance to react, the bear halted its charge, turned, and began walking toward the woods.

The bear's aggressive gesture had been a bluff. Thank God!

"It's leaving," I cried. "It worked." My heart was beating out of my chest; I was going to faint or cry or laugh! Relief surged through me. *Thank God, no one got hurt. We're all okay.*

I finally allowed myself to breathe and surveyed our group. Some of us were laughing, some of us still cursing, some of us crying. I'm sure all of our hearts were pounding. Amber looked incredulous, as if she didn't know where her energy and passion had come from.

"Whew, that was fucking close, people. Too close," I said, my body relaxing.

"Holy shit! I'm glad that charge was a bluff," said Cindy.

"It happened so fast," said Cook.

"Yeah," said Dillon. "No time to draw back my bow."

"Wow." Missy shook her head. "That could easily have turned out different."

"Yeah, but it didn't," I said. "We stuck together and we prevailed. Good job, everyone, especially you, Amber. You saved our asses!" I wrapped my right arm around her in a quick and casual embrace. "Feel better? Think you needed that, didn't ya, girl?" I whispered and kissed the top of her head.

"Maybe," she whispered. "But I think I need to go to my cabin now. I don't feel so great." She made for her cabin, walking quickly.

"Thank the good Lord," said Samuel, looking at the sky.

"Did we scare it away for good?" asked Rebecca.

I shrugged. "Who knows? But for a while, we had better keep on our guard when bleeding carcasses, or butchering them, for that matter. What'd you think Dillon, Cook?"

"Your guess is as good as mine," said Cook.

"I doubt it'd come back for more," said Dillon. "And we know what to do the next time, but yeah, I'd try to keep the blood to a minimum."

Most of us hung around talking about the incident for quite a while. No one seemed ready to do much else. I noticed Cindy was somewhat quiet, and she headed toward the cabins.

As she walked away, I pondered my growing interest in her. I felt guilty about it, but Pam seemed so far away. And it had dawned on me that I thought much more often of Alex than I did Pam. Of course, I worried about what had happened to her, but I hardly missed her. And I found myself wondering if I ever loved her.

There had been times during our marriage that I doubted we were going to make it. Pam and Alex were like oil and water. They misunderstood and triggered one another, and I had grown weary of the daily drama. And now, it seemed difficult for me to imagine continuing my future with Pam, even if we got back to our former lives.

I decided to catch up with Cindy to make sure she was all right. "Hey," I said, running up beside her and matching her stride. "You okay?"

She turned toward me and slowed her walk, tilting her head toward me. "You know, we've got to stop meeting like this." She had a smirk on her lips and her brown eyes were bright. "No, I'm fine. Just a little shaken."

"Yeah, me too."

"But you can protect me from the bear if you want." She hooked her arm into mine and we strolled toward her cabin. Her full hips swayed awfully close to mine as we walked. And I found myself wondering how great her marriage had been. *Should I ask? No, better not.*

I contemplated how short the walk was to the cabins. I'd have rather it went on a while.

Chapter 10

It took a while for the effects of our encounter with the bear to wear off. We became much more careful at night, most of us staying near the fire until we shut ourselves up in our cabins. But it seemed the incident had a subtle positive effect on our group. Something to do with the fact that all of us had come together as a unit and overcome a formidable threat. In our conversations over meals, we referred to the experience frequently, often with a shared air of satisfaction.

It was as though we had experienced a cathartic release as a group. True, it was Amber that had really given voice to our catharsis, and her outcry was driven in part by the dynamic between her and Rebecca. It was as if the bear represented whoever or whatever was behind our being here, and Amber's anger reflected all our shared anger.

The scare was the most concrete example of the growing change among our group. We had many opportunities to confront the challenges of our situation and had usually overcame them. It continued to be a slog to get through each day, but the sense that we were up to the task had an effect. Our family was growing stronger, despite our petty squabbles and emotional struggles.

Still, the weight of not knowing where we were, or why we

were here, continued to be a constant burden. We hoped that our planned excursion upriver would answer some of our questions. Yet I recognized that if Cook hadn't seen anything from his hilltop observation point, the chances weren't great that the expedition would see anything different on the banks of the river. I kept my negative thoughts to myself, however. I preferred that everyone believe I had just as much hope in finding someone as the next person. The truth was that with every long, hot, tiring day, I became more certain that this wilderness was our new home, and our new way of life. I was losing hope that I would ever see Alex again, or return to my old life.

In planning the river expedition, I decided I didn't want more than a few of us to be put at risk on the journey—besides, we wanted the raft to be small and light to keep it manageable as the crew pushed it upstream against the current. As our official explorer, Cook was the natural choice to lead the group. We selected Trey, too, because he had helped build the raft and was strong as an ox. And Missy. She was light, but strong in body and in mind. Besides, she wanted desperately to go on the adventure, and she was not a force to be denied easily. Missy reminded me so much of my Aunt Helen, feisty but gentle and caring too—both women had a lot of moxie. Missy had become one of my favorites.

Eileen and Rebecca had been experimenting with making pemmican, which Cook had described vaguely. It consisted of rendered tallow or lard mixed with meat, berries, and an assortment of other food items. Some recipes worked and some didn't, but they came up with a version that was edible and reasonably stable.

We gathered a sizeable stash of other provisions—apples,

bacon, a buckskin bag full of grain, and an assortment of vegetables from the garden, parceled it all together, and lashed it onto the logs of the raft. At least they wouldn't need to carry water since they could drink from the river.

The entire community stood on the bank of the river as the expedition prepared to set off. Their mission was to go as far upriver as their strength and victuals would allow and then float back downriver to home. And, we hoped, bring with them some news of the world.

Samuel and I stood knee-deep in the water and held the raft in position while the three of them—Cook, Trey, and Missy—climbed aboard.

"It's pretty wobbly," I observed.

"True," said Trey. "It was like that when we tested it. But if we all stay near the center and balance the weight, it's stable enough."

"Well, just be careful," I said, handing them their long poles. "Take no unnecessary risks. We want you back home."

"All right, old lady," said Missy with a wink as they pushed off.

Slowly, we pushed the laden raft out into the middle of the stream. The crew carefully positioned themselves at opposite edges of the raft and pushed upstream with their poles. We stood by the bank and watched them make their way laboriously against the current. The river ran straight for several hundred yards, and since their progress was slow, it was possible to watch their efforts for some time.

An hour later, the raft was still in view; everyone but me had returned to their daily chores. I was still watching and worrying. My biggest fear was that someone would get hurt. Our ability to provide medical care was almost nil, so even if the injured person made it back, we could provide little help.

When the raft disappeared around a distant bend, I felt an uneasiness in the pit in my stomach. Self-doubt taunted me. *What if something happens? I shouldn't have let them go. What if I have to watch one of them suffer or even die?* I felt panic well up.

"They should be okay," said a soft voice behind me. I turned to see Cindy approaching.

"Yeah," I said. "They can always drift back if need be."

"But you're still worried, aren't you? You see them as part of your new family and want to look after them."

I bit my lip and glanced down at my feet. "Yeah, something like that."

"I know you," she said. "You have a 'follow-the-rules' exterior, but you've got a caring heart."

I smiled to cover my sudden blush. "And what craziness would lead you to believe that?"

"Oh, I've been watching you. And I kind of like that about you," she said, her voice low, almost a whisper. She checked the bank, but no one else was there, so she stepped toward me. Her smile was mischievous, playful. She pushed her body against mine. Almost immediately I felt arousal brewing. Our time in the wild had had an interesting effect on my libido. Despite the hard work and anxiety, or perhaps because of them, rock-hard erections had become commonplace.

"Let's take a swim," Cindy said as she reached for the rawhide strip that held my buckskin trousers in place and toyed with it. I leaned my head ever so slightly toward her. The intoxicating scent of her skin washed over me. "Together," she added.

"Now?" I managed. My mouth was suddenly dry. I watched

her hand, and then glanced around to make sure no one was looking.

"Yes," she replied. "Now."

I moistened my lips. "What about Jason?" I thought that was her husband's name.

"Jason... is not here. Besides, he and I haven't been intimate for years."

Well, that answered my question. "I see."

Slowly her hand pulled on the knot that held my trousers in place.

"And Pam?" she asked, pausing.

"Well, she's not here, either."

"That's not good enough," she said, looking intently into my eyes. "Tell me more."

"I've never been unfaithful to her, but things are different now."

"Did you love her?"

"Not really," I said. That was my true response. I had affection for Pam, but nothing that would be classified as love since within a year of our marriage. I suspected Cindy knew, although I had no clue how.

She brought her face close to mine. "Okay," she whispered, and finished pulling on the thong. It released, and my buckskin trousers tumbled to my ankles. Gently, she grasped my exposed penis, now fully erect, and slid her fingertips up and down its length. Passion welled within and I pulled her close. My lips were on hers and I kissed her deep and long.

After a few minutes, she pushed me away and pulled off her buckskins. I stepped out of my trousers and threw my shirt off in one quick motion, tossing it to the ground. Again I pulled her toward me, kissing her passionately and pressing her breasts against my chest.

Never had I experienced such a compelling urge. I was part of nature's scheme now. Cindy's earthy scent, the fresh breeze on my skin, and the sound of her heavy breath altered me in a profound way.

The wilderness had become a part of me. My actions were completely beyond my control and I was oblivious to my surroundings. Cindy pulled me into the water. Its bracing coolness further energized every nerve in my body. Her breathing became a rhythmic heaving of her body. She seemed wild, almost animalistic. I felt unleashed, carried away. I stood up in the water, and Cindy wrapped her legs around my waist and inserted her tongue deep into my mouth just as I penetrated her. I cupped my hands around her buttocks and drew her to me again and again. Our breathing became louder and in sync.

Suddenly, and much to my dismay, Cindy released her grip on my torso and slid into the water. I was confused and not a little annoyed. It was an intense moment, so why had she fallen away? Then I heard a voice from the bank. I instinctively dipped down into the water and turned around. Christie was standing there with an apologetic smile.

"Sorry to bother you kids, 'cause you look like you're having so much fun. But you need to see this."

Chapter 11

Cindy and I followed Christie in silence. I was fuming at our interruption. Whatever it was could have waited.

Cindy took my hand and kissed it. "It's okay. We can finish later."

I nodded and snorted. "Damn, what timing!" Then, to Christie: "Somebody better be dying."

"Nobody is dying," she said. "At least, not yet." But she said no more.

We approached the grassy work area behind the meeting hall. Dillon, Ramiro, and several others were standing there, looking up at the sky.

"What's going on?" I asked, ready to get to the point. "What did you find?"

Christie pointed upwards.

"What? I see blue sky and clouds."

"Watch." Dillon loaded an arrow into his bow and shot it skyward. After fifteen feet, the arrow diverted, abruptly going in a direction perpendicular to its original path.

"Do that again," I said, instantly forgetting about my interrupted swim. Dillon shot another arrow and again it changed direction, this time heading more toward the left.

"How did that happen?" I asked.

"We don't know," said Dillon. "I took a shot at a bird flying overhead when I noticed it. If you shoot an arrow fifteen feet to either side the arrow isn't affected. You can shoot below this area and even above it and nothing happens. The arrow just sails straight through. But in that region, about thirty feet wide and about twenty feet deep, the arrow gets deflected. And it's not like it hits a surface and bounces off. It just moves in a new direction with no loss of speed. I've never seen anything like it."

I stared hard, but saw nothing. "How high up would you say this area is?"

"The lowest edge is about fifteen feet from the ground."

I picked up a piece of wood lying nearby and threw it toward the area. The wood reached a point and was suddenly heading in a new direction, without loss of speed.

I felt my stomach tighten. This was not normal, and I needed to understand it. For the first time for weeks, I was really afraid.

"Not work of Communists," observed Sasha in her imperfect English.

So here it was. The other shoe we had been expecting to drop. A strange phenomenon suspended in the air with no obvious support. It was not something natural. It was not a part of our previous life. It was likely connected to the reason we were here. If we got a handle on what it was, perhaps we would unveil the reality behind our situation. Even get an idea where the people we cared about were. And whether we would ever be going back home to sleep in a real bed.

"Let's build a platform," I suggested. "I want to reach that spot."

Ramiro looked around. "We would have to make something

from logs, I guess. You're, what, six feet? So to reach it, we would need a platform at least ten feet high."

"Yeah, but we'd better make it about twelve feet, so I can get a good reach." I contemplated the strange emptiness over our heads. "Let's do it now. We'd better find out what this is."

As we collected materials for the platform, I felt a new excitement. Fear gave way to the possibility that we'd soon discover the meaning of our situation and what had happened to everyone else. Maybe they could help us, or explain, or even return us to our old lives. Something was happening, finally!

I even felt a little vindicated. Whatever it was suspended in the sky wasn't due to terrorists or Communists. It was something else.

We spent several hours felling stiff saplings and lashing them together. The shadows were getting long when I climbed up on the platform. It felt stable enough. Still on my knees, I peered into the empty space where I knew there was something. The silence was heavy. We were all holding our collective breath.

I stood up on the platform and stared into the space above me even more intently, but I still saw nothing.

"Are you sure about this?" asked Rebecca. "It might hurt you."

"Toss me a stick," I said. "A big one." I was scared. But I felt willing to push through my fear. Whatever was going to happen was going to happen. I had to find out what this thing was and what was going on.

I grasped the end of the four-foot branch that had been handed to me and slowly extended it upward. Nothing happened at first, and then the end of the stick was moving in a different direction. Nothing pushed on the stick. The far end was just moving differently from the end I was holding. It looked bent, but there was no breaking of the wood. I tried thrusting it several times, and each time the forward portion bent, and then, as I pulled it back toward me, the stick returned to normal.

I looked down at the others, all standing nearby and looking up intently.

"I'll try to touch it. Be ready to catch me if something happens."

"Be careful," called Samuel. "It might shock you or something."

"I know!" I said with emotion. "But we need to see what it'll do."

"Okay, everyone," announced Christie. "Let's spread out in a circle and be ready to catch Charles if he falls."

Everyone formed a tight circle around the platform and assumed the ready position. For what, I wasn't sure. There was no way someone like petite Sasha would catch me if I fell in her direction. But it made me more secure knowing they were prepared to try.

"Okay, Charles, go ahead," called Amber.

"Carefully," added Cindy.

I reached my hand skyward while still kneeling on the platform. And then, abruptly, my hand was moving to the left. It wasn't jerked or pushed or anything. It was just moving in one direction and then in another. My elbow was still moving vertically, but my hand was moving horizontally. I pulled it back and tried it again and again, and each time the same thing happened. I fully extended my arm and paused to look at it—from all appearances, bent at a ninety-degree angle. But there was no pressure. No pain. I tried both hands and, without thinking it through, pushed my head and shoulders into the area. Again, the same thing happened. My upper body was moving in a perpendicular direction. My legs remained on the platform, but part of my torso was pointed parallel to the ground. This was the weirdest thing I'd ever experienced.

"Goddammit!" cried Dillon. "Does that hurt? Your whole body looks bent."

I was stretched up as far as I could go, yet, thanks to my body's painless distortion at a ninety-degree angle at my waist, my shoes were only a couple of feet away from my head.

After trying the same experiment several times more, I climbed down from the platform.

"How are you doing?" asked Cindy. She reached out and touched my waist, presumably to determine that I was still in one piece.

"I'm fine," I said. But I was perplexed. This was not the breakthrough I had hoped for.

Samuel and Ramiro got up on the platform and had the same experiences I had. Their arms and torsos bent in a right angle as they extended these parts toward the area. I stood watching in contemplation. The phenomenon puzzled all of us. Yet we were certain that it had something to do with whoever or whatever was behind all the events of our current situation.

Whatever the phenomenon was, I figured it had to be of alien origin.

"What the hell is it?" asked Dillon.

I shrugged. "I don't have a clue."

"It's like the structure of space-time is distorted in that area," said Rebecca.

Dillon and I both looked at her. My mouth dropped open. Everyone seemed to like Rebecca. She was young and a little spoiled, but polite, and usually tried to do her best to help out. But no one would have called her brilliant. Yet what she said seemed vaguely right. Space *was* being distorted.

"Or something like that," she continued, scrunching up her shoulders. "I heard them say that on some movie."

"For a minute there I wondered if you'd been holding back on us," I said, smiling at her.

"What do you mean?" she asked.

"Never mind. Look, everyone, let's find out if there are more of these around here. We have four bows. Make makeshift arrows—don't use the good ones, they'll get messed up—and go around the area shooting them into the air. We need to know."

"You bet, boss," snapped Samuel. This guy was unpredictable. He seemed always on the edge of an emotional explosion, barely contained behind his dark, simmering surface. But occasionally, after a show of disapproval, he would join in my suggestions with enthusiasm. Fortunately, this was one of those occasions.

We split up into four groups. Members of each group cut and shaped rough arrows while another walked around the community, firing arrows into the air. Another member retrieved the arrows.

"Hey!" called Sasha after just a few minutes. "There's another here."

She was standing on the little footbridge that crossed the creek which ran between the cabins.

"It's there," she said, pointing up. "I show you." She shot

92

an arrow skyward and, just as before, it veered off in a new direction.

"Creepy! It's right where we live," said Cindy, who was with my group.

We kept searching and kept finding more. By dinnertime we had discovered seven additional ones.

For lack of a better term, we called them "distortions", in honor of Rebecca's surprising comment. That made nine of them scattered around our little community. Nine that we found, anyway. One was less than twenty feet away from our dinner table, just hovering there, invisible, silent. No fuel smell, no sound, no shadow, nothing. Like thin air; but distorted thin air. And from what we could tell from shooting arrows around it, in a vaguely oval shape.

All this time, we'd felt so alone and abandoned. I didn't feel that way anymore. I suddenly felt exposed. Had they been there the whole time? How could they exist with so little evidence of their presence? Our situation made no more sense than before we found these fucking things.

Chapter 12

We sat quietly around the banquet table, eating a cold meal as the sun set. A fat-coated torch gave some light, and we kept looking up at the empty sky toward the closest distortion, maybe thirty feet from where we sat. I wasn't comfortable knowing it was there. I sensed the others were equally troubled.

Eileen poked at her slice of smoked pork. "I wish Missy and the others were back."

With the excitement of our discovery, I had temporarily forgotten about our reconnaissance mission. The thought of Missy jolted me back to reality.

"Maybe they found a town already," suggested Amber, her eyes alight with enthusiasm.

"We can only hope," added Harvey.

"What are those things?" blurted out Veronica. "I don't like them."

We all turned to look at Veronica, her eyes wide.

"They're creepy," said Michael, staring upward. His face was pale, eyes nervous. "There they are, hovering above us. Doing what?"

I had an idea what they were doing, but was struggling with whether I should say anything. I noticed Cindy staring at me.

"You've got it figured out, don't you?" she asked.

"Not even close."

"But... you have an idea?"

"Okay, Charles, spill it." This was from Christie.

My mind was racing, so I stood up and paced back and forth. I needed to talk this out for myself as much as for them. We needed to hear all options voiced in order to make our personal evaluations. It was times like this that one wished for paper to brainstorm and write it all down, but all I could do was talk.

"Here's the way I see things," I began. "Other beings visited us. I guess we can call them aliens from another world. The clacking noises and loss of communications were all part of a larger effort to subdue us. And while we were out cold, they set up this place in the middle of this wilderness and put us here. Heck, they may have created this wilderness by eliminating all towns and buildings in the area."

"But you're not suggesting that's true everywhere, right?" asked Michael. "Just around here."

"Maybe," I replied. "I don't know. But my thought is that we are part of an experiment. And the parameters of their experiment required them to change the land back to what it was originally before humans came along and altered it. That's why there are no signs of our modern civilization anywhere."

"But that would take years," said Samuel. "Eliminating concrete buildings and asphalt roads. Many years. I can't image we were asleep for that long."

"Maybe they had some means of speeding up the process. Look, I don't know what happened, but someone or something literally put us to sleep for a while, and maybe changed everything. Who does that? You tell me?" I put the question to them all, and waited. Silence.

"Our towns may be gone but we humans are still here," pressed Cindy. "Where do we fit in this revamped world?"

"Well, I'm conjecturing that the way these beings—or whatever they are—see it, we're just another species. They wanted us here, but apparently in a primitive state, to better mesh with the surrounding wilderness." I ran my hand through my hair. This had to sound as strange to them as it did to me. I supposed there were other conceivable possibilities—that we were part of an immersive computer program created by other beings, or that we were each fed drugs that created hallucinations that worked in tandem with others, but they were so far beyond the pale I couldn't seriously entertain them.

"And these distortion things?" asked Christie. "How do they fit into your scenario?"

I stopped my pacing and looked up toward the nearest one.

"It wouldn't make sense to conduct this grand experiment if they couldn't observe the results. Maybe those distortions hide observation chambers. Maybe these beings are inside them, where they can observe us. And they somehow distorted the space around them to keep them hidden and protected."

"What're you saying?" asked Amber. "That we're being watched?"

"Yes. That's what I am saying. That we are being observed as part of a study."

Everyone fell silent and looked up toward the distortion. The fact that no one said I was crazy surprised me. But the notion rang true. It made sense of our predicament when nothing else did.

"So, there are alien scientists up there in little viewing chambers. Counting how many times I take a shit each day," pondered Christie.

"Or tourists," I said.

"You mean we're like a zoo?" asked Veronica.

"Something like that."

Again silence. And we all stared up at the sky, pondering.

"What does that mean?" asked Eileen. Urgent angst was in her voice. "Are you suggesting we're stuck like this forever? What about our families? Our children?"

I shrugged. But since I had no clue, I figured I might as well be positive. "Even if my alien-observer theory is correct, there is no reason to believe that ours is the only human community. There could be many others, just like ours, scattered around. Perhaps our families could still be alive somewhere in other settlements like this one."

It was a thin hope. Even if there were other primitive communities scattered about, these would only make up a small percentage of the billions of people that had been on Earth before all this happened.

As far-fetched as my conjecture was, I could see that it had unnerved everyone. The possibility that we were out in the open and in full view of strange beings made us feel vulnerable. We cleaned up the dishes and quietly retreated to the privacy of our cabins.

In the dark but now familiar confines of my abode, I pulled off my garments and sat on the edge of my bed. My mind was spinning, both with the discovery of the distortions, and with second thoughts about revealing my conjecture to the others. I didn't want to undermine our morale by making everyone paranoid about being watched. I also wished Cindy would join me. The chance to re-ignite the flame we had felt earlier in the day would have been a welcome reprieve from the anxiety of our new discovery.

I pondered getting dressed and going to her cabin when there was a quiet knock.

Hopefully, I opened the door and looked out, but it was Amber.

"Can I come in?" she asked.

Without an invitation, Amber boldly stepped inside the cabin and sat down in a chair by the center table. I reached for my buckskin trousers and pulled them on.

"What is it, Amber?" I asked.

"I'm scared," she said. "Can I stay the night with you?"

"But... where would you sleep?"

"Right here. I'll just lay my head down on the table and sleep."

I sat down in the other chair and looked Amber in the eye. "Look, I understand you being scared. I've got the willies, too. But we've been here for over a month now and if there are aliens in those distortions then they haven't bothered us. There's no reason it should suddenly change."

"I know," she said. Tears welled up in her eyes. "But I'm still scared. I asked Michael, but he said 'no.'"

"You asked Michael to spend the night with you?"

She gave me a half smile. "He and I have... been together. Several times. We have something special. But now..." A tear welled up in one eye and rolled down her cheek.

"What did he say?"

"He says he doesn't want a relationship. It's crazy. Why wouldn't he want a relationship, with the connection we had?

And in this fucking place, there aren't a lot of options. Does that make sense to you, Charles? Why would he not want that?"

I shrugged. "Sometimes, men..." I wasn't sure how to finish my sentence. I didn't think that saying "just want to have sex" would help Amber feel better.

"So I've had it with him," she said, after watching me fumble for words for a few seconds. "I'm looking elsewhere. What do you think of Trey? He's kind of aloof, but don't you think he's cute in his own way? I've never been with a black guy."

"Um, I..."

There was another knock at the door. I opened it to find Cindy standing there.

"We have unfinished business to attend to," she said. "May I come in?"

"Hey, Cindy," said Amber, over my shoulder.

"Oh! I see you have company. Sorry."

"No," I quickly replied. "Amber was scared. I was telling her there was nothing to be afraid of."

Cindy took a moment, but she got the drift. "I see. Well, that's true, Amber. They just want to observe us." She stepped inside the cabin.

"I know," said Amber. "But it's the thought of them out there. Are you scared, too?"

"I suppose. Some."

"Then why are you... Oh. I'm sorry. Do you two want to be alone?"

I started to nod, but Cindy said, "It's okay, Amber. We're here for you."

"Can I sit here? And sleep?" asked Amber, looking frightened and younger than her years. "I'm wigged out."

"I'm scared, too," I said. "Cindy, please lie down beside me. I don't want to sleep alone." And I gave her my best pitiful expression, echoing Amber.

Cindy, perhaps a little miffed about Amber being in my cabin, hesitated.

"I'll do it!" said Amber. "I'll sleep with you."

At that point, there was another knock on the door.

"You've got to be kidding," I said under my breath. "Who is it?" I called.

"Are y'all in there?" came Harvey's voice from outside. "Can I come in?"

I let out a sigh. "Come in. And just prop the door open. I'm going to bed. You all can come and go as you please."

With that, I crawled onto my hard plank bed, lay back, and closed my eyes. The long, strange day had exhausted me. I hoped Cindy would climb into bed with me, but my three visitors sat around my table and chatted for some time before leaving me alone in the cabin, closing the door behind them as they left.

Chapter 13

The next few days were a strange brew of mixed emotions. The biggest concern was my conjecture that above our heads, invisible and mysterious, were alien beings, watching our every move as if we were chimps in a cage. The possibility that they were there never left our minds. Yet, despite this, everyone was excited about the prospects of the river expedition. Hopefully, Cook and the others had encountered a modern community on the banks of the river, and we could all return to some semblance of our previous lives—preferably one not involving alien observers. Often, someone was at the river bank, watching upstream for signs of the expedition's return.

Besides our concerns and trepidations, Cindy and I were swept up in the giddy heights of a new romance. We finally found time alone, and it was clear that, in these most unusual of circumstances, we had found a powerful physical connection. Our passion was of a level I had never encountered, and she said the same was true for her.

I was certain that our environment, where danger, exertion, and discomfort were a part of every hour, created an intensity and level of engagement we wouldn't have experienced in our previous lives. We were much closer to the natural order of things, surviving as we were on the edge of the wilderness. This intensity forced us to come to terms with ourselves, and made us better equipped to understand and connect with others.

Whenever she came near, my libido awoke and was often compelling. It was clear she felt similarly. When we acted on our urges, my will became utterly subservient to the animal within. I was swept up in mating fervor, and by letting nature take its course, I felt free and joyful, out of my body even if for a short time.

I wondered about the alien watchers. Of course, we didn't know for certain that they existed, but it seemed reasonable that observers were in the distortions. The nosy Little Perverts, as Rebecca had started calling them. Cindy and I often made love outside the confines of our cabin—in the river, on the beach, or simply out in the woods. What did the aliens think of us and our all-consuming passion? Were they learning something? Did they have anything to do with the intensity of our feeling?

As far as we knew, they had not interfered with us since we had all awakened. In fact, following the initial few days of uneasiness after discovering the presence of the distortions, we got used to the idea they were there and felt relatively little fear. The concern was small compared to the anxiety caused by the occasional howling at night, or the huffing of bears in the trees along the edge of the community.

But these alien Watchers, if they existed, had likely created our predicament. It was, as of yet, unclear what they had in store for us. And as our days unfolded, with all their hardships—collecting wood, preparing the food, and the multitude of maintenance-related chores, I noticed our original fear transform into something else, at least for most of our group. As we feared the aliens less, we resented them more. Real or not, it was easy to vent our frustrations on them.

These hypothetical beings—I imagined them as small, skinny creatures with abnormally large heads and bugged-out eyes, holding clipboards as they peered down at us—were seen as the source of our misery and unhappiness. For whatever reason, whether it was scientific interest or for entertainment value, they had made the choice to take our society and civilization away from us, and put us in these horrendous conditions. Every swipe of a mosquito and every boring meal of the same thing we had had the day before reminded me of the assholes hovering above us. Assuming they were even there, of course.

And then there was the question of our loved ones. If there were really creatures in those things and they had harmed Alex, they would be held accountable. I would make sure they regretted their callous actions if it was the last thing I did.

* * *

Five days after the river expedition departed, I was sleeping soundly, dreaming of large-headed beings hovering in the clouds, when a knock interrupted my sleep. A loud, urgent knock.

I heard Cook's voice outside the door. "Charles! It's Cook. Get up. We need you."

I sprang up and opened the door. "Cook. You're back!"

"Yeah, we're back, but Missy is hurt. Bad. She's been bleeding for hours. We've got to do something."

Cook knew I had no medical training. "We need Cindy," I said.

"Trey is getting her."

"Let's go." I followed Cook as he hastened toward the river. A vision of Missy pulling weeds in the garden came into my mind, then another of her smiling as she carried a plate of food to the table. She smiled a lot.

"What happened?" I asked.

"Upstream a ways, the river narrows through a small gorge. We were coming home but the current was strong in the gorge, so we were using our poles to keep the raft from banging into the sides. Missy's pole snapped as the raft surged, and she fell in. The raft pushed her up against a sharp rock and ripped a gash in her thigh. It's bad."

Missy lay on the beach beside the bank of the river. Trey was standing over her.

"She's mumbling again," said Trey, "but she's not conscious."

"Where's Cindy?" I asked and knelt down beside Missy.

"She's coming."

I placed my hand on Missy's forehead. I was worried she would be burning up from infection, but instead, her skin was cold and clammy. I felt for her pulse, but it was so weak, I had trouble locating it. I loosened the vines that held the crude bandage placed on her wound, and squinted in the moonlight to focus on the dark gash on her thigh.

Cindy approached and knelt down beside me. "The wound is still bleeding," she said, surprised. "How long has she been losing blood?"

"Hours," said Cook. "We tied the bandage as tight as we dared. She's been pale like this for some time."

Cindy felt her forehead. "She's in shock. We've got to get her to her cabin and staunch the bleeding."

I looked at Trey and Cook. "Let's carry her as carefully as

possible to her bed."

"Another mile and she's ours," said Missy. "Keep it going." This was followed by several indistinct sentences. She was talking out of her head, her voice low and weak. It didn't look good.

We carried her carefully to her cabin and eased her onto her bed. Cindy lit a torch, and I held it overhead.

"We must guard against infection," she said. "Cook, start the fire and get a pot of water boiling. When it's ready, bring me a small amount, but keep the rest boiling. Trey, give him a hand."

"You got it," said Cook. The two of them left.

Cindy looked at me. "We'll need strips of rawhide, and can you fetch the soap?"

I pulled off my shirt. "I'll grab a blade of some kind. How many and how wide?"

"Four should do it. About one inch wide. And put them in the boiling water. Send someone out for moss and boil that, too. We need a poultice."

Cindy spoke to Missy in reassuring tones, and I ran off to find a blade and soap. I sliced off strips from the bottom of my shirt and brought them to Cook. I sent Trey to collect moss for the poultice.

"The rawhide strips are boiling," I told Cindy as I re-entered the cabin with a container of boiled water. She took it from me, tested the temperature, and slowly poured the steaming water in a constant stream into the gash on Missy's thigh, rubbing vigorously with soap. She did this several times. Missy stirred each time, and I was glad she was out. It looked like it would be painful, but Cindy knew what she was doing.

"It's cleaned out," Cindy said. "But the gash is bleeding

pretty badly. If she keeps losing blood, we may lose her."

"What can I do?" I asked, panic rising up inside me. *I knew this was going to happen! We have no medical supplies, we have no medicine, and we don't even have proper bandages, Goddammit!*

"Stick your elbow out," she said, and she washed my elbow with the still-hot water. She did the same to her hands and then put them on either side of Missy's thigh and pressed the two sides together. "Place your elbow right here on the gash, and hold it there with firm pressure."

Missy moaned as I applied pressure, but she stayed still.

After about fifteen minutes, Cook came in with the strips of rawhide and the sterilized moss poultice. I released my elbow. The pressure had temporarily staunched the bleeding. Cindy kept the gash pressed together and lashed it with the rawhide and moss.

We then stood around watching while Cindy covered Missy up and continued to speak to her softly. I motioned for Trey and Cook to step outside.

"Do you think she'll make it?" Cook asked.

I shook my head. "I don't know. She's a tough one, though. And Cindy seems like she knows what she's doing."

"Yeah, she does," said Trey.

"Damn!" said Cook. "It was just bad luck."

Cook's face looked haggard for a young man. I was sure he felt some responsibility for Missy. I put my arm around his shoulders.

"I take it you guys saw nothing," I said.

"You mean signs of civilizations?" asked Trey. "Not a damn thing."

"We may have gotten thirty miles upstream," added Cook, "but saw no buildings, no roads, nothing."

"Well, something happened here while you were gone."

"What do you mean? Was someone else hurt?" Cook asked.

"No, nothing like that. It's...well, difficult to explain. You two look exhausted, so get some rest and I'll tell you all about it tomorrow. Cindy and I will do what we can for Missy."

"We are exhausted," said Cook. "We got virtually no sleep while we were gone, and it is damn hard work pushing that raft upriver."

"I'll bet," I said and slapped him on the back. "Good work, guys. We'll talk in the morning."

Cook nodded, and he and Trey left for their cabins. I came back inside and sat down beside Cindy. "You might as well retire, too," I said. "I can watch her for a while."

"I'll stay," she said. "We need to make sure she comes out of shock."

I wasn't optimistic about Missy's chances, so I was glad Cindy would stay.

Over the next few hours, Missy stirred little. She mumbled, but didn't move. Cindy and I held a few brief conversations, but we worried about disturbing Missy's rest, so were mostly silent.

I watched Cindy every time she leaned over Missy, gently touching her face, talking in soothing tones, and double checking the wound. She was completely confident and professional. Despite her buckskins, I could easily envision her in scrubs attending a patient in a modern hospital. Instead, here we were, in the middle of nowhere, with fucking moss and boiling water.

We shouldn't be expected to survive everything nature through at us out here. If alien sons-of-bitches really had put us here to watch us struggle, they should have given us more to live on—like a few medical supplies while they stocked our cabins.

Fuck them! People didn't die in our previous world from a gashed leg.

Settle down, Charles, Missy's not dead yet, and no one knows what those things in the sky are or why we're here. Still! Dammit! I cursed aloud, lost in my thoughts, startling Cindy.

"Sorry," I apologized, then stood up and paced, thinking.

"Why don't you try to get some sleep?" asked Cindy. "I'll stay up with her."

Missy's cabin was next to mine, so I took Cindy up on her offer and went to lie down. She had been with me earlier in the night, so as I lay on my bed, and took a deep breath, I could smell her scent mingled with smoke, dirt, and wood. As I drifted off, I heard crickets chirping in the woods and I imagined her next to me, her curvy figure pressed close, her scent wafting, and her skin soft and warm. How I hoped she could work miracles and save Missy.

I woke with a start, not remembering where I was initially, then it all came back to me. I threw back on my buckskins and ran to Missy's cabin to check on her.

She looked deathly pale in the morning sun.

"Will she will make it?" I asked Cindy as I looked into Missy's face. I had grown so fond of this feisty, opinionated woman. She had as much courage as anyone in the camp, and more moxie than most. *She can't die. Please don't die.*

"It's hard to say. I sure would miss her if she leaves us," Cindy said sadly.

"So would I."

There was a brief knock on the door and Samuel came in.

"I got the forge going right away when I heard. I fashioned

this." He held up a thin sliver of black iron. It had a small notch at one end and was sharp at the other. "With only low-grade iron to work with, I couldn't make it any better."

"A needle?" I took it from him and looked it over. It was larger than a modern sewing needle, but it should work just fine for stitching up Missy's gash. Samuel, whatever else he was, was damn good with a forge. "Excellent. But what do we use for thread?"

"More rawhide," Cindy said. "Just cut it thin."

I sighed and pulled off my buckskin shirt, which already exposed my belly button.

"We see enough of your ugly belly," said Samuel. "It would be kinder to the rest of us if we used my shirt."

I smiled at the barb, intended kindly.

"At any rate, we can't try to sew her up for a while," Cindy said. "Not until she regains consciousness. I wouldn't want to risk more blood loss until she's out of shock. But boil the rawhide."

"She spoke!" said Samuel.

I looked at Missy and saw a half-smile on her face. Her eyes were barely open.

"It's good to be home," she said in a feeble voice. She turned her head and closed her eyes again.

"That's a good sign," said Cindy.

"Odd to think of this place as home," said Samuel.

That was my sentiment exactly.

Chapter 14

The evening's exertion had exhausted Cindy and I, so during the following day, we took turns watching Missy and changing out her poultice, while the other caught up on sleep. Missy stirred frequently now, and even awoke for brief periods. She said little, but Cindy said she was out of shock. I felt much better about her chances.

Most of the others visited the cabin at various times, sitting with me or Cindy. Cindy had suggested the visitors speak softly to Missy in reassuring, comforting tones, even if she seemed asleep, and everyone did their best. They were relieved Missy was over her immediate crisis. But it was clear from their expressions that they were disappointed by the news brought back by the expedition.

Cook and Trey relayed to the others that they had found nothing but more wilderness in their thirty-mile trek up-river. I wasn't too surprised, given that there were no signs anywhere of other people. No trash in the water, no smoke plumes, no distant planes in the sky. If there were people left in the world, they weren't anywhere nearby. So the expedition's results just corroborated what I had expected.

But others had placed high hopes on the journey. Our sense of being alone became more pronounced when we heard the news, and our sense of vulnerability and resentment toward the Watchers increased.

In the late afternoon, Missy awoke for an extended period and even joked weakly with me for giving so much attention to her inner thigh. She drank water and ate bacon. I still worried about infection, but Cindy was being as careful as possible, keeping everything sterile.

With Missy out of shock, Cindy sewed up her gash the best she could using pieces of rawhide and Samuel's needle. With no pain relievers available, the experience was agonizing for Missy, and she blacked out for some time, causing me to worry all over again.

But Missy was awake again the next morning, and even sat up. Over the next few days, she grew progressively stronger. Thanks to Cindy's care, her wound never became dangerously infected.

Several days after the return of the expedition, while Missy was still convalescing, I sat on the bank of the river, talking with Trey and Cook. They had been told about the distortions, and Dillon had demonstrated their properties. I had shared with them my conjecture that these odd phenomena were protected observation chambers from which the beings who had subjugated the Earth studied us.

"So you think they turned the world into a wilderness so they can watch us?" asked Cook.

I nodded. "That's the idea. Am I crazy?"

"You mean the whole planet?" asked Trey. "A fucking planet-sized nature preserve?"

I shrugged. "Maybe."

"Fuck you!" Trey shouted, standing up and vigorously jutting his middle finger in the direction of a nearby distortion.

"Hey, Trey, better watch out," said Cook. "Don't get them pissed off at us. We're pretty vulnerable." He looked at me. "Is it possible they would do something?"

"Who knows?" I said. "Though it would be interesting to see them interact with us."

"I'd like to kick their asses," said Trey. "Come on down here, you bastards! I'll take you on."

Cook and I looked up toward the distortion, but nothing changed.

"Rebecca calls them Little Perverts, since they watch us do everything," I said.

"Bunch of wusses is what they are," said Trey as he sat back down.

I stood up and idly began throwing flat rocks across the surface of the river, trying to get them to skip. Then I threw one at the distortion, and watched its trajectory suddenly alter, just as happened many times before. "Clearly, my theory is just conjecture. If it's true, however, then there are implications we need to take into consideration. For example, it seems unlikely anyone is coming along to rescue us. And aside from getting us set up here, it doesn't look like these beings will get involved in our lives. It's up to us, and just us, to do what is necessary to ensure our survival"

"That might be part of their fun," offered Trey.

"Yeah," said Cook. "Or part of their study of human nature. They want to stress us."

"So we had better prepare for the colder months. And then, as spring approaches, we'll need to plant crops for next season. We have to be prepared to perpetuate ourselves."

"Yeah, I don't think these nasty buckskins will get us through the winter," said Trey, looking at his stained sleeve.

I frowned as I surveyed the filth covering my own buckskins. "We'll need warmer clothes and blankets, and the only place we can get them is to take them off of animals. Dillon and I have got to become more effective at hunting, especially deer, although the snares and trap lines have potential for smaller game, if we can get a little better at constructing them. And once we have the raw skins in hand, we have to become adept at tanning them so they'll remain pliable."

"Killing a bear would get us thick fur," said Cook. "Although that's a dangerous proposition."

"Let's trap them!" said Trey. "Use a bear fall. A big hole in the ground with sharp stakes at the bottom."

"Interesting idea," said Cook.

"I wish we could figure out a way to make cloth," I said.

"Yeah, but I don't see how," replied Trey. "We don't have cotton or wool."

"But what about flax?" asked Cook. "That's what they make linen out of. Does it grow around here?"

I shrugged. "We have to find out. Really, we've had it easy so far. They did everything for us—meat in the springhouse, crops in the field, the garden already going, tools forged. In a way, we were given a trial period. Soon, all that will change. Things will be much harder."

"It sounds like you're convinced your theory is true," said Cook.

I shrugged. "Somebody set us up here. Whoever it was, is either gone away or is up there, in one of those things."

Cook nodded thoughtfully.

"And winter brings illness," I continued. "Maybe we can figure out which plants are medicinal. Anything anyone can remember will help."

"Don't ask me," said Trey. "I don't have a clue about that stuff."

"I don't think any of us do," I said. "So the only way we can survive is to acquire the wisdom that our ancestors took centuries to discover and to work very hard."

"Fuck," said Trey. "We've been given the shaft."

"We can survive," said Cook. "We can do it."

Trey nodded. After a minute, he raised his fist to the sky. "Damn motherfuckers!"

I looked up in the direction of the distortion and sighed. "Life will never be easy again."

Chapter 15

Later that evening, we were all pleased to see Missy hobbling to the dinner table, holding Dillon's arm.

"You'd better get the lead out," I said, "or you'll miss the grub."

"You eat mine and there'll be hell to pay. Even one-legged I can still kick your ass."

"Good ol' Missy," Cindy said. "Glad to have you back."

"Have you heard?" asked Amber. "About the... things?"

"Yeah, I heard all about them. But I still don't understand it."

"There's one right here," said Rebecca. "Watch." She threw a stick at it, and Missy watched it suddenly change its trajectory perpendicular to its initial direction.

"It's got little green aliens in it," said Amber. "They watch us like little perverts."

Missy stared in the direction of the invisible phenomenon.

"How many are there?" she asked.

"We've found nine around the camp," I said. "But we've come across two more out in the woods. One out beyond the wheat field, and another near the salt lick."

"Does that make sense?" asked Trey. "Why would they have observers in the woods if we're the experiment?"

"Well, it would make sense if they see us as just one part of the bigger ecosystem," suggested Dillon. "They are studying our world, not us in particular."

"Right," I added. "Placing an observation chamber near the salt lick would give them the opportunity to see lots of animals, not just humans."

"It's a nature preserve," observed Missy. "I'll be damned."

"If my crazy theory is correct," I stressed. "But it seems to fit the facts pretty well."

Now that we were all back together again, the moment seemed right to talk about our future. Winter was coming and we had to consider the long haul.

"Given what we now know about our predicament, it's a good idea to talk about our work responsibilities," I said. "Some of you don't like what you're doing. And some of you don't have enough to do. I propose..."

"God, man!" said Samuel, standing up and looming over me. "Can't we enjoy a quiet moment with our wounded comrade without you trying to boss us around?"

"He's right," said Eileen. "I don't want to talk about that stuff right now."

"Sorry... well, when do you want to talk about it?"

"How about never?" said Rebecca.

"Everything is going along fine without your interference," said Samuel.

Cook stood up and looked at Samuel. "Everything has been fine so far thanks to Charles's leadership. But winter is coming, and life will be hard. We've got to take that into account or we won't make it."

"I'm just... fucking... tired of it!" cried Samuel, slapping his palms down hard on the table. Everyone jumped and stared at him. We'd never heard Samuel curse.

This time I stood up, speaking in the stunned silence. "What would you have us do? Just ignore the situation?"

"Charles is right," said Missy, who was sitting next to Samuel. Samuel spun toward her, his face red with anger. But much to everyone's relief, he contained himself. Without a word, he stomped away from the table.

"It's just a lot to take in," said Missy after Samuel had walked off. "Emotions are running amok. Just go ahead, Charles. We know you have our best interests at heart."

Missy's calmness amazed me. For a moment, it had seemed as if Samuel would strike her. But I followed her advice, and we took the time to go over all the chores, both current ones and new ones we expected to have to deal with as winter neared.

I assigned most of us to do basically what we had already been doing, with a few minor tweaks. "Now listen," I added, standing before our dinner table. "I make no claim that this is a balanced allotment of tasks. Some of you will have little to do while others are working their asses off. It will be expected that everyone will lend a hand for the others when possible. If we don't do this, we won't make it. Especially the first few years while we're learning everything we need to learn."

"Years! We won't be here for years," wailed Eileen. "We'll find the others."

"We might," I said. "But we must assume we will be here indefinitely. Because if we don't prepare, we die. Hard times are coming, I assure you."

"It's already fucking hard," offered Amber. "How I would love to wash my hair."

"Or shave my pits," said Rebecca.

"Or sleep with air-conditioning running. Just imagine," added Amber.

"Ooh, what about a Coke with ice?"

"With Doritos! Cool ranch flavor!"

"Oh my God."

"Girls, that kind of talk is no good," said Missy. "Best to appreciate the good side of life."

"What's fucking good about this life?" exclaimed Rebecca.

"Our life sucks," said Trey. "Thanks to those damn aliens up there watching us."

"Forget about the aliens," persisted Missy. "Besides, it's just a theory. Try to live in the moment and appreciate the little things. A good meal, a cool dip in the river."

"But Missy, you almost died," said Harvey. "Aren't you pissed at whoever put us here?"

Missy shrugged. "I'm not happy about it. But it is what it is."

"Missy is right," I said. "Whoever is responsible has taken us away from our friends and families, and if I could get my hands around their little green necks, I would squeeze long and hard. But I can't. So let's do our best to forget about the Watchers. If we don't, it will eat at us. So we must continue to do what we can to survive. Not for their entertainment, but for our own sake. Heck, we could be the last humans on Earth."

"Ooh," said Amber, giggling. "What if we're part of a reality show on some alien TV station?"

"Well, then I can see why you would want to wash your hair," replied Rebecca. "It looks like a greasy blanket."

Amber jumped to her feet. "You know what, Rebecca? You're a fucking bitch!"

"Dammit!" cried Eileen. "How can the two of you be so immature about this? Don't you realize? Our families might be gone. Don't you care about that?"

"Sorry," said Amber, quietly.

We all looked at Eileen's plump face as her eyes welled us. "Why is this happening?"

Christie and Cindy tried to comfort her as the tears poured. The rest of us drifted away from the table without further comment.

Chapter 16

The next morning, Dillon took down our first deer. It was a kill shot from almost directly overhead, near the trail to the salt lick. We had wounded several, but not sufficiently to take them down—they had bounded away, taking our arrows with them. That afternoon, Dillon spent time with Christie, explaining to her how to prepare and bleed the deer carcass, and to remove its skin. That same morning, I'd sat less than fifty yards from him and had missed a prime shot, so I resigned myself to using the last couple of hours of daylight to hit the practice range. We depended on my archery skills, so they needed to improve.

My practice session didn't start out so well. I shot all my arrows, but didn't get close enough for any of them to be a threat to the target. Our bows were barely adequate, and arrows not much better.

God! What happened to the days of going to Walmart and buying what you needed? I pulled out an arrow out of the ground, checking the end for damage, then looked up at the sky. Before the alien Watchers stuck us here, my life was easy. And now? Toil, worry, rigging whatever we can to make things work, hoping to stay alive.

Winter's coming, so it's gonna get bad. I've got to get better at hunting.

After a few minutes of practice, Missy came by the practice area and stood watching me.

"Yay, you got one!" she said, after I bounced one of my arrows off a swinging piece of wood. "I can taste the venison steaks already."

"Well, I'm getting there. In the meantime, rest your hopes on Dillon."

"Ah, Charles. Don't undersell yourself."

I gave her a smile. "Never."

Missy watched me take a few more shots, then said, "Charles, I never thanked you and Cindy for taking care of me. Without you two, I wouldn't have made it."

"Thank Cindy, not me. She's the one who fixed you up."

"There you go again, Charles."

I had drawn back the bow to take a shot, but stopped and looked at her. Her face was thinner but still round and her cheeks were colorful again. Her smile was huge and kind, as always. I felt a bit of relief because we were all safe and healthy again. For now.

"Okay," I said. "You're welcome. This place wouldn't be the same without you. We can't let you get out of all this fun."

"Yeah, yeah," she replied. "And I love you, too."

"Ooh!" I cried. "Dead center." I watched the piece of wood swing back and forth, carrying my arrow with it. "I'm getting dangerous."

"Well, I'm glad we had this special moment," she said.

"Yeah, well, I love you too, and I'm going to back it up by going over to the salt lick right now. I'm on a roll."

"Now? Isn't it kind of late?"

"We've got a little daylight left," I said. "It'll do me good to get in the woods. It helps me think."

"Well, be careful. And come back before it gets too dark. That bear was huffing around the cabins last night."

I gave her a nod, grabbed a handful of good arrows, and walked to the bank of the river. The salt lick—by far the best option for hunting—was on the other side. We had set up a braided vine rope along the shallow ford that extended from our beach area, so crossing was now relatively easy, but we still had to tie our clothes on top of our heads. Also, the current was deceptively strong in the middle section of the small river, so a tight grip on the rope was important in the chest-high water.

After climbing up the far bank, I brushed off as much water as possible and donned my buckskins. The salt lick was about a hundred yards away, and I made for my favorite perch in a beech tree, near the rock outcrop where the salt-laden mineral extrusions were found. As I approached, I heard the tell-tale sound of skittish deer bounding away. Although they had run off, it was a good sign. They would typically return, and sometimes sooner than expected.

I relaxed and waited, comfortably on my perch, a wide branch about fifteen feet above the ground. The breeze was blowing toward the river, so I was downwind of the salt lick. The deer would have to approach the mineral extrusion via a trail that went about twenty yards away from my position.

The problem was not only to hit the deer from that distance, but to do so with sufficient force to penetrate its hide, always a challenge with our primitive instruments. The best target to aim for, Dillon told me, was just below the shoulder of the animal. A good shot there, and the deer wouldn't run very far. No need to follow a blood trail for miles, or haul a carcass back a long way through dangerous woods with the scent of fresh blood wafting in the air.

"Dillon took one down with these damn bows and arrows," I said to myself. "I should be able to, too."

Over the next hour, the shadows deepened upon the forest, but the deer took their sweet time. Then, with just a few minutes of sufficient light left, there was brush movement and light cracking of ground litter. I made out two doe coming down the trail toward the lick. They were walking cautiously, as if they sensed danger in the tree tops. I drew back the bow as they approached the closest point in the trail, but now that they were so close to the salt lick, they abruptly picked up their pace.

I decided not to waste the arrow and perhaps merely wound a deer, and hoped they would pause at some point for a stationary shot. Just as the thought passed through my mind, a howl penetrated the forest, coming from no more than a couple of hundred years away. A wolf. Both deer froze in their tracks, searching the woods and sniffing the air.

It was pause I was hoping for. As I drew back my bow and aimed at my prey. Things were moving in slow motion, and I felt confident, alive. This time I would kill this animal. I stopped breathing. Every muscle in my body was tensed. And time stood still for one second.

It was now or never. I released the arrow. It flew true and, for the first time in all my efforts, it hit the deer firmly in its side. A tad higher than I intended, but it was a kill shot, and I absolutely knew it when it left my bow. The doe took several wobbly steps and collapsed, flailing about on the ground. The other doe bounded away.

Adrenalin was pulsing and my heart was racing. I couldn't

wait to drag that thing back to camp and, with victorious bravado, sling it down. I felt like beating my chest like a gorilla. God! What a surreal life I was leading.

I began to descend, but froze when the howls of several more wolves reached my ears. And they were close. Shit! The blood of the deer's wound could draw them to my kill. An involuntary chill ran through my body. I knew I had better stay put. I held my breath again.

Moments later, I heard crashing in the woods all around me, and watched several wolves come into view, staring hard around them and sniffing the air. I suspected they were aware of my presence, but weren't sure where I was. I didn't move a muscle. Then another wolf approached. It was a magnificent creature, larger than the others. And while the fur of its comrades were various mixtures of white, gray, and black, the fur of this animal was a solid isabelline color, more yellow than gray. This wolf stopped and sniffed the air, too, and brought its eyes up, locking them on me. I didn't move. Despite being safe on my perch, my heart pumped. A low-pitched growl seemed to seep out of the yellow wolf's massive chest, giving me a cold chill. But it then turned it's attention to the deer, which was still flailing. I saw the big wolf rip the doe's throat open in one vicious jerk. This was a signal for the others, and they all tore into the warm flesh of my kill.

Now what? As I watched them tear at my deer, I weighed my options. I had three arrows left, and considered taking shots at the pack. Wolf hide could be tanned, although I had no idea if their meat was good to eat. However, with the fading light and the excited movements of the pack, I would be lucky to wound one or two, and would probably piss them off in the process. If so, would that induce them to stick around? Was I going to lose my first kill, and be stuck in this damned tree all night? I decided my best option was to wait until they finished devouring the deer carcass, which was fast disappearing, and hopefully, once sated, the wolf pack would wander off.

There were many wolves and the doe was small, so dinner didn't last long. Once they had devoured the meat, they seemed in no hurry to leave. Darkness was descending.

Then a voice called for me from the river. Anxiety surged over me even before I understood the words.

"Charles! It's getting dark. You'd better come back."

It was Missy! She was close—too close. I was certain she had crossed the ford to this side of the river! *What is she doing on this side? Oh my God, no!* My eyes went straight to the pack of wild animals below me. All the wolves stopped their incessant pacing and perked up their ears, looking toward the river bank.

"Missy!" I yelled. "Wolves! Go back! Go back! Run!"

Immediately, the wolf pack converged at the base of my tree and looked up at me, growling and pawing on the tree trunk.

"Wolves?" Missy yelled. She was closer now, maybe fifty yards away. Her voice got the pack's attention once again. "Are you okay?"

"I'm okay!" I cried. "Go back across the river! Now! I've got their attention! Hurry! Run!"

Suddenly the big yellow wolf, obviously the pack leader, stopped looking up at me and gazed toward the sound of Missy's voice. My stomach sank. *Do something, Charles!*

"No! Hey!" I screamed loudly. "Here I am! Look!" I started jumping up and down on my branch, making it shake to get

125

their attention. A couple of the wolves looked up at me, but the leader took off. The others followed.

"No!" I heard myself yell. In desperation, I stood there on my limb and watched them all go toward Missy. "Hey, you assholes! I'm coming down."

I climbed down a branch or two, trying to give the impression I was descending. Several of the wolves running toward Missy stopped and looked up at me, but the yellow wolf, after pausing for a moment, continued running toward Missy and was lost in the shadowy trees.

"What did you say?" cried Missy.

"Run, Missy, run! They're coming! Run! They'll kill you!"

I descended to the lowest branch of the tree and listened intently. Maybe, by some miracle, she would get back over the river in time, or the stillness of the night air was deceiving me and she wasn't actually as close as I thought.

My immediate vicinity was now clear of wolves, so I jumped down. As my feet reached the ground, I heard Missy's scream. Then growling and distant splashing in the water, and then, in a terrified voice that would forever be etched in my brain, she called out my name.

I ran toward the sound, drawing my bow. I wasn't sure what I would do when I got there, but I wouldn't let them harm Missy if I could stop them.

When I reached the bank where the vine cable was tied, I saw neither Missy nor the wolves. But then, in the fast fading light, I made out several dark shapes in the river twenty yards downstream. The wolves were growling and tearing as they swam, and in their center was another shape. Smaller. Lighter. And still struggling.

"Missy!" I screamed, and ran down the bank, but thick

rushes impeded me. I couldn't get a shot from here, so I ran back to the vine cable and splashed into the water to cross to the other side. I don't remember feeling the water. I was running as fast as I could and screaming. "No, no, no! Missy? Missy!"

"Help!" I cried at the top of my lungs toward the cabins as I ran up the beach and pulled back my bow. I let fly an arrow at the fast-moving cluster of dark bodies, but had no idea if I hit anything.

"What's happening?" cried Cook, who was the first to appear.

"The wolves have Missy! They're in the river. There!"

I pointed to the dark blob, now further downstream.

"They're killing her!" I screamed. "Arrows! We need more arrows!"

Dillon came running with arrows and his bow. He handed some of the arrows to me and we took off after the pack. From the corner of my eye, I was vaguely aware of others rushing toward the river bank.

On this side of the river, the rushes were not as thick, so we ran along the bank. By now, I could barely make out the dark blotches in the river, but could hear them splashing. There were no more screams. I prayed that Missy was just unconscious.

We found an opening in the rushes along the bank and took several shots at the cluster. One wolf whimpered—somebody had struck home. The dark shapes moved toward the far bank. We shot more arrows at them, but I heard no further indication of success.

I stopped and stared into the dim shadows, straining to make out anything. I was out of breath, my heart was pounding, and my legs were trembling.

"They're pulling Missy into the reeds," I said. "We gotta swim for it."

I was easing myself into the water when Dillon's hand fell on my shoulder, holding me back.

"It's no good," he said.

"No!" I cried. "We've got to stop them." But I knew the truth. I had known it when I was in the tree.

"It's too late," Dillon said, his voice grim. "She's gone, Charles. She's dead." He squeezed my shoulder. My head felt heavy, like I couldn't hold it up, so I backed up out of the water several steps, and bent over. Then something rose up from inside, forcing me upright. I couldn't let this happen. I couldn't.

I looked back toward the opposite bank. I saw little, but the wolves had clearly pulled their prize up onto the bank. The only sounds were occasional growling and yelping. "Okay, let's cross at the ford. We can approach them while their attention is on Missy."

But Dillon was shaking his head before I could even get the words out. "It's no good, Charles," he said. "It's pretty dark and there are too many. They might attack."

"He's right," said Cook, joining us.

"We can't just..." I stared into the darkness. Over the sound of the running water I heard the tearing of gristle and cracking of bones.

Missy was gone.

Chapter 17

As I stood, sopping wet on the river bank, my head swirled with grief, guilt and anger. In shock, I stared in the direction of the pack. It was completely dark as we walked slowly back to the camp. Cindy took my hand. She seated me in front of the fire in the outdoor kitchen, but I continued to shake. I was still trying to process what had happened. Missy was gone.

My stomach was in convulsions, and I couldn't sit still. I stood up and began pacing around, thinking about what had happened. Eventually I vomited in the woods and felt a little better. No one said a word. Finally, I returned to the fire. Someone brought me water. Cindy sat next to me. I looked around at all the worried faces and then back at the fire.

"Tell us what happened," said Cook eventually.

"She was worried," I said, gazing into the flames. "She came to see about me. The wolves were there. I had taken down a deer, and they were eating it. They heard Missy's voice."

Cindy put an arm around my shoulders and her other hand on my thigh. My legs trembled under her touch. I couldn't focus my attention. All I could see in my mind's eye was Missy being taken down by a pack of wolves. I couldn't believe this had happened, while I stood by in a fucking tree.

"They tore her to pieces. While she was alive, they ripped her apart. I tried to warn her. But she came anyway. She was worried about my welfare."

Tears were streaming down my face now. Others around me were crying.

"Better take him to his cabin," said Cook to Cindy, speaking quietly. "Everybody else better get inside their cabins, too, until we can size up the situation in the daylight tomorrow."

I let Cindy lead me to my cabin and, as if I was a child, she undressed me and put me into bed. She climbed in with me. I rolled over onto my side and let the sobs overwhelm me. I couldn't control myself, and at this point I didn't even care. Cindy spooned against me despite the heat. I eventually fell into a restless sleep, with visions of Missy, or maybe it was my Aunt Helen—I don't know which—drifting in and out of my dreams.

* * *

The next morning, Dillon, Cook, Trey, and I crossed the river with our bows and a handful of arrows. We saw nothing of the wolf pack near the ford, so made our way down the bank to where they had pulled Missy's body out of the water. The grass was brownish-red, but nothing else remained. Not even a shred of buckskin. They had either consumed everything or taken it away.

We made our way to the salt lick, and the story there was the same. An area of bloodstained leaves marked the place where the doe had fallen, but except for bits of fur and one large bone, the carcass was completely gone.

"They don't leave much," I observed.

"They probably dragged the bodies off somewhere," said Cook.

"I doubt it," said Dillon. "They just eat everything. Their jaws can break up bones."

"Well, they wouldn't have gotten far," I said. "We'd better grab supplies and get going."

"Say what?" asked Trey.

I looked at the other men. I sensed their hesitation, but didn't understand it.

"The wolves killed Missy. We have to go after her killers," I said, not understanding their confusion.

"I don't get it," said Dillon. "Are you worried they may attack again?"

"Look, boss," said Trey. "If we go after a wolf pack armed with nothing but homemade bows and arrows, we're inviting another attack."

"Wolves don't stay in one area," added Dillon. "They roam their territory. They shouldn't be a threat to our community anytime soon. In fact, I doubt you would be able to keep up with them if you did follow them."

I looked at Cook.

"Tell us what you're thinking," he said.

"The fucking wolves killed Missy! That's what I'm thinking!" This was a stupid conversation. Didn't they understand revenge?

"Is it about payback?" asked Trey.

"Look, will you join me or not? I'll go alone if I have to. I'm not just going to let them do this and get away with it."

They all looked at each other.

"Count me out," said Trey.

"Animals kill because that's what they do," said Dillon. "There is no desire to harm for harm's sake, only a desire to meet their needs. Revenge makes little sense. There's no point."

Cook let out a sigh. "Okay, I'll go with you," he said. "I can't let you do this alone."

"Thanks," I said. "Now let's get them. Especially that yellow motherfucker."

"A yellow wolf?" asked Trey.

"The leader," I said. "He's big and mean, with yellow-gray fur. I want him."

"Sometimes the alpha is female," said Dillon. "Are you sure it was a male?"

"Male or female, I don't give a fuck. I just want it dead."

* * *

Back at the cabin, I was packing up a few things when Cindy came in.

"I don't understand this," she said. "I loved Missy just like you." Her voice cracked. I knew she was trying not to cry. "I worked with her in the garden every day. We talked and cried together. But going out there into the wild just to hunt down wild wolves because they did what they do to survive? Why put yourself at risk? And me? What about me? What about us?"

"I've got to do this," I said, not looking at her as I wrapped up a bundle of pemmican. She didn't understand—she couldn't. She didn't hear the tearing of Missy's flesh in the dark.

"Can you even track a wolf pack?" she asked. "And what if they attack? Can you and Cook destroy an entire wolf pack with your arrows?"

"We'll figure it out."

"What if Missy had died from eating a poison berry? Would you hunt down the bush that grew it and kill it, too? This makes just about as much sense."

I took her by the arm. "I'll be careful, I promise. Two or three days out, that's all. If we don't get him by then, we'll come back."

"Him?"

"Yeah. Him. Her. The big yellow wolf. It was their leader and led them to Missy."

Cindy pulled her arm away. "This is a side of you I don't understand."

Chapter 18

Cook and I started out that afternoon. We didn't want to let the wolf pack get too far ahead of us. Cindy was right in that neither Cook nor I possessed the requisite skills to track a wolf pack through the forest. In fact, without Cook, I would've soon become lost in the woods. We headed north-northeast, with the distant mountain range to our right. Cook had explored in this direction for several miles and suggested we follow a small creek that meandered through the area.

We had no particular reason to believe the pack had traveled in the same direction as the creek, but it was possible. At least the creekbed offered an easy means of returning to the camp without getting lost once we headed back.

We kept up a steady pace all afternoon, almost jogging at times. The pack would move fast, so we, too, needed to move quickly. Cook never complained and, in fact, we spoke little.

Our time in the wild had conditioned us. We were stronger and leaner, so our stamina levels were beyond where they had been in our previous lives. I remember running six miles on blacktop, wearing expensive name-brand running shoes, with an air-conditioned house and ice-cold Gatorade waiting for me at the end of the run. And I thought I was in shape then? I chuckled thinking about that now. That was another life. I was different now. Like my ancestors, I was an integral part of the circle of life—nature in the raw.

As we jogged along, I glanced up at the sky, wondering if we were passing under a distortion. Missy was the first of us to go. Were they entertained by her grisly demise? I squeezed my fists tightly as I imagined the alien Watchers hovering in the sky.

An image came into my mind of Missy the first time I saw her, outside my cabin, and I felt that familiar prickling behind my eyes. The lump in my throat formed immediately, and tears started. I let 'em flow. They mixed with the sweat.

This was real life. Not like all those raw ugly things we tried to hide in our old lives. Putting on a happy face so we didn't have to explain how empty we felt inside. But out here, there was no pretense. There was no time or place for it. We were on the hunt.

We hunt. We hunt. In my head, these two words kept time with my steps and I fell into a comfortable cadence. We kept the pace going until darkness threatened, but saw no sign of the wolf pack.

After stopping for the day, we spent an hour collecting a large pile of wood from along the creek bank, and got a hearty fire going. We thought it prudent for one of us to stand guard, arrows close at hand, while the other rested. We had no bed rolls, so we slept on the forest litter. I had finished standing guard on my second shift and was drifting off to sleep when I heard Cook's voice.

"Charles. Wake up."

I sat up, immediately wide awake. "What is it?"

"Listen."

I tried to focus on the surrounding sounds. There was

the crackle of the fire and the cacophony of insects, but then a long, lonely howl reached my ears. It was a long way away—several miles. But it was there.

"It's coming from the east," said Cook. "In the morning, we'll leave the creek bed and head in that direction."

I nodded and looked up at the full moon. "I'd say we have two more hours of darkness before break of day. Let's head out as soon as it's light enough."

"Okay, boss," said Cook, smiling. "We'll get that sucker."

The next morning I roused myself from my restless sleep and was raring to go. But Cook hesitated.

"I can't make out the mountain range," he said, pointing toward the northeast. Thick morning fog obscured their profile.

"But surely that mist will burn off after a while," I said. "Then we will be able to see the mountains. So let's go ahead and get started."

"But by that time, we could be way off track. If we want to get back home, we have to go due east and we need to be able to see the mountains to do that. We don't want to get lost out here."

"Okay," I said, letting out a long breath. "That makes sense." I pulled out some pemmican, and the two of us quietly chewed while staring into the surrounding forest.

I knew Cook wasn't happy about this particular adventure. I knew it made little sense to him. Yet he had come along. He was a good friend. I felt the urge to say something, but I hesitated. In my old life, I had never thought about my buddies this way. They had my back, sure. They might offer some "can't miss" investment advice, or walk the dog while we travelled. But this was different. Cook was willing to risk his life to back me up. This was another level of dependable.

Our life was unforgiving. I may not get many more chances to say something. I didn't with Missy.

"Cook, I want to say something. Well, first, thanks for coming with me. I would have gotten lost in these woods without you. But also...thanks for understanding. For tolerating my crazy obsession."

"Well, we all loved Missy. And although I'm not sure why you feel compelled to risk your life to hunt down and kill a wild animal, I'll have your back, just like you would have mine."

I smiled at Cook. "Never doubt it."

Cook's comments had struck a chord within me. I didn't know where my family was or even if they were alive. But something powerful now existed between many of us in our little community. The bond I had with Cindy, Cook, and several of the others was much like a family connection, and even stronger in some respects. There were family members I wasn't sure I would risk my life for. But I wouldn't bat eye should I need to risk my life for these guys.

Soon, we were on the move again, with the sun peeking through the mists, giving us occasional glimpses of the mountain range. Our muscles warmed up as we again picked up our pace, trying to stay headed toward the east, with the peaks now slightly to our left.

"It's impossible to stay headed exactly east," said Cook, "but since the creek is behind us and running perpendicular to our course, we'll eventually reach it on our return, even if we veer off a degree or two."

We crossed several more small creeks, one of them at the bottom of a steep canyon. We climbed up its opposite side and onto an exposed and barren area, the bare rock broken up only by the occasional red cedar. Here, the land fell away to the southeast, and from our elevated position we had an unobscured view in that direction for many miles.

The landscape before us was an expanse of forest-covered hills, and in the distance, I detected glitters from a watery surface. Probably our river, just further downstream.

"If you were a wolf, where would you go?" I asked Cook.

Cook pointed his bow to the left, along a wooded ridge that ran off of the elevated barrens.

"Let's stick to that ridge," he said. "It looks like it goes a few miles. When we get to the end, we make camp for the night. And then, if there are no signs of the pack, we head home. Agreed?"

There had been no more howling since the previous evening, and no abandoned carcasses. No tracks in the mud along creek beds. The woods seemed endless and empty. The futility of our quest was becoming apparent, and my commitment was wearing thin.

"Agreed," I said.

The woods along the spine of the ridge were sparse, and we made good progress with little effort. As we neared the point where the ridge dropped into a small valley, we set up camp again, stacking up lots of wood.

We had started working on the fire when we both froze. In the distance, a long howl drifted across the landscape. It was far away, yet the hairs on the back of my neck stood up. It was them. We hadn't lost them.

Cook and I looked at each other, and just as I was about to speak, I heard a noise in the underbrush close to the camp. My heart pounded. Was it an attack? Cook and I both reached for our bows and loaded an arrow. The noise came closer. We pulled back our bow strings and pointed our arrows in the direction of the sound, which had come from a thick area of brush twenty feet away.

We caught a glimpse of movement. My eyes opened wide, my muscles readied for action.

Then we saw a flash of tan fur and a delicate, graceful movement into a clear area nearby. It wasn't a wolf. It was a deer, feeding in the fading light and oblivious to our presence.

Cook lowered his bow, breathing a sigh of relief. I, however, let my arrow fly. My arrow struck the unsuspecting deer in the middle of its chest and dropped it.

"Why did you do that?" asked Cook, surprise in his voice. "It's too far to carry the meat back."

"I know," I said, and hurried over to the deer to make sure it was dead. It was still thrashing, so I slashed an artery in its neck so it would bleed out quickly. "It's not for us. It's for baiting our trap."

I had realized there was no way we could keep up with a wolf pack on the move. And even if we did, they would likely attack us. Sure, that would give us an opportunity to take shots at the wolves, but it was a dangerous option. They could attack in a group and when we were unprepared. The obvious alternative was to induce them to come to us, but under circumstances in which we had the upper hand. We had to set a trap.

Cook and I roasted a piece of the fresh venison for our dinner. We then took out our blades and shredded the deer, making the corpse as bloody as possible, and hung it five feet off of the ground, the blood dripping and pooling below it.

We split up our stash of arrows. He took eight and I took

nine. We climbed up separate trees that provided us with a good view of the bait. And then we waited.

My position was strategically solid. I could see the deer carcass and had a good shot along the obvious access lane between two large maple trees. As darkness descended, my vision became impaired to the point where a shot at a moving wolf near the carcass would be dubious. But as I expected, the full moon rose over the horizon a few hours later, and the higher it rose, the more light it cast into the baited area. Our eyes were already accustomed to the moonless night, so this was more than adequate to take a decent shot.

The limb I was resting upon was far from comfortable, and I discovered, to my chagrin, that an ant trail meandered inches from my leg. There was no suitable place to relocate, so I had to tough it out, swatting at the small black critters in the dark and shifting my sitting position often. For the next few miserable hours, as the full moon ascended and the light grew stronger, we waited. I heard Cook, who sat in a tree thirty feet away, doing his own share of moving around and shifting position. It led me to wonder if we would be detected and perhaps scare off the wolf pack.

Just as the setting moon was a few degrees of arc from the tree line, threatening to blanket us in darkness once again, there was movement in the woods all around us. I froze as the familiar fear returned. There was no way the wolves could reach me, but to have this pack of vicious killers so close at hand was unnerving. But then I saw the yellow wolf, moving into an area of bright moonlight as it neared the deer carcass. I thought about Missy, and her body being pulled out of the river by these same wolves, and my fear became suffused with anger. I watched the pack gather around the dangling bait, dancing back and forth in a circle, unsure how to access the meat several feet over their heads. A few jumped up at it, nipping at it, sharp teeth snapping shut with a loud and powerful snap. *Those jaws could easily break my bones if they caught me.* Soon, the other wolves were all playing the game, tearing small shreds of flesh off the lower portion of the carcass.

The moving figures made difficult targets, but I aimed for the group and let go. I heard a quick yelp and all the wolves froze, looking intently around them. At that moment another arrow flew from Cook's tree and struck one wolf square in the midsection. He fell to the ground, but was not dead. He began whimpering and reaching with his mouth in a vain attempt at pulling the offending shaft from his side. I reached for another arrow and reloaded, but now that the pack had stopped moving, the woods were quiet and the wolves picked up on the sound of my movement. They all stared up at me. The yellow wolf, who was half a head taller than the others, took a few steps toward my tree, staring straight at me, its growl low and menacing.

It was the wolf that led the pack into the water to attack Missy. And it would rip my throat out in an instant if it had the chance.

"This arrow's for you, motherfucker," I said, aimed, and let it fly.

And then a remarkable thing happened. The yellow wolf moved to the left during the arrow's brief trajectory, and the arrow struck the empty ground where it had just stood.

Was it that the yellow wolf, its reflexes honed by a successful life in the wild, had somehow sensed the arrow coming toward it? Did it react to the twang of the bow? Or was it just pure chance? I didn't know.

Disturbed and even annoyed, I grabbed more arrows and took shots at the pack in rapid succession. So did Cook. We heard several wolves give yelps of pain, and a couple of them went down, but the overall effect was to make them even angrier. I called to Cook, "I'm down to one shot! Whatcha got?"

"One good one, one broken one," he called back.

"We haven't killed too many," I said.

"Nope. But we pissed them off good."

The sound of our voices brought the wolves to the bases of our two trees. They circled, looking up and growling. The yellow wolf was still alive and well.

"Remember the old days, when wolves were afraid of humans?" asked Cook.

I shook my head. "Not anymore. Not enough of us around these days, I guess."

"We'd better save our arrows," said Cook. "For the trek home. Though I don't expect these guys to leave soon."

I didn't think so, either. The sounds of pain from their fallen comrades had upset the pack, and they were furious. They would get at us if they could. I sat back for the long wait. I counted seven active wolves, although one was hobbling badly. In the dim light, I saw an additional three dark forms lying around the deer carcass, their movements feeble.

An hour later, day broke, illuminating the scene. Three wolves were down. Two of them were still alive, but probably would never rise again. The third was motionless. The hobbled wolf was sitting, licking the arrow protruding from his hind leg. I suspected he was bleeding badly and would join his friends before long. But that left six healthy, angry wolves, including one super-wolf leading them. Plenty of killing power for the likes of Cook and me.

After a few more hours, the remaining members of the pack returned to their game of tearing off bits of flesh from the deer carcass, and sniffed curiously around their immobile companions. The yellow wolf, however, ignored the game and returned to standing and staring up at me, occasionally snarling or growling.

His eyes glowed with a red hue. They were full of anger.

I had a clear shot and was tempted to use my last arrow to bring the sucker down. But it had gotten under my skin. I wondered if it would simply shift aside as the arrow flew. Part of me realized that the previous dodge was just a fluke, but I wasn't completely sure. And why did it stare at me and not at Cook? Was it making this personal? Well, so be it. It was already personal on my part.

I wondered about the extent of their patience. We had pissed them off by shooting at them. And with the deer carcass at hand, they had food. I feared they would try to wait us out. The prospect of sitting on my uncomfortable tree limb for days on end was not appealing.

"It doesn't like you," said Cook, now visible in the gathering daylight.

"The feeling is mutual," I said, looking down at the yellow demon below me. "It's the one that led the pack to Missy."

"We'll be here for a while," said Cook.

"How much pemmican do you have left?"

Cook rummaged around in his bag.

"Enough for a day or two, I guess. If I stretch it out."

"Yeah, same here."

Over the course of the next hour, the pack dislodged the

deer carcass from its limb and devoured most of it. This settled them down. They sat on the forest litter, their bellies full. But they still watched. I no longer saw movement from their wounded comrades. Our arrows had done their work. Three dead. The hobbled wolf got up occasionally, but moved slowly, and would make pathetic whimpering noises as he tried to get about. It was striking how much a hurt wolf sounded like an ailing pet dog.

The yellow wolf broke off its stare to wander over to its hobbling comrade and sniffed at the arrow, licking at the wound. It looked at the remains of the shredded deer corpse and suddenly bounded away, running through the woods. Its comrades watched for a moment before they followed, crashing through the undergrowth, with the hobbling wolf closing up the rear.

Chapter 19

We listened to the sound of the wolves bounding through the brush, moving further away. I couldn't believe our luck. They had taken off, leaving a half-eaten deer carcass and their fallen comrades behind. It struck me as peculiar behavior for a wolf pack, but I was no expert.

"Cook," I said, trying not to speak too loudly. "What's going on? Did they really leave?"

"They have definitely left," Cook said. "I'm not sure why they did, but they left."

"Should we make a run for it?"

Cook listened for a minute.

"God, yeah," he said. "Let's get the hell out of here."

My legs were painful and stiff as I climbed down from my tree. Once on the ground I realized it may take some time for my leg muscles to adjust. They felt weak, and I felt exposed and vulnerable should the pack return.

"Let's move," said Cook. "Back up the ridge and then due west."

"We're outta here."

We started slowly, but it didn't take long for my legs to loosen up as we jogged along the ridgeline. A few miles later, back on the barren plain, we slowed down to a brisk walk, striking due west by keeping the distant mountain range just behind us and just to our right.

"Well, we got a few of them," said Cook.

"Yeah," I said between breaths, "but I wanted that big alpha."

"But this is enough. Right?"

My resentment centered on the yellow wolf, not its henchmen. It was the one I wanted to take down. But we had missed our chance. How could I ask Cook or anyone else to strike out again? Perhaps one day the yellow wolf would visit our community, and I would get my chance. Time to let this lie and get back to our group. I had other responsibilities, like preparing for winter.

"It's enough," I said.

As the day neared its end, we had seen no sign of the wolf pack and I was feeling good about our chances. The pace, the stress, and the lack of sleep the night before had exhausted us. Fortunately, we found the creek bed without difficulty, and since it contained an ample supply of driftwood along its banks, we decided it would be a good place to camp for the night. We stacked up a huge pile of wood and got the fire going just as the dark of night settled across the land. We kept the fire blasting bright, with one person standing guard at all times. It meant our exhausted bodies would not get much sleep, but if we got through the night, we would make it home the next day, and could rest to our heart's content in our snug cabins.

At first, time passed without incident. But then, a few hours before daylight, I heard the sound that sent chills down my spine. Howls filled the night air. They came from three different wolves, spaced out and perhaps a mile away.

I awoke Cook. He listened and was immediately alert.

"They followed us!" he said.

"I wonder if they somehow knew we would come down from the trees if they left us."

"What should we do?" he asked, looking up in the nearby trees for suitable perches.

I mulled it over. If we climbed back up on a limb, we would be back where we were the night before, with one day's less food. Perhaps the fire would keep them at a distance, but eventually it would burn out.

On the other hand, daylight was only two hours away and home was less than a day's hike.

"Let's make a break for it," I said. "The moon is bright, and we can follow the creek without losing our way."

Cook nodded, and in a matter of minutes, we were crashing our way through the thick undergrowth along the creek bank. We were unencumbered, but because we often got tangled up in the thick growth, the going was slow. We decided to step into the dark water of the creek, which never rose above our calves, and splashed over the flat rocks at a reasonable pace.

"They might lose our scent if we stay in the water for a while," suggested Cook.

Daylight came with no incident, so we left the cluttered creek bed, which, with all of our splashing, made me feel conspicuous. With the creek visible in the morning light, we were able to pace along it, beyond the thick underbrush, but close enough to see the stream.

It was nearing noon when we saw them. I looked to my left, and there was the yellow wolf, perhaps thirty feet away and moving alongside me on a parallel course. There were noises behind us, and I caught glimpses of the rest of the pack.

"They're here," I said, now hurrying and breathless.

"I know," said Cook. He had his one good arrow out and was loading his bow. I did the same.

The pack shadowed us for an hour while we kept up as fast a pace as possible. Then they moved in closer. One gray-brown wolf bounded to within ten feet behind us and gave a low growl. Cook spun and released his arrow, hitting the wolf square in the chest. It fell down and yelped pathetically, distracting the others as they gathered around their wounded comrade. Cook and I hurried onward.

"Better make that last shot count," Cook said. "We still have about five hours to reach home."

"We won't make it," I said.

"We have to try."

If we kept jogging along the stream, we would be doomed when the wolves made their move. Our only chance was to make a stand, with a big fire at our back. We couldn't stop them for long, but maybe for a while.

"Stop!" I said. "While they're distracted with their wounded comrade, let's gather wood—there's plenty along the creek. We need to get a fire going. We can take one down with my arrow, and if they attack, at least we would have the fire. We have our hand blades, and we can make spears. Perhaps we can do enough damage to discourage them."

Cook nodded. "Okay. If they rush us while we're on the move, we don't have a chance."

"Let's do it. Fast!"

Quickly, we gathered the wood. We heard the wounded wolf crying several hundred yards away, still occupying the attention of his brethren. While Cook worked on starting a fire with his bow, I ran around collecting more wood. Within ten minutes, we had a significant stack of wood and a blaze going. I had never moved so fast in my life.

I stood beside the fire, catching my breath, when I heard cracking in the forest in several places around us. Cook was standing up and using his hand blade to sharpen a long stick. His motions were quick, hectic.

"If you have the chance, make me one, too," I said.

I was holding the arrow in my bow with the string taut. I wasn't about to set it down.

Cook held the sharpened end of the stick in the fire. "It will harden the point," he said. "Plus, any flames still on the wood may scare them off."

The fire was growing, and Cook and I stood with our backs to it. I pulled out a flaming branch from the fire and held it in front of me. "Firebrands should help keep them away."

There were five wolves now, and they circled around us about fifteen feet distant. I watched the yellow wolf. It seemed its eyes were on me exclusively.

I pulled up my bow to take my aim, and it immediately flinched back and stepped further into the woods.

"Somehow, that fucker knows when I'm aiming at it," I exclaimed.

A solid black wolf veered off from the circle and approached, moving straight toward Cook at speed. Cook readied his spear, but this was a clear attack, so time had come to use our last arrow. I fired as the black wolf leaped toward Cook. Cook's spear caught it in the chest and broke. My arrow struck her on the hind leg. A painful wound, but not a killing shot. It yelped and hobbled away. Again, the other wolves backed away.

"We need more spears," I cried. "And plenty of firebrands at hand's reach."

We took our hand blades and hacked at a few nearby saplings. We took two or three apiece to the fire and sharpened them, then burned the points to harden them. As I held one of my spears in the fire, I noticed a stiff breeze had come up, blowing the smoke sharply away from us. I looked up in the sky.

"Oh, no," I said. "Look."

Cook looked up at the angry, dark clouds bearing down on us. The winds were picking up, and I heard distant thunder.

"We'll could lose the fire when that rain storm hits," he said. "Looks like nature is conspiring against us."

"What should we do?" I asked.

Cook shrugged. "We're more vulnerable if we run. At least here, we have the creek to our backs. Fire or no fire, we have to fight or die."

I thought of Cindy and our cluster of cabins, our home. It was merely a few hours away, and we were at the end of our rope. I wondered if everyone had been right. Did I put Cook's life in danger for the sake of irrational demons that drove me? Or was it just bad luck?

In short order, the wolves returned and once again circled us. The black wolf had dislodged the arrow shaft from its hindquarters and joined the pack, despite the bloody gouge on its chest from Cook's spear stab. It was us versus Mother Nature and five determined wolves. It didn't look good.

Just as the first heavy raindrops hit our faces, the yellow wolf broke off from the circle and made straight for me. I yelled at the top of my lungs and thrust my crude spear into its thick neck as it came. It yelped and retreated a few steps, but shook off the pain and came at me a second time. I reached behind me, picked up a firebrand, and held it in front of the wolf. It stared at it and at me, growling. It moved suddenly to the side and tried to get around it, but I was too quick for it. It stopped and growled more. I saw its muscles flexing, and watched the raindrops dampen my firebrand, reducing the flame. I sensed the beast, despite the dwindling flame, was about to launch itself at me. I gripped my spear tightly. This was the moment of truth. If I could just take it down before the others got to me...

Then a bolt of lightning blazed across the sky, followed by a loud clap of nearby thunder. The yellow wolf yelped at the sound, flinching to the ground and looking up at the sky. Another bolt seared overhead, and a tremendous thunderclap followed, vibrating my bones. The yellow wolf backed up several feet and cowered low on the ground, whimpering. It was strange to see this animal, vicious in appearance and disposition, so afraid of the sound of thunder. Its comrades, not so fearful, gathered anxiously around their leader, uncertain what to make of the situation.

Another blast of thunder, this time directly overhead, and the yellow wolf's nerve broke. It dashed into the forest, searching for safe haven. The rest of the pack looked back at Cook and me and then bolted after their leader.

It was a striking and unexpected sequence of events. Our pet dog in Indianapolis was fearful of thunderstorms. At the first sound of thunder, even distant thunder, he would seek me out and bury his face in my lap, removable only with much force and sharp words. But to see this big alpha wolf similarly afflicted would have been almost comical under different circumstances.

"This is our chance. Let's move!" I said to Cook.

Keeping our spears but nothing else, we took off along

the creek bed. There was no telling how long the thunder would distract the big wolf, so we ran through the rain at full stride. After a mile or so, utterly exhausted, we slowed to a jog. We listened for the distinctive sound of the wolves crashing through the forest around us, but there was none. We ignored our weariness and kept forcing one step in front of the other. In less than two hours, we had covered the last miles to home.

We staggered into the village, tossed our spears aside, and collapsed. Lying on my back and breathing heavily, I looked up to see Cindy's concerned face peering down at me. We'd made it. I smiled.

"God, it's good to see you again," I said.

Chapter 20

After twelve blissful hours of uninterrupted sleep, I pulled my sore body from my bunk and went out into the offensively bright daylight. I found Cook already up, sitting with most of the others at our big table and chatting about our adventure.

"Here's the great hunter himself," said Christie, giving me a smile. "Glad to see you back."

"Glad to be back. Though I wish we had had more success."

"Cook said you got a few of them," said Dillon. "Honestly, I was surprised you even found them."

"Ha!" said Cook. "They were pretty intent on finding us. That big yellow wolf doesn't like Charles."

"Well, the feeling's mutual," I said. "And if I get another chance, that sucker is going down."

"But even so," said Trey, "we appreciate what you guys did. Killing those wolves won't bring Missy back, but it makes me feel a little better about her loss."

"Yeah, me too," said Christie. "I can hardly bear to think about Missy's last minutes of life. How horrible it must have been."

"My God!" cried Eileen. "Don't even talk about it."

Samuel, who was standing by the group with his foot on the bench, shook his head. "I don't get it," he said. "Cook and

Charles run off into the wilderness with homemade bows and arrows to give a wolf pack payback. Am I the only one that sees that as lunacy?"

"No, you're not!" said Cindy, with a surprising sharpness to her voice. "It bordered on insanity. I loved Missy as much as the next person, but how does it make sense to go after animals in the wild because they killed her? They had left the area and weren't a threat anymore."

"They could come back this way," said Cook.

"Maybe," replied Cindy. She peered at me. "But tell me, Charles, is that why you went after the wolf pack? To protect us from later attacks?"

I shrugged. "In part. But mainly I wanted to get the bastard that took Missy away from us."

Cindy threw her hands up in the air. "You see? Insanity."

Later that evening, as Cindy and I sat in my cabin, there was an awkwardness between us that had never been there before. She said little, and so did I.

A few of her things were lying about the cabin. During our silence, she got up and gathered them together.

"I need a few days alone," she said. "Got to think things over."

"C'mon, Cindy. Is this necessary?"

She stared down at the bundle of items in her hands, her face distorted with puzzlement.

"This is a part of you I don't understand," she said. "This reckless resentment seems so different from the kind, generous part of you I have seen so often. I've just got to sort it out."

Over the next few days, Cindy kept her distance. During her absence, I tried to reflect on what concerned her. About why I felt a personal resentment toward the wolf pack and, in particular, the yellow wolf. It seemed natural. I loved Missy, and they took her away from me. If it was wrong to feel that way, I didn't understand why.

But I was ready to try to understand. I missed Cindy and wanted her to be happy with me again. I decided to approach her after dinner and try to talk it out. During the meal, she sat at the opposite end of the banquet table, and Samuel plopped down beside her. I watched from the corner of my eye as they engaged in conversation. He seemed to have garnered all her attention. She did not look my way even once.

But I was not to be deterred. She lingered around the fire with Samuel after dinner, still in conversation, so I stationed myself along the trail to her cabin and waited. My plan was to sit down with her in her cabin and make it clear I was ready to do what it took to make things right.

I was somewhat surprised when I saw Cindy walking with Samuel toward her cabin, still in conversation. A little embarrassed, I stepped into the shadows as they walked by. My hope was that Samuel was just being a gentleman and was walking Cindy to her cabin door. Once he left, I would knock.

But to my chagrin, he stepped inside with her.

What were they doing in there?

If they were just interested in talking, surely somewhere outside would do just as well. I knew Cindy had an active libido, but would she really invite Samuel to her bed so quickly? The thought galled me. It was time to get things out in the open, so I went and knocked on the door.

Cindy opened the door partly, and looked at me through the opening. "Now is not a good time, Charles. Come back later."

"I know you have Samuel in there with you. But I think you and I should talk before you do anything rash."

Suddenly, the door pushed open all the way and Samuel's dark frame filled the doorway. "She said it's not a good time, copier salesman. So get lost!"

"I'm not talking to you. That's my girl you have in there with you."

"Not anymore," Samuel barked. "Get lost or you I will make sure you will regret it."

"Samuel!" cried Cindy. "Please...just back off." She turned to me. "What is it Charles? Why are you here?"

"I've been thinking a lot. About us and about why I do things. I wanted to talk to you about it. I wanted to fix things."

"I'm not sure you can, Charles."

"Cause he's a fucking wacko!" spat Samuel. "Chasing wolves through the woods."

"Fuck you, Samuel. Are you really trying to take my girl from me?"

"I had my eye on her before you did. I can take her if I want."

"Stop it!" cried Cindy. "I'm nobody's possession! Now Samuel, please leave. I want to talk to Charles alone."

"What? Are you kidding me?"

I was tempted to make some retaliatory remark, but realized if I wanted Cindy's ear, I had to remain civil. So I bit my tongue.

"Please, Samuel," repeated Cindy. "Leave us."

Samuel let out an exasperated sigh, and stomped away a few steps before turning. "If you get tired of that loser, you know where I am."

Before I could reply, Cindy pushed me inside the door.

"Just let him be," said Cindy. "Tell me what is on your mind."

"I will, but tell me. Were you going to …"

"Going to what?"

"You know, you and Samuel."

"What! You think I would jump from your bed to his in less than a week? What kind of woman do you think I am?"

"But why did you bring Samuel to your cabin?"

"Because we were having an interesting discussion and the mosquitos were eating us alive. My God, Charles."

I looked sheepishly at the ground. She was right. The mosquitos were really bad out tonight. "Sorry." Then I took a breath and looked up into her eyes. "But I want to know what it is that made you unhappy with me. I want to understand it."

"Okay Charles. I will try to explain it to you. But listen carefully, or you will lose me."

I sat quietly for a good hour listening to Cindy. But her general theme was fairly simple—she did not want to be with someone that could not let things go. By being a hard ass about rules, by taking revenge on nature, and by being resentful about those that put us here, I was unable to enjoy the good things in life. And despite our circumstances, there were good things to appreciate, including the new special connection she and I had.

As she enumerated my failings, objections rose up in my mind. But I could see the time was not right to voice them. I swallowed them and nodded.

I was glad I did. The days after our conversation, Cindy softened up. She came back to me and soon, we were back to or previous life of sleeping together and frequent love-making. I kept to myself a recurring dream of piercing the body of the yellow wolf through the heart with my arrow and watching it bleed to death in agony before my eyes.

Missy's tragic death hung over our little community for quite some time. We often investigated the surrounding terrain for any sign of unfriendly visitors, such as tracks in the muddy banks along the river or scat among the nearby trees. Nighttime was particularly stressful. We listened intently to the sounds around the compound, and even walking between cabins and the work areas made us feel vulnerable. No one stayed out in the fields or in the garden after dark.

The distracting fear pushed thoughts of the strange distortions further from our immediate concern. We never forgot they were there, and we still didn't understand them, but they didn't interact with us in any way. Not knowing what the beings looked like or anything about them made it easier for us to think of them abstractly. To me, they became a kind of disembodied consciousness hovering several feet above the ground, not unlike the notion of the Christian God watching from on high.

Even though I no longer feared them, I often considered them during my more contemplative moments. And the more I thought about their intentions, the less sense they made. Okay, it would make sense if we were some form of entertainment. That we were odd little creatures trying to survive, and the visitors in the observation chambers got pleasure from watching us struggle—much like a reality TV show, as Amber had suggested.

But if we set aside the "Earth as a zoo" idea, we had to assume these beings were, in fact, studying us to learn about us. To learn how we would live without technology. To learn how we would react to life's challenging struggles. How would we develop? How would we adapt to the primitive technology while embedded in a world in which nature reigned supreme? Perhaps they had subjugated other cultures, and we were just part of a comprehensive interstellar study of indigenous peoples.

But it still didn't work out. Why would they be interested in our particular set of challenges? While it was true we didn't possess modern technology, they gave us *some* technology, albeit of a rustic sort. I remembered an episode of a TV show mocking the Amish for deciding that their preferred technology, the technology of the Victorian era, was deemed the "correct" amount of technology. It was its arbitrariness that made it comical.

So why were *we* given *this* amount of technology—crude iron implements, log cabins, and grain production? Why would a society struggling in our particular way interest the aliens intellectually? Wasn't it equally arbitrary?

Perhaps the level of technology we were given was the most primitive level of technology that we, citizens of our modern age, could use to survive. Maybe they wanted us to be pushed to the limit, testing our determination and ingenuity, yet keep us around. Maybe that was the experiment. Perhaps it made sense. Yet if they knew where our breaking point was, then they would already understand us pretty well. So what would be the point of this big experiment?

Heck, maybe they *did* just enjoy watching us suffer.

On one late morning as I was returning from a hunt at the salt lick and lost in my thoughts, when I happen to almost step upon Amber and Ramiro having sex underneath the distortion next to the wheat field. As they covered themselves with their buckskins, Amber smiled and said they were just

159

giving the nosy "little perverts" what they wanted.

I hurried on and left them their privacy. But again I worried about the difficulties of pregnancy and raising a child in our circumstances. So far we had been lucky, but that couldn't last.

Cursing at a nearby distortion became common whenever some aspect of our miserable lives annoyed us. Sometimes we spoke to them, as if we were certain that beings were inside watching us, asking why they would do this to us. They were often the scapegoats for anything unpleasant that happened.

Those damn aliens. They were indirectly responsible for the loss of Missy. They were responsible for the mad itching of my scalp and skin. They were responsible for the stink and sweat in which I slept every night. For the never-ending sequence of tedious chores, from cleaning up to cutting and hauling wood, to threshing grain, to maintaining ourselves and our settlement, to rendering fat for candles, to hunting, skinning, tanning, and smoking the deer we killed. Every day was labor-filled and hard. And when we had down time, there was nothing to read, no computers, no TV, just each other.

Those fucking bastards.

The more my resentment grew, the more difficult it became to keep it hidden from Cindy. Strangely enough Cindy and others seemed to be okay with our plight. They took it in stride. Cindy missed her children, and her oversized breasts often made her miserable in the heat, but she seemed to thrive. It pleased her to weed and otherwise tend our garden, setting aside and drying seeds from the various vegetables for next season. I saw the excitement in her eyes whenever she would figure out some new use for a plant. And she seemed proud of Dillon and me as we became more skilled at taking deer, admiring the carcasses we brought in and complimenting the two of us.

That something as mundane as a slain deer would have such an energizing effect on not only Cindy, but everyone, was surprising. There was a growing confidence and enthusiasm for what we were accomplishing. We were figuring it out. Ramiro had increased his supply of fish, mostly due to his clever fish traps. Our hunting efforts provided a steady stream of fresh meat. We bathed and cleansed ourselves with Rebecca's lye soap, although it was mushy and sometimes too caustic. And as the days got cooler, Cindy brought in an assortment of "taste-tested" berries. She had tried them herself to determine their value as a food source or other uses. A small purple one caused vomiting, for example, which could conceivably be of value.

All of us appreciated the ripe berries. Along with the honey, they added flavor and sweetness to our otherwise bland diet. It was amazing that a bit of sugar would be so savored. I reflected on the sweets and drinks we used to enjoy in our previous lives, and how far the sugar in them could have been stretched to sweeten our current diet.

And while the welcome relief of the cooler days further buoyed our growing morale, they also foretold what was to come. We couldn't ignore what the approaching winter meant. Our greatest concern was the tiring task of harvesting the ripening grain. We had found two wrought-iron scythes hanging outside the workshop, and put them to use, constantly sharpening them. The implements were balanced over one's shoulders while walking into the grain, swinging the blade back and forth. It took practice to get the hang of the motion, and the effort took its toll on the back muscles, tiring them quickly. But Michael and Harvey, the two assigned the responsibility of seeing that the fields were harvested and the grain collected, were young lads, and their muscles responded. They were both completely lean now, with toned and tanned upper bodies.

Once we felled the stalks of wheat, we tied them up into bundles and carried them to the flat work area next to the storage bins. We took the old grain out of the silos and stored it in the clay pots Amber had made out of a reddish mud from the river bank. The new grain stalks had to be thrashed against a stone until all the kernels were removed. Then we gathered the individual grains and tossed them into the bins. We dried the ears of corn in the sun, stripping off and storing the hardened kernels.

Typically, our meals were comprised of either a bland porridge made from the wheat kernels, or tortillas made from flour or cornmeal, sometimes filled, sometimes not. The tortillas often had tiny bits of stone in them that were more than just an annoyance. If someone's tooth cracked, there would be little we could do about it in our circumstances, except live with the pain. Worrying about medical emergencies, including dental issues, plagued me constantly. What would we do? It was coming. It was inevitable.

As the forest foliage became tinged with red and orange, preparing warm clothes and bedding for the upcoming winter became an urgent concern. We knew of no way to make cloth, as there were no sheep or cotton plants. But thanks to Dillon's good memory, we were able to master the art of tanning our accumulating stock of buckskins using tree bark from the cypress trees growing along the river. We boiled the reddish bark in a clay vat for an hour before steeping the buckskins in the reddened water. This step was necessary, or the skins would become stiff and rot.

We figured the requirements of winter dictated two sets of buckskin clothes per person as a minimum. That way, each person could double up—wear both sets—if it got particularly cold. Also, two sets of fur-lined moccasins for each person, and two buckskin blankets for the upcoming cold nights. It took several full-grown deer to make one buckskin suit, and since there were sixteen of us, we needed to kill, skin, and dress around sixty-four deer. And blankets required half that many again. Dillon and I were kept busy stalking the salt lick.

Fortunately, our aim and stealth improved steadily, as did our skills at making our archery equipment. And there seemed no end of the parade of game that came to the lick to satisfy their mineral needs. We smoked the deer meat to preserve it, and sometimes mixed the meat with fat and berries to make pemmican. Deer rib bones and smaller bones were sharpened and used for spear points and other tools. Unfortunately, wild deer are lean beasts with little fat, which would have been so valuable around our village.

There were a few other fur-bearing animals in our general area, such as beaver, that we occasionally took with our traps and snares. But beavers are small and their pelts insufficient for clothing us. The big prize would have been to kill a bear, and we managed to take down an adolescent. But it possessed relatively little fur. We used the beaver and bear fur for various special needs, such as hats and gloves.

As the colorful woodland foliage became brown litter covering the forest floor, the days shifted from cool to cold. Yet Cook continued his forays into the surrounding wilderness. In fact, with the leaves falling from the trees, he found more vantage points from which to scope out the land. It wasn't unusual for him to be gone a night or two during his wanderings. I often worried about him being attacked by a bear or a wolf pack, but he said he was accustomed to the discomfort of sleeping up on a tree branch, where he was relatively safe.

Despite his persistence, he found nothing to give us the slightest glimmer of hope. Every indication suggested that we were alone in the middle of a vast wilderness. This did not stop many of us from discussing and planning a sojourn downriver. I desperately wanted to get away, to find out what had happened, and to see if there were others alive. But I was in no hurry. Winter was coming. It made no sense to strike out into the wild before the milder days of spring. But venture out we would.

Chapter 21

Winter hit with its full intensity. It was worse than any of us had imagined. Not because the temperatures were extreme—they seemed similar to what I would have experienced back in Indiana—but because the cold was everywhere, constantly permeating our lives. Our only defense was a warm fire. We kept fires going in our cabins, in our outdoor kitchen, and in the meeting hall where we took our meals. But fires meant labor in the form of collected firewood. And as the weeks went by, we had to travel further and further into the surrounding forest to find it.

Veronica now spent her entire day collecting wood. But the kitchen fire and the fire in the meeting hall had top priority, with much smaller amounts allotted to each of the sixteen cabins. So no one had fires blazing big in their cabin hearths unless they wanted to fetch their own wood. A fire in your cabin kept you warm if you sat next to the hearth, but the warmth was never constant in the rest of the cabin.

At night we wrapped up in our buckskin blankets on our wooden plank beds, but as the fires dwindled out, we were never securely snug like we were on mattresses in our former lives.

We couldn't spend all our time in our cabins, either. There

was too much work to be done outside. As the temperatures dropped below freezing, the creek and the edges of the river iced up. Swimming in the frigid river was only for the hardy, so we adopted the practice of hauling clay pots of water into the cabins and dumping them into a larger clay vessel, which we used for most of our personal cleaning. Fetching clean water and supplementing our personal allowance of firewood became additional annoying chores that we had to attend to every day. At least there were no fields or gardens to tend to in the winter.

We had managed to accumulate enough tanned buckskins to give everyone two outfits, and double buckskins were warmer. Yet they were less than ideal. They were stiff in the morning cold and accumulated lice. If they ever got wet, they became slimy and miserable. But the work still had to be done, no matter how unpleasant the weather.

As we got further into the winter and the temperatures dropped, a surprising thing happened. Cold was our constant companion, but we stopped thinking about the cold. It wasn't that we didn't feel it—it was more that we didn't care as much that we were cold.

I remembered reading about some poor child who had been lost in the woods and reared by wolves. He was eventually returned to civilization, and the boy, who had lived naked in the forest, loved to dash outside when the freezing weather came, discard his clothing, and play with the snow. The author's point was that when it comes to the cold, our bodies are heartier that we realize. Now I was convinced, too. The cold was pervasive, but so what? Carry on and ignore it. And we did just that, just as we had done with the alien Watchers in the sky.

There was one traditional means of staying warm that many of us employed. Cook and Christie, both of whom I admired a lot, had become good friends soon after our time here began. Their connection had grown over the months. During the depths of winter, they hardly ever slept apart. Trey and Rebecca were another constant pairing, and that seemed in the natural order of things. They were both beautiful people with good natures, though they were both particularly unhappy in our primitive circumstances.

Most of the others would take advantage of evening company intermittently. Poor Amber, craving love and having no clue how to find it, often made the rounds with the other men, who soon tired of her. I worried about the effects of so much rejection, but she seemed to take it all in stride.

I figured her romantic pursuits probably mirrored the ones she had in her previous life, but it was still sad to see. I felt fatherly feelings toward her, and was tempted a couple of times to sit her down and have a talk with her about how she was conducting her life. She needed to realize she was being used. Didn't she have more pride in herself?

I had talked to Alex about sex when he was about thirteen, but Amber wasn't a pubescent teenager. Ultimately, I decided that it wasn't my place. Cindy didn't want to get involved either. So, we all just watched it happen.

In fact, interpersonal drama was the least of our problems. There wasn't much time for it, with survival being the top priority.

Sometimes groups of friends would gather in one cabin, all huddled together under several buckskin blankets in one bed, chatting the night away. Eileen, Ramiro, Sasha, and Veronica often did this. Michael and Harvey, who had become best friends, often spent the night in the same cabin, while Samuel and Dillon almost always kept to themselves, Amber's visits constituting the most frequent exception.

Cindy and I put the little hiccup of my wolf pack adventure behind us, and our relationship continued to deepen. Sex was a huge part of it. The cold and the vigorous outdoor life continued to do wonders for our libidos. With our bodies so easily accessible, with nothing but loose buckskins covering us, making love required nothing more than loosening a leather thong. We made love in our cabins and even outside in the cold. Cindy seemed to have an insatiable hunger for sex, and I, too, was sexually charged in a way I had not been since my twenties.

But our carnal appetites didn't obscure our deeper connection. I found my feelings for her growing stronger than anything I had ever felt for Pam. I would lie awake at night, Cindy sleeping contently beside me, and listen to her breathing while I worried about her welfare. With no medications beyond a few medicinal plants that Cindy had discovered, we were vulnerable to disease. An infection or ailment that would have been simply treated in our previous lives might now kill us, or at least cause us agony for long stretches of time. We had one advantage over our pioneer ancestors, though: we had all been immunized in our previous lives as part of standard health protocols.

I took comfort in the fact that Cindy seemed to be of hearty stock. I was inclined to suffer from digestive tract ailments due to our rustic diet, but she wasn't similarly affected. I constantly admired her attitude, and how she flourished with the hard work. She said more than once that she enjoyed it. From time to time, I even wondered if she *preferred* it here. On the face of it, it didn't seem plausible. Life was still dismal and difficult. The daunting prospect of our entire future spent living this way would get anyone down. Yet Cindy seemed okay with it. She seemed happy with life.

I often wondered if Alex would have liked her better than Pam. He was a good kid, despite being self-centered, which I guess was normal for kids his age. Pam had resented my attention to Alex's needs and claimed I spoiled him. There had never been a genuine friendship between those two. But Cindy was a much more nurturing and self-confident person than Pam. I was inclined to believe that Alex would have warmed to Cindy's good nature.

Thoughts of Alex, even in the hypothetical embrace of a loving new family that included Cindy, always left an empty pang in my stomach. I had to believe he was alive and safe back home, or if not, somewhere in this expanse of wilderness in another community similar to this one. But not having any idea was profoundly disturbing. And what was worse was that his memory faded with each passing day. How long were we asleep? How old was he now, if he was still alive? And what did he look like?

Sometimes it made me so angry that I felt the need to strike out. I didn't want to take out my resentment and bitterness on the others, especially Cindy, so I'd leave camp for the day, taking my bow and arrows, ready to kill anything I saw.

If there was no game at hand, I'd exhaust my quiver aiming and firing at the distortion near the salt lick. Then I'd find the arrows and do it all over again from another angle. And then again. Over and over until I was exhausted. It was a lot of time to waste, but if it made me easier to live with, so be it. Sometimes you just have to get it out of your system. And I always felt better afterward.

With the forest clear of most of its foliage, we saw much further into the trees. One crisp, clear morning, the land had a fresh blanket of snow. I wandered through the woods just past the cornfield, looking for deer tracks. I took a shot at a distortion hovering nearby and watched the arrow veer suddenly in another direction, as it always did. As I was retrieving the arrow, I glimpsed yellow in the distant woods—a flash of isabelline fur. Armed with plenty of arrows, I ran for the spot, but saw nothing but trees. There were no tracks anywhere in the snow.

"Bastard!" I muttered.

Chapter 22

One early spring morning, Cindy had gotten out of bed to coax the cabin fire to life. I pulled myself up and sat on the edge of the bed, watching her nude form as she stood in front of the hearth. My scalp was particularly itchy, and Cindy caught me scratching away.

"Damn lice," I said.

She smiled and came over. "Let me see if I can help."

She combed through my hair with her fingers, pinching out the lice. Then I noticed her look curiously at one before tentatively putting it in her mouth.

"What are you doing?" I asked, astonished.

"It's bitter."

"You just ate a lice!"

"A louse, you mean. I saw a TV show on ape colonies that pick lice from each other's fur and eat what they find. It's an additional source of protein."

"Gross. And you decided you would copy ape behavior?"

"Yeah." She shrugged off my disgusted expression. "They're not so bad. Wanna try one?" She snickered and extended her pinched finger and thumb toward my mouth.

"No thanks," I said, scowling.

Cindy shrugged and continued to pull out my lice and eat

them.

"Our lives are different," she said after a few minutes. "We're becoming different beings. Get used to it."

"I don't want to get used to it."

"Aw, come on, sweetie, it's not that bad."

"It's pretty bad. And I can't ever forget those alien assholes put us in this predicament and now they watch us suffer."

"Well, that's assuming your crazy theory is right about the nature of the distortions. But even so, all of that is out of our control. We have each other, and we're all getting much better living our new lives. Remember your promise to me. Can't you let it go?"

I stood up and began pacing, getting angrier with every step. How could she accept this? "Whoever 'they' are, they did this to us. And maybe to Alex and your children! And everyone else, for all we know. How can you just let it go?"

Cindy looked at me and I saw the disappointment in her eyes. It was our usual practice to make love in the morning once the fire hearth was ablaze, but now I was aggravated, and not in the mood. Not that I blamed her for any of this. But damn, I wished she was more pissed off about it.

"You know what?" she said, picking up her buckskins. "I'll wash up in my cabin." She rubbed her hand through my hair. "I'll see you at breakfast."

"I'm surprised you have any appetite left," I said, trying to lighten the mood. "You ate quite a few lice." She walked to the door without a reply. "That's weird behavior," I called after her as she closed the door. "Just saying," I added weakly, and mostly to myself.

I stood there feeling guilty about my display of agitation. I looked at the large clay vessel that held the chilly water I had dumped in there the night before, and at the fire struggling for life.

"The hell with this," I said.

The river had never completely frozen over, although several feet of ice had formed along the shore. But with the onset of spring, the ice was thinning and there were plenty of sections of bank that were now clear of ice. I decided to take my first dip of the new season.

I walked to the beach, steeled my nerve, and dove in. The chill of the flowing water was invigorating. I used lye soap to wash my skin and hair, scrubbing vigorously with the river sand, something I'd been unable do during the winter months. Fully refreshed, I got out and put on the set of buckskins I had washed and hung out to dry the day before, and walked to the outdoor kitchen with a spring to my step.

For the moment, I appreciated Cindy's point of view. Life wasn't so bad. A frigid early morning dip was something I never would have done in my old life. But it made me feel good.

Eileen was setting the outdoor table for our breakfast, which I was pleased to see. It was the first time that season we would eat breakfast outdoors. It was still cool out, but our breath no longer condensed and, really, I didn't care about the cold anymore.

Cook, Christie, and Trey were already sitting at the table while Eileen worked the fire, cooking up the porridge with a few eggs.

"It's good to eat outside again," I said, smiling at them all.

"And look what Christie has," said Trey. Christie held out several small pieces of a brown-amber substance.

"Is that the maple sap?" I asked.

"Yep," she replied, "and it tastes pretty good. There's enough for each of us to add a few pieces to our cereal."

"Yum," I said. "Good thinking."

"The maple sap really flows at this time of year," added Trey.

"Yeah. One of the catch-pots is half full," added Christie. "I checked this morning."

"Did I hear we're having maple cereal this morning?" said Cindy, walking up to the table. "That sounds delicious!"

Trey laughed and shook his head. "Isn't it funny how the little things mean so much more now?"

"It's true," said Cindy. "It's too bad we weren't able to appreciate them in our former lives."

"Oh, no, not that again," said Cook, in a mock-appalled tone.

"I have to admit," I said to Cook. "It is a glorious, fine morning, and I'm excited about my maple cereal."

"Hmm," he replied. "Should I presume we're content staying here, and we should set aside our trip downriver?"

"Hell no," said Trey. "This ain't my idea of paradise. We're going downriver."

"Still plenty of time to discuss it," I said. "We shouldn't leave for at least a month. Or even two."

"It's fucking crazy," said Christie. "We've seen no sign of anyone else. No one has spotted a plane in the sky. What is it we hope to find?"

"A way out of this hell," said Trey. "Some kind of civilization with some technology. That's all I ask. I can't stand this." He reached over his shoulder and extended his middle finger, pointing it toward the sky. It was an old drill by now, and everyone understood for whom it was intended.

"We don't know what we'll find," I said, "but we've gotta try."

"It might get us killed," said Cindy.

"Anybody who wants to stay, can," I replied. "It's voluntary."

Cindy frowned. "Well, like you said, plenty of time to discuss it. But I'm not convinced it's a good idea."

I looked at Cindy with concern. It was impossible not to consider trying to get out of our situation and finding out what the hell happened to everyone. I would have to work on her reluctance. I had to convince her I wasn't chasing another yellow wolf.

That evening, a roaring fire made the cabin toasty warm. Cindy and I had made love and tossed the buckskin blanket off our bodies, lying there and cooling off. I reached over and took her hand.

"You are coming, aren't you?" I asked her.

"What?" she asked.

"The expedition downriver. Will you join us?"

"I don't think so, Charles."

"But we'd be gone for quite a long time. It'd be hard without you."

"I love you, Charles, and I want to support you. But that doesn't mean I should throw my life away chasing something that probably doesn't exist."

"That's a bit overly dramatic, isn't it? If we find nothing, we'll simply work our way back, either upstream in the rafts or walk back along the river bank."

Cindy shook her head slowly. "You think so? Let's work this out. For every day you travel downstream, that's equivalent to, what, four days working up against the current? If you bushwhack on foot through the foliage along the river bank, it would take at least that long. Now, I figure you would want to go downstream for at least one week before giving up and heading back. Probably longer than that."

"*If* we find nothing."

"Okay, right. *If* you find nothing. So you come back after a week. That means you'll be traveling back for a month or more. I doubt you can survive that long in the wild, either pushing those heavy rafts upstream or walking through the woods."

Her concerns about walking back were legitimate, if not overstated. We would have to hunt and fish along the way, since we couldn't carry enough food. Plus, since we would have to sleep out in the open, we would be vulnerable to animal attacks and the weather.

Returning upstream made more sense. We could carry more supplies, and even a buckskin tent. We could tie the raft off and sleep on it at night. The only factor was the weather, and possible cataracts in the river. But as long as we were willing to sweat, we would make it back home.

"We would have to come back on the rafts," I said. "We can do it."

Cindy shrugged. "Maybe. If you had enough supplies on board. But suppose you're a week downstream and haven't found anything? What would you do? I doubt you would stop. You would feel compelled to keep going—another week. Maybe two. Your greatest danger would be your dislike of our life here motivating you forward. You would push it beyond the point of no return."

There was truth in what she said. It would be hard to give up on the expedition, to accept that there was no one here but us. The temptation would be to keep going—to find somebody, somewhere. Until we reached the fabled "point of no return" and beyond. With no supplies, we would die before we returned. But hell, what would be lost?

Wasn't it worth trying? Wasn't it worth getting out of this miserable life?

Chapter 23

Over the next two weeks, Trey and Michael were back on task building rafts. These were to be sturdier versions than those the expedition had taken upriver the previous summer, and their design benefited from Trey and Cook's experiences. They had cleared an area along the river bank among the rushes, chopped and collected bundles of bamboo to use instead of logs, and had strapped them together to form four rafts. Trey and Michael had propped them up on free logs so that once the rafts were loaded and ready to launch, it would be a simple matter to roll them into the water.

They had built little shelters on the rafts, designed to keep our supplies dry when bad weather loomed. Several of us, including Dillon, Ramiro, and Christie, had come to look over the finished product, and were milling around the river bank. I expressed my concerns about their awkward size and maneuverability. They seemed a little big for our small river. Plus, I kept thinking of Cindy's warning about needing to push the rafts back up river if we found nothing. But no one else seemed to be concerned. Everyone was hopeful we would find a town, or at least a farm or trading post.

I was examining Trey's container of pine pitch, which would be used for sealing the wooden shelters, when I heard Cook's voice singing out over the river valley. He had been on an overnight trip downriver, scouting for potential obstacles to our journey downstream.

"Hel-lo. Hel-lo. Hello, people," his booming voice called out. "Look what I found."

It wasn't Cook's habit to announce his return in such a manner, so it got everyone's attention. We looked toward his voice and, a minute later, Cook came walking into the clearing with two strangers at his side. We stared with our mouths agape. Strangers!

The man and woman wore rough, filthy buckskins very similar to our own. The man was short and stocky, with black hair and a wide face. Tattoos covered his arms and neck. The woman was thin, with straggly blond hair. Her skinny legs were bowed, and her smile showed several missing teeth.

"Greetings, everyone," Cook beamed. "I would like you to meet Jackie and Daryl." He turned to his companions. "These are my mates. This is Trey, and Christie, and Michael, and Dillon, and this guy is in charge of our group. His name is Charles."

Mechanically, I extended my hand, shaking my head in disbelief.

"Where do you come from?" I managed.

"From downriver," replied Cook, still full of himself.

"Our community is about twenty miles west of here," said Daryl. "Straight downriver."

"How big is it?" blurted Christie. "Is it a town?"

"No," said Daryl. "There are sixteen of us."

"And they know of even another community," added Cook.

"That's right," said Daryl. "Our site is at the fork of two rivers. We made it up river on the north one and discovered

179

the other settlement. It's a little closer to us than you guys, only fifteen miles. But the south river, this river, has a big cataract a few miles from here, so we never got this far before now."

"That's where I found them," said Cook. "I was looking over the rapids when I spotted them doing the same thing. Good thing we didn't send our rafts down."

The others began barraging them with questions, but I cut them off. "Please come into our camp and get something to eat and rest. I'm sure it's been a tiring journey."

"Oh, this guy does this sort of stuff all the time," said Jackie, speaking for the first time. Her voice had a thick rural accent. "But me? I sure could use some vittles."

I led Daryl and Jackie to our outdoor kitchen and sat them at our dinner table. Christie went to fetch Eileen to get grub going.

They sat at the table and waited to be served. They tried to politely answer our questions, all the while looking around our community with interest.

"Is anyone in your group from Jersey?"

"Do y'all have shampoo?"

"Have you tried going downriver from your site?"

"I must say," said Jackie, looking at the cabins. "There isn't much difference between your place and ours. Sixteen cabins placed near water. A few utility buildings and some fields."

"Were you given any technology?" I asked. "Besides primitive stuff. Or medicine? Do you have medicines?"

"Nope," said Daryl. "We've had to do everything ourselves, except for a few basic tools made from raw iron, and no medicine at all."

"Same thing at the other village," said Jackie. "Sixteen cabins, although two of their people croaked last winter. They're up near the foot of the mountains. It's a bit colder up there."

"They died?" asked Cindy. "Of what?"

"Oh, something went around. No medicine to fix 'em up, and they didn't make it."

"It could happen to us at any time," I said, half to myself.

"We lost someone last fall," said Christie. "The wolves took her."

"Wolves!" said Jackie. "That's awful."

"Sorry to hear that," added Daryl.

"Thanks," I said. "We all miss her."

Everyone was awkwardly quiet for a few moments.

"So how far have you guys explored?" asked Trey. "We went about twenty miles upriver, but found nothing but more woods."

"Oh, we've tried," said Jackie. "But we haven't found diddly-squat. I mean, beside the other group and now you guys. What I mean is, we haven't found anything from before."

"I've been downriver a ways," said Daryl. "And a fair distance into the woods around, but they're thick around there. I recently spotted a big lake about ten miles north of us. Exploring it will be my next adventure. It's under the shadow of the mountain, but far east of the other settlement."

"A lake might be a good food source for us," suggested Jackie.

"But no sign of the old world?" I asked.

"Not a single thing," Daryl replied.

"Have you..." I began, not really sure how to phrase my question. "Have you noticed anything peculiar around your camp?"

"Oh, yeah," said Jackie. "We know about them. At least, we do now."

"We missed them at first," added Daryl. "But the folks at the other community—Shady, we call it—realized they were there. And they told us about them. Once we looked for them, we found them everywhere."

"Have you figured out what they are?" asked Rebecca. "Have you seen anyone in them?"

Jackie and Daryl looked at each other, and Jackie shrugged. "I don't know if we should say anything," said Daryl. "We have ideas about them, but you should talk to Phil about that."

"Who's that?" I asked.

"He kinda runs things down our way," he replied.

"Well, we know all about 'em," chirped Amber. "We figured it out a long time ago. There are aliens in there, just watching us."

"Yeah," added Rebecca. "A bunch of little perverts, watching what we do."

"Right," said Jackie, nodding her head. "That's a notion we have too. They're studying on us." She chuckled. "They *are* a bunch of damn perverts."

Amber pointed up to the sky, toward the distortion near the banquet table. "There's one right there. We try to forget about them."

"So you call the community up the north branch of the river Shady, eh?" I asked. "What do you call yours?"

"Hobbes," said Jackie. "Don't really understand why. Phil will tell ya."

After we finished up the meal, I gave Daryl and Jackie a tour of our community, showing them our freshly sowed fields, the products of Samuel's workshop, and some of the things we made, from soap to bows and arrows and tanned buckskins.

"Wait till you meet Howard," Jackie said. "Very creative

fellow. Said he always wanted to be an engineer. He's got all kinds of plans on how to improve things."

"Really!" I said. "Sounds very interesting. I'd love to meet him."

"You guys should plan on coming downriver. Maybe next week even," said Daryl. "I'll let our folks know to expect you, and some folks from Shady can come down, too."

"It'll be a regular jamboree," said Jackie.

I turned to look at Cindy with the most excitement and optimism I'd felt since we'd arrived here. Maybe this was the beginning of the end of our situation. "So, what about it? Are you ready to go on a little trip?"

Chapter 24

The next morning, Dillon and I escorted Daryl and Jackie back to their raft, which they had beached just the other side of the cataract. The hike was long—about five miles one way—but since it was still early spring, the undergrowth of the thick woods was light, so walking was easy. It was good to get out in the world after the dark winter months.

It struck me as I warmed up and started enjoying the feeling of movement how weird that felt. *It's good to be out in the woods. What the hell?* In our old lives we hardly noticed the change of seasons. Who cared, unless you were vacationing and enjoying the scenery? One season morphed into the next, and the only difference were the clothes you wore and the sports you watched. How long ago was that?

As much as I longed for the comforts of my old life, I couldn't help but think sometimes this was the way we were meant to be. I often imagined our ancestors living in hunting and gathering societies, and wishing I'd paid more attention in my college classes. How did they survive? How did they evolve to become the civilization we used to know? How did they learn about medicine? If we didn't find a way out of our circumstances, we would have to figure all that out.

The cataract itself was impressive. There were two noisy

areas of surging turbulence, filled with jagged rocks, with a short gap of calm between them. It was clear that navigating the cataract on a raft would be highly risky.

Before departing, Jackie and Daryl gave us a few pointers for the trip downriver to their settlement, and what signs to look for to know we had reached it. We gave them a hand as they launched their raft, and downstream they went, soon out of sight as they rounded a sharp bend.

Dillon and I made a close inspection of the cataract, considering all the possible routes through it, and convinced ourselves that any attempt to navigate its foamy recesses on a raft was folly. A trip downriver would require ferrying our conveyance two hundred yards along the shore to bypass the obstacle.

On the trek back, I reflected on the fact that we had found others in this crazy new world. That we were not alone. And if there were two more communities out there, there might be more. There could be hundreds, even thousands, scattered across the landscape. Pam and Alex might be alive and well in one of them. The possibility buoyed my spirits.

We would visit these two communities, get to know them, and systematically launch our explorations until we found other communities. We would combine our ingenuity and resources and grow strong. When there were enough of us, we would somehow strike back at those beings who had taken away our civilization and, once again, seize control of our destiny.

I couldn't deny that we had learned a few things during these extreme changes to our lives. The next time through, during the process of rebuilding our world, we should alter a few things. Create a civilized world with a deeper connection to nature. A world in which we never lost touch with how to do things, ensuring we could make, with our own hands, anything we needed.

Bah! I thought, rejecting that line of reasoning after considering it. *That's bullshit. We had to give up those things to gain the advantages of our technology. To free ourselves so we could focus on science and literature. To create art and entertain ourselves. It's a reasonable trade-off. And we don't need a race of meddling aliens to teach us otherwise.*

During the week that followed, we prepared for our visit to Hobbes. Since the community was twenty miles downstream, we supposed it was possible to reach it in one day, as long as we began our journey on the opposite side of the cataract.

The first step was to get a raft on the other side. We streamlined two of the rafts, shedding their cabins and other unnecessary weight. Eight of us took the lightened rafts downstream to the edge of the cataract. There, we lifted one raft out of the water and dragged it along the bank toward the other side of the cataract, the side closest to Hobbes. Since there was no path, we tried to force the raft through the close-packed vegetation along the bank, but the bamboo bundles of out which the raft was made constantly snagged on small trees and vines as we pushed forward. After a hundred yards of this, about halfway through, we took the time to use our rough axes to clear a path, hacking saplings and undergrowth along the way. This delayed us several hours, but we made it to the other side, where we secured the raft near the bank.

Afterward, all eight of us returned to the homeward side of the cataract and climbed onto the remaining raft, and with our poles pushed ourselves five miles back upriver. We got home just as night descended, exhausted but full of excitement.

Now we were set. With a raft stored on the opposite side of the cataract, visiting our new neighbors was a straight shot downstream.

The debate over who should go was intense. Everyone wanted to, but the raft was most stable with only four travelers. In the end, I decided that Cook, Cindy, Samuel, and I would make the trip. Cindy was hopeful she would learn a few new things about plants. Samuel, who was accomplished in the workshop, wanted to share what he had learned with their blacksmith. Cook was our lead explorer. And as community leader, I was expected to go and meet Phil, the leader of Hobbes. In a half-joking way, Trey and Rebecca accused me of favoritism by selecting Cindy over them, but I assured them there would be plenty of other trips, and that they would go next.

The next day, the four of us got an early start. We stood on the raft and relaxed as we glided the five miles downriver to the rapids, occasionally using our poles to keep the raft away from the bank or impediments in the river. Once there, we beached our raft at the head of the rapids, carried our few supplies along our newly-cut path to the raft waiting on the other side, loaded up again, and continued our leisurely drift downstream.

Along the way, we noticed occasional creeks merging into the river, causing it to swell, becoming wider but slower. The river bank itself changed little, full of thick forest and large patches of rushes and cattails. We saw deer and other wildlife from our vantage point in the middle of the river, but never a sign of human habitation. But that did not stop all of us from gazing around us every foot of the way. There was always hope.

After several hours, we reached a bend marked with a series of massive sycamore trees draped over the water. Upstream beyond the bend, we could see that the river widened. It was obvious another river merged with this one. Daryl and Jackie had alerted us that the community of Hobbes would be on our left, on the peninsula formed by the two converging rivers.

Then we saw it—an opening in the rushes with several poles inserted into the ground, each one with a tattered piece of buckskin attached to its top. And nearby, a raft was secured on the steep bank.

We had arrived at another community. The idea made me giddy.

Hobbes didn't enjoy the luxury of a beach. The Hobbeseans had cut down the rushes and weeds in an area along the river bank, so pulling the raft up the steep slope was a challenge. We stretched out our overworked backs, looking around curiously, and walked inland.

I didn't want to surprise anyone, so we yelled "Hello" as we walked. A minute later, a group of curious, buckskinned people surrounded us. It was a new experience to be in the midst of unfamiliar people. It put me on the defensive. Yet there was no animosity in the faces of those around us. Just friendly, curious smiles.

Jackie and Daryl were there in the group. Everyone was talking at once, but Jackie, who apparently considered us her property, yelled, "Hey! Will everyone please shut ya trap?"

"Now," she continued in the subsequent silence, "let me introduce everyone. This is Cindy, and Cook, and, what's your name, hun?"

"Samuel."

"And this is Samuel. And this is Charles, who's in charge up

188

there."

"Well, he thinks he is," snapped Samuel.

"Oh, hogwash!" replied Jackie. She then went through the names of the Hobbeseans standing around her as we continued to walk inland. By the time she had finished, we were standing in the center of their community, too distracted by curiosity to remember many of their names.

One individual who stood out was a plump-cheeked man with flushed skin and a jolly smile on his face. Jackie informed us he was Howard, the aspiring engineer who had big plans for their community.

"He's from Shady," added Jackie. "Him and those two over there. That's Spence and Helen." I noticed that the attractive young couple were holding hands.

"Very pleased to meet you," I said, shaking Howard's hand. "I look forward to hearing about your ideas."

"Oh, you'll hear about them all right," said Jackie. "He won't stop talking about 'em."

"She's probably right," added Howard, smiling. "But it's because I believe they'll make our lives so much better."

"I like the sound of that."

"Are you planning on visiting our community?" he asked. "We're up the other river, the North River we call it, about fifteen miles."

I shrugged. "I'm not sure. We didn't pack extra supplies or anything."

"I wouldn't worry about that," said a tall, lean fellow walking up to the group. He wore a raccoon hat, Davy Crockett style, with the bushy tail dangling from behind. "We can fix you up with plenty. And you can ride to Shady with those three."

"That's Phil," said Jackie, elbowing me in the side. "He's the one that runs the show around here."

"I'm just another guy trying to survive," said Phil, offering a shy smile. "But I try to suggest things that make sense."

"How do you do?" I said, shaking his hand. "I'm Charles. This is Samuel, Cook, and Cindy."

Phil's eyes paused on Samuel. "So you're the magician in the workshop we've heard about?"

Samuel shrugged. "I do my best. But I believe I've found my God-given vocation. I didn't do it in my former life."

"Hopefully, we can all exchange our various areas of expertise with one another," I said. "The more minds, the more resources."

"Indeed," said Phil. "I couldn't agree more. But come. The day has been long. Let's dine, and then we can chat the night away if we wish."

The trip down hadn't really been that tiring, but grub sounded good. As we sat down at their big dinner table, which was very similar to our own, I couldn't help comparing the relative merits of our two communities. As they served the food, I realized we all took Eileen's cooking skills for granted. The bland grain and meat dish they served us, virtually unseasoned, was not up to her standards. But we were all famished and soon cleaned our plates.

After our meal, we sat around the fire with many from their camp, exchanging questions and information late into the night. They listened with envy to our description of our salt lick, which not only meant that hunting involved much less exertion, but that we had a supply of a salt-like substance for our food.

"I've got it!" said Jackie, raising her hand. "We'll call their place 'Salty', after the salt lick."

"Yeah," said Howard. "Makes sense. What do you guys think?"

I shrugged. "Sure."

"I like it," said Cindy.

"Okay, Salty it is," I added. "And I was told why the other community is called Shady—it's under the shadow of the mountains. But why is this place called Hobbes?"

Phil chuckled. "Well, it comes from the philosopher Thomas Hobbes. Have you heard of him?"

"Not really. I took a philosophy course once, but not much stuck with me."

"I've heard of him," said Cook. "What was his famous line?"

"In a state of nature, the life of man is solitary, poor, nasty, brutish, and short," said Phil. "Something like that."

"Yep," I said. "That about sums it up."

"Well, not necessarily the solitary part," added Cindy, taking my hand in hers. I put it to my lips and kissed the back of her hand with a wink.

The conversation continued for several hours, and despite our excitement at meeting new people, it became evident that neither our group nor theirs had all that much new to say. We had all been presented with similar challenges, and we had all, more or less, dealt with them the same way—buckskins for clothes, spears for fishing, clay for containers, tallow for candles.

Howard shared some of his ideas for improving our communities, many of which were beyond our current capabilities. Once exception was his plan to build a brick kiln. I really liked the idea. Once we had bricks, we could build many new structures that would be warmer and free of insects.

"We can make brick ovens, storage buildings, and even a

191

latrine," said Howard.

I rubbed my chin, intrigued by these prospects.

But then our discussion took a different note when the subject of the distortions, with their possible inhabitants, came up.

"There's one right there," said Jackie, throwing a piece of wood in the general direction of a nearby distortion.

"We've found twelve of them around Shady," said Howard. "But nowadays we try to ignore them."

"We were totally unaware until the folks at Shady told us about them," said Phil. "There are thirteen right around us. We were pretty riled up for a while, but we're gradually getting used to them."

"We found about the same number around our place—Salty, I should say," I said. "Even found some in the woods, not close to cabins or anything."

"Yeah, we found some, too," said Phil. "Not sure what that means."

"There're a lot of things I'm not sure about," I said. "I understand that some of you share our opinion about these things—that they're observation chambers from which beings of some kind watch us. Yet I couldn't say why they want to watch us. If they were zoologists, and wanted to study our species earnestly, why would they give us this particular amount of technology? Why not the technology cavemen used, or feudal Europe? And surely they would have known we would discover their observation chambers, and that the discovery would impact the way we conducted ourselves."

"Well," said Phil. "Perhaps they expect us, over time, to forget they are there."

"Maybe," I said. "But I still can't help wondering if there's something we missed."

Phil scratched his chin. "Like what?"

"Think about it. These alien beings come across our world and find us interesting. Rather than, say, destroy us and exploit our resources, they turn us into an object of study. They eliminate all vestiges of our civilization, such as cities and highways and dams and whatever, but they don't want to eliminate us. We are part of this world, this ecosystem, even if we exploit it for our own benefit. So they set us up in small, non-intrusive communities here and there."

"That seems the way of it," said Howard.

"Right," I said. "So we suppose they monitor our behavior from these distortions in the air. But maybe they don't watch just *us*, which is why they have these observation chambers in the middle of the woods. Maybe these things are set around the world so they can watch all life forms—near water holes in Africa, in the upper canopy of the rainforests, even deep in the northern oceans—who knows? Perhaps alien visitors somehow can transport to the distortions watch us like we're some kind of zoo. Heck, maybe schoolchildren take field trips here to watch the intelligent apes."

"We've taken to the habit of calling them "little perverts," said Cindy, "because they watch us do everything."

"But what about all the billions of other people on Earth?" asked Howard. "Any ideas what happened to them?"

I shrugged. "In other communities scattered about. Or they were destroyed. Or stuck in some huge holding area, still asleep like we were."

"There's a lot we don't know," said Phil. "But, why did you say we're missing something?"

"Because it doesn't make sense! Why put us in these

communities? If they simply wanted to learn about us, what was wrong with studying us in all of our glory? If it's their view that we're a blight on this planet, why not just wipe us out? Surely the world would be better off without us humans to stress its ecosystems."

"Well then, *why* did they put us here?"

I looked up in the general direction of the closest distortion and felt a wave of hate.

"For their pleasure," I uttered with disgust.

"What pleasure?" asked Helen. She was still holding Spence's hand.

"The pleasure of watching lesser life forms struggle. The same reason kids pull the wings off flies, to watch them try to survive. They want to stress us to see what we'll do. They don't seem willing to help us. I suspect they would watch every one of us die, if that's how things end up."

"Hmm," said Phil, rubbing his chin. "If that's true, it would answer a question that's been troubling me." He blew his noise with a loud honk into a filthy piece of buckskin. "If they set us up this way to study us, and we tip the cart by building improvements, would they interfere?"

"What do you mean?" Cindy asked. I saw the familiar worry wrinkles form on her forehead.

"Well, suppose, for example, we bring all three of our communities together to make one larger town. That's something we've been discussing. The worry is that these alien observers wouldn't want us to do that, and take measures to correct it or punish us."

"Or if we fire bricks and build better buildings. What would they do then?" pondered Howard.

I sat quietly as the others discussed the intentions of these beings. I didn't care if they didn't like us changing things. We should do what we believed would best ensure our survival, and if they messed with us, then so be it. But I didn't think they would, and I for one was willing to take that chance.

Chapter 25

That night, the four of us went to sleep in a cabin our hosts had prepared for us—Cindy and I on the bed, Cook and Samuel sacked out on the floor on buckskin blankets. When I awoke the next morning, I went for a bracing dip in the still chilly river, and joined Phil as he prepared breakfast at the outdoor kitchen, standing over the fire.

"Hi there, Mr. Salty. Hungry?"

"Yep," I said. "You crack those eggs for us?"

"We did," Phil replied. "Although I wish we had some of that salt from your salt lick to season them."

"Sorry we didn't think to bring some. Next time."

We stood staring into the climbing flames.

"I like the idea of combining all our communities into one village," I said, breaking the silence. "I mulled it over all night and it makes sense. With all of us together, there's more we can accomplish. Damn the Watchers."

Phil poked the fire and looked up at me.

"Then let's do it," he said.

"We should probably use our location," I suggested. "Since we have the salt lick. Keeps a steady stream of game close at hand."

"True," he replied. "We have no salt lick, but I suggest

Hobbes is the sensible choice."

"Why so?"

"Well, we're downstream of both Salty and Shady. If we plan on dismantling our log cabins and moving them, it'll be a lot easier going downstream with the logs."

"That's a good point," I said.

"Plus," he added, "have you noticed the breeze? Since we are on a peninsula between the two rivers, the wind blows constantly across it. Helps keep the mosquitoes at bay in the summer."

I looked around the surrounding land and appraised it. Plenty of room for more cabins. And Phil's point was valid. Carrying the heavy logs from the cabins upriver to our place would be an immense chore, especially with the cataract blocking the way. Besides, what difference did it make where we lived? We could always journey upriver if we needed more salt or game.

"I'll discuss it with the others when we get back, but you might be right."

The denizens of Hobbes set aside their chores and we lounged around the entire day, getting familiar with each other and telling story after story of what had transpired. My adventure of chasing the yellow wolf across country seemed to resonate with some of the Hobbeseans. Others thought it odd.

The next day, we began our journey up the North River to Shady—about fifteen miles upstream with no rapids blocking the way. It was us Salties and Howard on a simple, light raft—Helen and Spencer volunteered to stay behind. The five of us used poles to push the raft upriver against the current. Toward the end of the second day, under the loom of a huge forested mountain, we reached Shady's tiny beach.

Again, we experienced the excitement of meeting new people. Howard introduced us to Carmine, a heavy-set, sweaty former attorney. As we were chatting about the trip, a squat, middle-aged woman barged into our conversation.

"I'm Beatrice," she said. "That's my man you're talking to."

"I see," I said. "Hello."

"Yes, this is Beatrice," said Carmine, letting out a long sigh.

"The word is that you and—" Beatrice nodded her head toward Cindy in an ungainly gesture, "—her are an item. Is that true?"

"Beatrice, please!" said Carmine. "Let them get refreshed before you start with your meddling questions."

"I just want to know," she whined.

"We'll talk later," I said, putting her off in as polite a manner as I could muster. Howard introduced us to all the others, and we sat down to a companionable dinner. But the journey had thoroughly exhausted us—getting here was much more difficult than going downstream to Hobbes—so we chatted for only an hour after dinner before retiring.

The next morning, we got a better look at the place. Sixteen cabins, placed on opposite sides of a small creek, with a meeting house, workshop, and other auxiliary buildings. If it weren't for the looming mountain and the slightly cooler temperatures, the community would be a clone of Salty.

Cook, Samuel, and I spent the day discussing with Howard and Carmine the logistics of combining our communities, while Cindy grudgingly agreed to let Beatrice show her around the community. I would have hell to pay later, but we needed to cover a lot of ground, and it quickly became obvious that wouldn't happen with Beatrice hovering around peppering us with random questions.

Everyone seemed to be enthusiastic about all of us living in a bigger community, and, surprisingly, no one seemed to have any concerns about the alien Watchers getting upset with us for changing their arrangements.

We were eager to get back and get the move started, but the notion of getting back on the raft and going downstream to Hobbes, and then pushing another raft twenty miles upriver from Hobbes to Salty, was a tiring thought. Cook, who had kept close attention to our position relative to the mountains as we journeyed upriver, estimated that we were only about fifteen miles away from home, if we cut through the forest.

"We would be home in two days if we bushwhack across land," he said. "And if we miss it by walking too far east or west, we'll eventually reach the river, as long as we keep south, and just follow the river path home."

We all agreed, and the next morning, the four of us set off through a tall, mature hemlock forest with little undergrowth. We made good progress. Near the end of the day, just as darkness descended, we reached a creek.

"Look familiar?" asked Cook as he looked around.

It was the same creek near which Cook and I had defended ourselves from the wolf pack months earlier. We piled up a healthy stack of firewood and we rotated keeping guard throughout the night.

During my shift standing guard, I was certain I heard wolf howls. But they were far away and barely audible. Who knows, I may have imagined it. The entire time, I thought of the events surrounding Missy's awful death. I rehearsed in my mind, time and time again, how I could have done things differently. Why, for example, did I have to go hunting that night?

The next morning we followed the creek to the south without further incident and reached Salty with a few hours of daylight to spare. The others were so excited to hear about the news of our journey, they could hardly contain themselves. We spent hours answering all their questions. Before we retired, I asked everyone to consider the proposal of combining villages and moving everything to Hobbes. No one had the least reservation. I looked up at the nearest distortion and pondered.

That evening, as I lay my weary head down with Cindy beside me, I reflected on all the recent developments. We had traveled across extensive tracts of land and were able to get around without getting lost or worse. We were about to pool together our resources and skills and become stronger than ever before. Things were changing fast, and conditions would soon improve. Assuming, of course, that the Watchers left us alone.

And let them try stopping us, I thought, full of bravado. The idea of disrupting what they had set up gave me great pleasure. We would grow and flourish again, despite their efforts to keep us down. Fucking bastards. I looked forward to the day we would pay them back for what they had done. We just needed a little time.

I looked down at Cindy and watched her breathing peacefully as she slept. I fell into a soft sleep, feeling more confident and optimistic than ever.

Yep, I thought. *I'll take good care of her and the others.*

Chapter 26

Everyone's excitement levels were high as we dismantled the cabins for the move downriver. Taking them apart was not particularly challenging. The notch-cut logs were held together with wooden pegs, so we simply disassembled them, taking care to carve identifying numbers on each log. We took only the cabins. The workshop and other auxiliary buildings at Hobbes were sufficient for all of us, so we left those at Salty intact.

Once they were moved to the beach, we tied the large cabin logs into bundles of four, and let a group of these bundles drift downstream with the river current, following along in a raft to make sure they didn't get snagged along the way. Getting the heavy, water-logged timbers around the cataract required great effort. We had to untie the bundles, then several of us had to carry each individual log along the path to the far side, and reassemble the bundles.

But progress was steady, thanks to our enthusiasm. We had a sense of salvation from our predicament, a kind of liberation. To live in a larger community, where we could pool our resources, promised a significant improvement in the quality of our lives.

Yet, there were other feelings mixed in with our excitement, including a surprising sense of nostalgia. Despite the months of discomfort and hardship, our community had come together and overcome many obstacles. We had learned to survive in these surroundings and had become accustomed to the way we lived—from tending the gardens and trapping fish to knowing where to hunt for deer. We knew we would return often, however. The gardens, fields, fruit trees, and especially the salt lick of our former home would still be of value to our larger community.

There was a darker, more sinister emotion mixed in with our enthusiasm. As we took the cabins apart, it began to concern everyone that we were changing the way of things, and that those who had put us here might not like it. Perhaps the alien observers wanted us to stay in our small communities having to struggle to survive, and as a consequence of violating their design we might all go to sleep one night and not wake up again.

But the concern didn't stop us from carrying on. Besides, they didn't leave us an instruction manual.

The days had changed from cool to pleasantly warm by the time we had erected our new homes at Hobbes. Those from Shady were building their cabins alongside us, completing their last one only a few days after we had finished. According to Howard, it was mid-May. He had followed the precession of the sun since last winter, and had counted the days since the winter solstice, so he had a good idea of the date.

And there we were—a city of forty-five souls. It seemed a metropolis compared to the way we had lived until now. With new people, and the forest awakening with the warmer weather, we walked around with smiles on our faces. It was a happy, exciting time.

We considered changing the name of our new community. I had suggested "Camp Defiance". It would be a strong reminder to never forgive those who had destroyed our world. But to my surprise, few of the others were enthusiastic. In the end, we stuck with Hobbes.

The first order of business was to figure out how our new community would be run. Two days after the Salties and Shadies had settled into our new homes, Phil invited Howard and me to his place, and the three of us sat down for a powwow. He had fixed his place up by decorating the walls with the skulls of small animals he had found in the woods. Decorating my cabin never entered my mind. I also noticed his collection of raccoon pelts piled in a corner.

We discussed how we should run the community. We talked about who was good at what and whether changes were needed as to how we allocated the responsibilities. But we didn't feel the need to reinvent the wheel, at least at this stage. Spencer was excellent at making pottery and utensils, and would be in charge of Amber and the others doing the same. Eileen was the best cook, but now she would now have assistants to help prepare the larger meals. We assigned leaders in other activities, but everyone pretty much kept at what they were doing.

I worried, however, that the larger size of our village would affect our work ethic.

"We are a larger group now," I noted. "Should we be concerned that it will be easier for individuals to slack off? To fall between the cracks?"

Phil took off his raccoon cap and scratched his scalp. "I don't think so," he said. "Everyone realizes the situation we're in. It's a case of contributing or we all suffer."

"Yeah, I agree with Phil," Howard said. "I don't believe it'll be a problem."

"But what if it does turn out to be a problem? Shouldn't we have rules in place before hand? They may deter people from attempting to do less than their share."

"Charles, we may be the leaders of our communities, but we can't let that power go to our heads," said Phil. "People participate in our system because they want to. Nothing compels them."

"You're wrong about that. Everyone needs this community. If someone doesn't take part, they can be asked to leave. That's what gives the leadership of our community its leverage."

"I gather that you are suggesting rules for punishment." Howard stated, his eyebrows knitting together and crossing his arms.

"I don't know." I replied. "I just want to make it fair for everyone. If there are rules for everyone to follow, everyone gets treated equally, right?

"Hmm. Maybe we should not go there, at least at first," said Howard. "Let's see if it's necessary, then we can revisit the idea."

I shrugged. "We need rules. We're better off with them."

"Look," said Phil. "We're just discussing work allocations today. Let's address other problems if and when they arise."

"Okay, fine," I said, spreading my hands. "We'll just see how it goes."

Despite my concerns, it soon became clear that Phil and Howard were right. Over the days and weeks that followed, neither I nor Phil nor Howard noticed anyone attempting to get out of doing work. I did worry that, as the drudgeries of our day-to-day existence continued, the community-wide sense of participation would wear off. But for now, I had underestimated the character of my comrades. I had at least expected some territorialism on the part of the original Hobbeseans, but noticed little of that. Everyone cooperated and seemed happy to have new friends around.

The first order of business was to select an overall leader through a general election. The only candidates were Phil, Howard, and myself. Each of us gave a speech to the assembled group about their views on how we should proceed. In my speech, I returned to the idea that we needed to have rules, though I decided to avoid any mention of specified punishment. I guess people, on the edge of survival, value rules. I won the election by two votes over Phil. I immediately assigned Phil and Howard as seconds-in-command.

"Way to go, copier salesman," said Samuel, slapping me on the back. I was never sure how to take his remarks. He had been extra surly around me in the weeks following the incident at Cindy's cabin. But things had leveled off. Amber had been spending a lot of time with him in the evenings, and I figured that helped. But I suspected he still fancied Cindy, and resented me for being with her.

But I was in an affable mood. "I promise to keep taxes at a minimum," I said. "As in zero."

"A reasonable policy," Samuel returned.

As we settled into the routines of our new community, the advantages and disadvantages of our location quickly manifested themselves. The cross-breeze that Phil had mentioned was noticeable, even though at this time of year the heat was still mild. And the rivers bordering two of the three sides of our triangular peninsula created a sense of security.

But there was a slew of logistical challenges. The food

sources at Hobbes were sufficient for its initial population, but now that it was nearly tripled, regular trips to the fields, orchards, and gardens of Shady and Salty were required. Our steady walking back and forth soon formed established paths through the woods, allowing one to make the journey on foot in one long, tiring day.

We needed to expand the garden and grain fields at Hobbes, which would require that we clear an area of heavily forested land just west of the current fields. Howard had big plans for the timber that would be harvested as we cleared the forest. It was his idea to build a palisade wall to enclose the third edge of our peninsula, the side not bordered by a river. We hoped this would keep hungry wolves and bears away from our cabins—unless, of course, they were hungry enough to swim across one of the rivers.

Howard also urged us to construct footbridges over the two rivers so we could easily access the opposite banks. Around Salty, the South River was shallow enough to wade across as long as one held on to a vine cable. By the time the river meandered its way downstream to Hobbes, augmented by numerous creeks, it deepened significantly. The North River was also too deep to be easily waded.

Initially, the denizens of Hobbes simply felled trees across the river, stretching from bank to bank, and used a vine cable as a handhold. Most times one made it. Sometimes not. The waters weren't dangerous, but a dunking meant wearing wet buckskins for hours until they dried out. Howard's bridge proposal was readily accepted.

As the elected leader, I spent much of my time supervising these projects with Howard. But I found time to walk the woods with my bow and arrow in hand. My successful kills were few and far apart, especially compared to the easy pickings at the salt lick back at Salty, but it gave me a quiet time to reconnect with myself.

Dillon and the other hunters continued to develop the hunting equipment. We now had strong bows, made from cured wood, with well-crafted arrowheads and feather fletching. The hunters' skill at using the equipment continued to improve. We often had enough venison for our meals, despite the larger population.

As the days wore on, my busy schedule meant I had less time for Cindy. She was busy, too. She had picked up a few tidbits of knowledge about local plants from the others, and had become a fanatic about learning all she could about them. She would spend hours roaming the woods collecting specimens, or building racks on which to dry them out in the sun. She seemed to flourish. I had never seen her so happy, healthy, and beautiful. She was the best thing that had ever happened to me in my life, bar none. We were soulmates in every sense of the word. I'd never been as close to any other human being. Even Alex.

I tried not to think about him even as his memory faded. There was a void now, intensified occasionally by bitterness toward the Watchers—those vague entities I believed hovered above us, enjoying our struggle.

One night, with a full moon in the sky, Cindy and I lay together on my bed, exhausted. Earlier that day, I had supervised the construction of the first section of our palisade wall. We had erected about twenty feet of the wall and needed one hundred and eighty feet more. That was a long way to go, but it was a beginning.

Because we were both tired, our libidos were at bay. Instead, we lay there companionably, listening to the sounds of the forest and waiting for sleep to come, when I heard a long, chilling howl. I sat up in bed, listening intently. After a few minutes, I heard it again. It was distinctive—low, threatening and familiar.

"It's him," I said. "I know it." I jumped up and started to put on my buckskins.

"Who?" asked Cindy. "It's who?"

"That damn yellow wolf. I recognize its howl."

My bow was propped against the wall. I picked it up and collected a handful of arrows.

Cindy jumped out of bed and grabbed my wrist. "What are you doing?" she asked. Concerned puzzlement distorted her face. "Are you really going out into the middle of the night to confront a wolf pack?"

"I'll get Cook. They sound close, and the moon is full. If we hurry, we might get a shot." I looked her straight in the face. "I've got to. For Missy's sake."

"No!" she cried, this time taking both my wrists and holding tight. "No. No! Do not do this. Do you hear me? Do not do this, Charles," she said slowly and with a slight hint of threat.

"But Missy…"

"Missy is gone! She wouldn't want you to commit suicide in the middle of the friggin' night pursuing a wolf pack. Listen to me, Charles. Do not do this. For me. For us."

Silently, I paced back and forth across the cabin floor, holding my arrows and bow tightly, my stomach in knots. She was telling me she would leave me if I went after the yellow wolf. But I couldn't help it if she didn't understand. Without a word, I went out the door.

I reached Cook's cabin and knocked. Cook answered the

door.

"Did you hear it?" I asked.

Cook nodded.

"It could be them," I said.

"Maybe," he said. "Maybe not."

"We should find out."

"He's not going!" called out a voice from inside the cabin. It was Christie. "You go get yourself killed if you want to," she continued, "but Cook is staying put."

Cook looked at me sympathetically. "Sorry, Charles. Can't do it this time."

"Great," I said. "Just great. Okay, I'll go by myself."

"I wouldn't, Charles. It's crazy."

"Whatever," I said, and stomped away. I walked toward the edge of the forest and peered into its dark recesses. I was standing in a recently cleared area and had an unobstructed view of the sky. The moon, close and bright, looked down at me. It seemed alone and cold, like a torn and bleeding body floating in a nameless river.

I suddenly felt tired, old, sad, and alone. I looked around me. Beyond this community was a dark and wild expanse of wilderness. I couldn't do this alone. Would no one help me? Had everyone just forgotten about Missy?

I sat down on freshly hewn stump and dropped my head. *I can't do this. Cook's right, this is crazy.* I had to try to let them go. Missy, Alex, Pam, and their memories were fading with every passing day in this remote enclave, and I couldn't do anything about it. I couldn't change it. I felt defeated and haggard. I started crying, something I hadn't done in a long time.

I sat there for a long time, alone with the wild world

imprisoning me, toughening me, teaching me, taunting me, and providing me what it does. This was the way of my life for now, but the future could be different. I had to figure out a way to make it different.

I looked again into the wood and heaved a heavy sigh. The wolves may have escaped my wrath today, but it wasn't over yet.

With a weight in my gut, I made my way back to my cabin. Cindy was gone. Feeling alone and misunderstood, I climbed into my bed and found restless sleep.

Chapter 27

I awoke at first light and took a stroll around our little community. We had cleared enough of the forest for the garden expansion and had moved most of the timber to the three-foot deep ditch that served as the foundation for our palisade wall. We had marked the boundaries of the new grain fields, but much work lay ahead of us, using only our primitive tools to fell the trees.

Not far from the edge of the newly cleared area we had discovered another distortion. The woods seemed full of them.

In the dim morning light, I stood and looked over our progress. There was little wind this far from the apex of the peninsula, so a cloud of hungry morning mosquitoes assaulted me. I slapped at my neck for the twentieth time and looked up with irritation at the invisible space where the newly-discovered distortion hovered. There they sat in their observation chambers, comfortably observing my misery as I swiped away.

Surely they realized we were working hard to improve our lot. Did they enjoy watching us strive? Would we reach a particular point, just to have it all jerked away from us? To be put to sleep and to wake up back in our original cabins?

It would be hard to go on if that happened. Yet it seemed possible that exactly that *would* happen.

I picked up a stone from the freshly turned dirt and threw it hard at the distortion. As usual, it abruptly veered into a perpendicular path.

Bastards! Perverts!

If they would eventually interfere with our progress, I didn't want to wait. I didn't want to give them a show and then have it all taken away. It was time to force them to reveal their hand. Time to make it clear to them who we were. We would not acquiesce. We would not quietly follow their plan.

It's time they felt the heat for a change.

As the idea took hold in my head, my conviction grew. I decided to bring it up to the others. It was time to poke and prod until the Little Perverts squealed.

* * *

Our communal dining area at Hobbes included three long banquet tables with enough seats to accommodate all forty-five of us. There were usually two fires going, and four cooks preparing food and serving it out, with Eileen in charge. That morning, our breakfast was the usual gruel of wheat and corn, flavored with salt we had gathered from Salty's lick. It was filling, but bland and, due to repetition, boring. The only highlights were a few bits of dried maple sap and Veronica's honey. She'd become our resident apiarist, and had discovered a few new hives at our new location.

I finished my serving and walked to a dais we had built near the head of the three tables. I stepped up on the platform and looked out upon the faces of Hobbes. The conversation quieted.

"I would like to urge a new initiative," I said, "and I would like everyone's cooperation."

"It depends on what it is," said Phil.

"Perhaps you should have discussed new initiatives with us first," suggested Howard.

"Sorry, but it occurred to me this morning. We have, against our will, been placed in these deplorable conditions. And perhaps the culprits are just sitting there, in their observation chambers, watching us suffer." I turned toward the nearest distortion as if in presentation, lest they had forgotten who put us here. "And I think it's time we strike back. It's time we show them our displeasure."

"But we're not even sure what those things are," noted Christie.

"And to what end?" asked Cindy, frowning up at me, "and how?"

"Yeah, what's the point?" asked Phil. "They didn't bother us when we combined our communities. Why kick the hornets' nest?"

"Why? Just look around you! We are forced to live on the edge of survival in this wilderness, all because they fancy it. They have taken away our loved ones and probably our civilization. We are obliged to make it clear we find it unacceptable. Don't you agree?"

"I don't know," said Phil. "Life could be a lot worse. Especially now."

"What do you propose?" asked Cook, always a logical guy.

"Let's see if we can get a reaction. Let's start by building a big bonfire under one of their chambers to see if smoke has any effect. If it doesn't, then let's construct a platform so we can build a fire directly underneath the thing. Let's burn them out, the motherfuckers," I bellowed and shook my fists at the sky.

"I like the sound of that," said Trey.

"That's stupid bullshit," said Samuel. "Why in God's name would you want to provoke them?"

"Fuck 'em," I replied. "Fuck them for what they have done to us and our planet. We've got to fight them somehow. Plus, we should know if they will react. We don't want to put in all this hard work on new projects just to have our efforts wasted."

"Fire and smoke," said Howard, stroking his chin. "What else did you have in mind?"

"Whatever," I said, shrugging my shoulders. "You're our engineering guy. Do you have any ideas?"

"Everything gets diverted. I don't see what we can do."

"Let's build our latrine under one of them," suggested Carmine. "Maybe we can stink them into submission."

Carmine's comment got a chuckle, and I should have been grateful for the lighter attitude, but I was frustrated by many in our group. They seemed to be okay with the way things were. They were settling for what we had. I hadn't anticipated such lack of enthusiasm for my new plan. I felt good just thinking about burning the little bastards alive.

"How about water?" someone suggested. "Can we figure out a way to douse them with water, maybe from the river?"

"Wouldn't it just divert?" asked Christie.

"Only one way to find out," I replied. "Or what if we figured out a way to drape some kind of screen over the distortion, so they couldn't see? Wouldn't they have to come out and remove it? We would have a chance to speak with them."

"How can we do that?" asked Phil. "We don't have cloth."

"Use vines and leaves. Let's see if we can get a rise out of the bastards. What do ya say?"

"I'm with you," said Trey. "I'd love to piss 'em off."

"Kick 'em in the balls!" growled Beatrice.

"Beatrice!" exclaimed Carmine, looking at her with astonishment.

Phil stood up. "You're our elected leader, and it looks like you have some support for the idea, so we'll go along with you if that's your call."

"I think it's a stupid idea," said Cindy. She stood up and marched away from the table.

"Look, everyone," I said. "We can't just sit here and let them do with us what they want. We have to fight back. In whatever way we can."

"Okay, boss," said Samuel. "We'll try it your way. But if it backfires and we all get punished, this is on your shoulders."

A backlash was a real possibility. But that was better than not knowing anything.

I nodded. "I understand."

* * *

That evening, after we finished hacking at the trees standing in our future grain fields, several of us used the branches to build a big fire under the closest distortion while the others watched. We kept it going all night, using lots of green leaves and uncured wood, creating a thick column of smoke. The column spilt and diverted as it neared the edge of the distortion, drifting up along its edges and giving us a ghostly glimpse at its basic shape—an oval, like a giant invisible egg in the sky.

The next morning, we switched shifts and kept bathing the distortion in thick smoke until after lunch. We observed no change. No little men popped their heads through the haze and yelled at us to stop. It was anticlimactic to say the least.

It was time to escalate our aggression.

I assigned Trey, Spence, and Veronica, all of whom were sympathetic to my plan, to build a sturdy structure with a platform positioned four feet below the distortion, and by the next day we had built the crude edifice. We layered the platform with a bed of small stones to prevent the fire from burning the wood underneath and then piled fresh wood on top of the stones and lit the fire. Soon it was raging, and we climbed up the side of the platform frequently to toss on fresh wood. For hours, the fire blazed away, the tips of its flames tickling the bottom of the distortion.

They have to feel the heat, I thought, standing there watching the elevated bonfire burn. The smoke was not as thick as before, since that was not our intent, but I watched the tendrils of smoke divert in weird paths around the distortion. But it was the heat for which I had high hopes. Perhaps enough heat energy would get through to make the alien Watchers uncomfortable.

Howard walked up and stood beside me.

"What do you say?" I asked. "Any chance this will have an effect?"

Howard shrugged. "I doubt it. If these areas are shielded by distorting the space-time fabric around it, then all physical processes would follow the same path, including heat energy."

"But we don't know that for certain."

"No, we don't."

Veronica and Spence chopped and collected wood, while several of us kept climbing up with more pieces and feeding the fire. As night approached, we had accumulated a sizeable stockpile of logs, and we set up shifts to keep the fire going. I was scheduled to tend the fire at dawn so sacked out in my cabin.

Trey knocked on my door as the early light dappled the forest.

"Any sign of activity?" I asked as I pulled myself out of bed.

"The fire is out," he said. "The platform got pushed over."

"What?"

"Come see."

I followed Trey to where we had built the platform. Standing there were Veronica and several others.

"It was my shift," Veronica said. "I had just put more wood on the fire, and went to the bathroom, and when I got back…"

"You mean you went to visit Daryl at his cabin," snapped Beatrice.

"Whatever!" returned Veronica. "The fire was going good when I left. But while I was gone someone pushed the platform over."

"Any idea who?" I asked.

"I saw nobody."

I turned to see Cindy walking up. She had been sleeping in her cabin since the night I heard the yellow wolf. "Do you know?"

"Nope," she said. "I know that some of us don't care for your plan."

"Reservations are understandable, but this… Why protect the alien perverts?"

Cindy looked down at her moccasins. "Some folks here are of the opinion that these beings are acting for our benefit."

"What?" I asked, gaping at her. "How could anybody think… " I shook my head and let out a deep breath. Now was not the time to discuss it.

"Let's make sure the toppled fire is completely out. I have to figure out what to do."

I started back to my cabin, and Cindy came up and took my hand. "May I join you?"

"You would be most welcome," I said, smiling at her.

Back in my cabin, I sat on the edge of my plank bed and rubbed my face with my hands. Cindy sat next to me, caressing my back.

"What do I do?" I wondered aloud. "Should I find out who pushed the fire over? Or just ignore it?"

"Even if you found out, what good would it do?"

"I bet it was Samuel, that ass."

"Who knows? I say ignore it."

"I guess the fire wasn't working, anyway. We'll try water next."

Cindy lay back on the bed and let out a sigh. "You do that. Whatever you've got to do, Charles."

I looked at her and took her hand. "Thanks for your support. But I suspect you're not entirely on my side."

"That's not true!" she replied with surprising emotion. "I *am* on your side. I have doubts about your motivations, as you know. But that doesn't mean I'm not one hundred percent your ally."

"Thanks." I kissed her hand. "I guess I have one thing to thank the alien Watchers for. If they hadn't put us here, I never would have met you."

"See?" she said. "They're not so bad."

"No, they're bad. And I still intend to make it clear to them we are of that opinion," I said.

"Ah, jeesh!" she said, blowing a lock of hair from her

forehead and reaching for me. "Shut up and kiss me. I'm horny and tired of all this talk." She kissed me hard and moved her hand to my crotch. I dropped my buckskin trousers and pulled her close.

Chapter 28

We never discovered the party responsible for pushing over the fire platform. I had my suspicions, but decided it was in everyone's best interests to ignore the event. I continued to promote our efforts to vent our discontent toward the distortions in the sky, but specified that involvement was on a voluntary basis. It seemed a sensible approach. Yet perhaps this strategy further enhanced the schism I later discovered was growing within our little society.

Over the next few days, the volunteers picked up the pieces of the toppled platform and rebuilt it near the river, where a distortion hovered a few feet from the bank. Howard constructed a system in which he mounted a long lever on a fulcrum. He attached a reed basket to one end and a vine rope to the other. We placed a deerskin pouch full of water in the basket and, while others pulled on the rope, we lifted the pouch to the level of the platform. There, others stationed on the platform doused the distortion with the water.

It didn't take us long to realize this approach had no effect. The water diverted, occasionally soaking the person tossing the water. After a few hours of effort, our enthusiasm waned, including my own. It seemed nothing we did mattered.

Later that evening, Cindy and I lay in bed together. I felt

low, so I was glad of her company. The thought running around in my head was that we were all insignificant. We had been placed in these communities against our will, given what others had decided we should have, and then made powerless. Nothing we did seemed to affect those responsible. We couldn't hurt them or even annoy them. There was no way for us to express our defiance. I was close to despair.

"Don't be so down," she said, her arm draped around my drooping shoulders. "There is an alternative."

"What? Settle for what we have? Be content and forget their transgressions? Is that your suggestion?"

"Yes," she said, nestling her head against my chest. "That's exactly what I'm suggesting. Think about it. Like you say, nothing we do affects these distortions. True, they may be beings in them watching us and studying us. But otherwise they don't interfere. So we are simply living our lives and trying to survive. Let's carry on and value our time on Earth." Then she took my hand in hers, and kissed it. "Together," she added.

I sighed and nodded. What she said made sense. But I couldn't help what I felt. Every day we toiled and sweated in our fields. We turned earth with a hand-operated plow, felled trees with primitive axes, and planted every seed laboriously by hand. We all remembered how our lives used to be. How food was conveniently picked up off a grocery shelf and plopped into a microwave. No planting or weeding or grinding. The alien Watchers, if that was what were in those distortions, were responsible for these changes. If our suffering was simply to sate their curiosity, well, that fucking pissed me off! Damn them.

But what choice did we have really, other than carry on?

Maybe our old lives were not so much better. We went through the motions of living often questioning the meaning of it all. But at least that life was more comfortable and made sense some of the time.

The age-old question of our reason for being here wasn't new. It was just that the sages of our old civilization had come up with some pretty good philosophical and spiritual explanations to help us navigate and feel like we had a purpose. But what was the purpose here? This was the rub for me. Had we never known our previous existence, this wouldn't be nearly so difficult to swallow, and like Cindy, maybe I could just accept this situation, adjust, and become more content. I did love her, even if I sometimes hated this lifestyle. Maybe there were some positive aspects. The sex was certainly like nothing I'd ever known. And I was healthier in a lot of ways, my senses were keener, and my mind less distracted by trivia. Sometimes I did feel more connected to the world around me. And I was a truly a part of an ecosystem which I had come to know intimately.

I looked into Cindy's kind eyes. "You may be right, but it's hard for me to see it that way."

She leaned up on her elbows, looking at me tentatively. I'd come to know her well. She was struggling with something.

"What is it?" I asked. "You can tell me."

"There is another reason you should let go this campaign to bother the Watchers. I've gotten wind that a faction of our community is not happy with your aggressive tactics against the beings. They're questioning your leadership."

"Yeah," I said. "I've noticed the grumbling."

"It's more than grumbling."

I sneered. "If they want to fire me, then fine. I would be

happy to let someone else run things. This is not an easy fucking job."

"Plenty of folks are on your side, so they aren't interested in firing you. They're considering separating."

My forehead crinkled. "Separating? Forming their own community? That's crazy. The more of us together in one place, the better off everyone is. We just joined communities for a reason!" *What were they thinking?*

"Yeah, that's true. But they don't agree."

"What would they do? Head back to Salty or something?"

"Maybe."

I felt irritated and couldn't lie still. I got up and paced the cabin floor a few times, and then sat at the table, watching the shadows from the torch light play on the far wall. I started considering everyone in my mind. I had a pretty good feeling who liked me and who didn't.

"Samuel is behind this mutiny, isn't he?"

"He's a part of it, but there are many others. Even Christie and Dillon."

That surprised me and even hurt a little. I considered both of them good friends. But the only one who really mattered was Cindy, and she was hard to read about this particular issue.

"And you?" I asked, unconsciously holding my breath. I'd always rather know where I stand with people.

"Me?" she asked playfully. Then, without hesitation and a smile, "I'm with you, lover boy." She came over and put her arms around my shoulders, kissing my ear, sending pleasant chills down my body. Her hair cascaded onto my chest. God, how I loved her scent. I reached up and patted her clasped hands.

"But, if you were on your own?"

Cindy bit her lip and moved around to look me in the eyes, and nodded. "A lot of what these separatists believe makes sense. They like it here. I do miss my family and I worry about them constantly, and I miss the conveniences and some comforts of the old life for sure. But I like a lot about our new life too. I like coming home from a hard day's work, eating simple food from our fields, and actually connecting with others. I didn't do that in my old life. I was rarely present for people, face to face, eye to eye, and moment to moment. I was too distracted. I didn't know myself there—my true self. Here, I do.

"Then, at the end of the day, coming back here to lose myself in passion with you before sleeping like a log. I'm alive and in the present, and what I do daily has a clear purpose. I am a part of this community, this clan, this…" she paused before continuing, "…this tribe. That's what it feels like. A tribe. We belong to a tribe now. I don't worry about money, retirement, traffic, or my boss. I just worry about what's before me and what needs doing. This lifestyle keeps me present. I wasn't anything like that in my old life. But I didn't realize it until I wound up here."

"You don't think about what we lost? The way it used to be?" I asked incredulously. It seemed like that's all I ever thought about.

"Do I miss shopping and driving in cars and keeping up with my friends on Facebook? No, not really," she said without hesitation.

I could hardly believe it. "Really?" I asked, looking her in the eyes. "Really?" I said it more deeply, as a genuine question. I wanted her to explain it to me.

"Really," she said definitively. "Think about it and tell me what you're missing Charles. Working in the rat race, so you have enough money and stuff to keep up with the neighbors? Where the majority of your time is spent in front of screens, in a moving vehicle, or involved in all the drama that world creates? I was miserable, but I didn't know why. I thought it was these!" She cupped each large breast in either hand. "But it's not. It was that lifestyle. Maybe we weren't meant for all that technology and the disconnection that resulted from it. Have you ever thought about it like that?" She held my gaze, looking intently.

I bit my lower lip. "Fair enough. And I agree with a lot of that. But shouldn't it be our choice? They..." I jabbed my index finger up and outward, indicating the aliens, "...just picked us up and put us here, with whatever they deemed we needed to barely survive! How can you say that's okay?"

"Maybe they're trying to help us," she offered meekly.

"What do you mean, help us? Help us do what?"

"You won't like to hear this, Charles, but sometimes I wonder if they are trying to help us see how harmful life was before we were placed here."

"Like what?" I asked. "What were we doing that was harmful?"

"Well, I don't know all the details, but what we were doing to the planet for one." It was her turn to pace and talk now. "Destroying the friggin' ozone layer was harmful. Wouldn't you agree? Then there were all the chemicals we used on food. I didn't really think that much about it and just bought organic because I knew it was better, but here..." She stopped to make her point. "Now, I see *how* things actually grow—the way they're supposed to, without chemicals and pesticides.

Charles, we were poisoning our own food supply! And pumping our meat full of hormones, then eating it and feeding it to our children and causing cancer to proliferate. Then throwing drugs—more chemicals—at the cancer trying to stop it! It was insane!

"Or how about the fact that the majority of us were so anxious and unhappy that we were on medication? We were depressed, addicted, or committing suicide. Or mass shootings." She stopped her pacing and opened her hands. "Charles, don't you remember all the shootings? Every time you turned around there was one on television. We were going crazy, Charles! We were making ourselves crazy in that life."

Her passion had gotten her out of breath. I'd never seen her this way before.

"Okay, all good points," I agreed, "but this isn't the way to help us. Giving us no choice, and very little to live on. Forcing us. No, I can't see how forcing us into this situation is helping us. It's just moved us back in time, and now we have to get back there and recreate what we know is possible. Rebuild what we had. I can't be happy here like this and I can't see them as helpful. Period."

"Okay. Well, all I know is that we seem stuck in this predicament. Our lives can still be fulfilling and even pleasurable, but we can't let our resentment, hate, and bitterness consume us."

She stood in front of me, positioning her face inches from mine. "Can you try that, my love? Just be here with me and enjoy our life together?"

I looked into her soft brown eyes. I did so love her, and I didn't want to argue anymore. It didn't feel right to argue with her.

I nodded slowly and let out a long sigh. "It's hard. But, as I promised you before, I will try. For you, because I love you so damned much." I kissed her, then cupped each of her breasts in either hand and dropped to my knees, feigning adoration. "And these?" I said as if in awe. "How could you blame anything on these lovely ladies?"

She swirled away playfully and moved towards the door. "Well, we spent all our time this morning talking, so I've got to get to work now. See you tonight." And she was gone.

I too had to get to work. My mind was already busy considering who was against me, who was for me, and what that meant for our future.

Chapter 29

It fell upon my shoulders, as leader of the tribe, to keep our people working together as a unit, happy as possible under the circumstances. My aggressive assault upon the distortions had caused a rift among us, and although I didn't fully appreciate the point of view of those who took a softer stance toward our alien subjugators, I directed the community's attention away from the distortions and toward improvements.

Most of the creative energy behind these efforts came from Howard. He pushed hard for us to construct a brick kiln, arguing that we could build energy-efficient and insect-free structures if we used bricks, including ovens and fireplaces in our dwellings that would do a better job of drawing out the smoke. He experimented with various recipes for the bricks and the mortar used to seal them.

In the meantime, we used crude, sun-dried versions of bricks to build the kiln. We also worked on a community latrine, footbridges over the North and South Rivers, and continued to make progress with the log palisade, a labor-intensive and time-consuming enterprise. But we all antici-pated a sense of security from having our corner of wilderness, the river peninsula formed by the convergence of the two rivers, walled off from the surrounding woods.

The shift in emphasis did the trick. Everyone seemed to be on the same page, and Cindy said she noticed less grumbling about my leadership. Every day we worked until the sun went down, hacking trees, clearing branches from the trunks, and positioning them into the base trench. The days ended with us exhausted but pleased with our progress.

Even while all this new activity was going on, our regular day-to-day chores still needed attention. I was returning from a luckless hunting outing with Dillon and Wally, a hunter from Shady, when we found everyone gathered around the three banquet tables. It was mid-morning—everyone should have been hard at work on their various responsibilities, so something was up. As I got nearer, I saw Cook and Daryl sitting in their midst.

The pair of them had left two days earlier on an expedition toward the range of mountains to our north. Their mission had been to investigate a large lake we had previously glimpsed in that direction from afar.

As we walked up, everyone turned their heads toward us.

I smiled at our explorers. "Hi, Cook. Daryl. Glad to see you made it back. Did you find the lake?"

"We did," Cook said. "Its closest edge is only about eight miles from here. But that wasn't all we found."

"Nope," said Daryl. "We found another community."

"Really?" I put my hunting gear down and looked intently at them. "More people? That is good news! Is it like the others?"

"Yes and no," replied Cook. "It's a primitive settlement with log structures like ours. But it's bigger. And more adapted."

"Yeah," said Daryl. "They've got it together."

"Do they know anything about what's going on?" I asked.

"Well, this woman named Ursula is in charge of the place. She's pretty knowledgeable," said Daryl.

"They say she knows all about plants," chimed in Cindy excitedly, who was sitting next to Cook.

"Yeah," continued Cook. "She knows about a lot of stuff. And they do things differently there. Their whole attitude is different. They call their community Acceptance."

"Interesting," I said again, rubbing my beard. "The lake is eight miles, you say. How far to the community?"

"Two miles further along the bank of the lake, near where a small river flows out. That river must merge with this one downstream." Cook gestured toward the East River, which was what we had taken to calling the merging of the North and South Rivers.

"Ten miles? Well, that's not far. An easy day's hike. Let's plan a visit."

"Don't have to," said Cook. "They're coming here. Ursula said to expect her and a few others from their community in four days."

"So there are more people out there," I mused. "Who knows how many more settlements there are?"

"Awesome," said Cindy.

"Oh, my God, this is so exciting!" said Amber, giggling.

"We should receive our new neighbors in style," added Cindy. "How about a big feast?"

I turned to Eileen. "What about it, Eileen? Are you and your staff up to preparing a big meal?"

Eileen smiled with pleasure. "It'll be like having guests over for a holiday dinner."

"What about it, boss?" said Cook. "Get out there and bag us a turkey, will ya?"

* * *

Everyone was excited about the visit from newcomers. And it wasn't just because they were new. If the rumor was true, these folks were different. They had this survival thing down. They knew more than we did. Maybe they even understood why we had been stuck in this wilderness. Others' hopes seemed to be running high, but I was cautious. I didn't want new ways of thinking to worsen the schism in our group.

We worked hard on getting Hobbes ready, cleaning it up and preparing a big meal. We slaughtered a pig and killed several deer. There were a few vegetables from the garden ripe enough to serve, mainly radishes and beets. And we placed clay containers on the tables, some containing salt fresh from Salty's salt lick, honey in two pots, and clumps of dried maple syrup in the others. Eileen tried her hand at making apple pies, using green apples from the orchard, sweetening them with honey, and then sprinkling them with maple syrup granules.

"Better not eat too much of this pie," said Eileen, looking over her final product as I walked up to her. "The green apples might upset our tummies."

"It looks delicious," I observed.

"Too bad we don't know what time our guests are arriving," Eileen said. "It would be fun to have everything spread out on the table."

"It would be," I agreed. "But this will be an impressive meal. I'm not sure we ever ate better, even in the old days."

There was truth in what I said. We didn't possess the range of seasonings and foods we used to have, but our tastes had changed over our months in the wild. Just a little seasoning was enough. And eating extremely fresh fish or meat was something we had rarely enjoyed before. Plus, there was something about hard work and eating outside that elevated one's enjoyment of even simple food.

"God, I hope they come," said Eileen. She was a constant worrier.

"Well, if they don't, we get this incredible meal all to ourselves."

It was just then I heard a cacophony of voices calling out from the North River footbridge. It had to be because our guests arrived.

I looked at Eileen. "Time to shine. Start getting everything ready, and I'll go meet our visitors."

Cindy came running up. "I think they're here," she said. Her eyes were wide with excitement.

"I think you're right."

We walked to the footbridge and found two men and two women surrounded by a mob of Hobbeseans, all chattering at once. One woman stood out among the others. She had a striking, weatherworn face, with moss green eyes, long eye lashes and streaks of silvery gray running through her long, dark brown hair. She wore a buckskin skirt, but her tunic seemed to be made of coarse cloth. Her body was sleek, with sinewy muscles. She exuded strength, both physical and spiritual.

The questioning chatter ceased as we walked up, and the woman looked at me with confident eyes. She had to be Ursula.

"She's beautiful," whispered Cindy.

I couldn't have agreed more. She was older than Cindy, and lacked Cindy's curvy figure. But her beauty ran deep and drew me toward her, as I was sure it did to all those around her. Immediately, I felt a touch of something akin to threat. *No, not threat, Charles, don't put something there that's not.* She just had a presence. Something I couldn't quite put my finger on.

"I'm Charles Beck," I said, extending my hand as she walked toward me. She took a second to look me up and down, gave me a slight smile, and took my hand. Her grip was calm, relaxed, but firm. "And this is Cindy."

Ursula paused to survey Cindy before directing her gaze at me again, and speaking for the first time. "I've heard much about you," she said. "I'm Ursula, and this is Chelsea, Tom, and Jason. I hope our visit today has not inconvenienced you or your people."

"No, no." said Cindy. "We're so excited to have you. We have many questions."

"And I will give you all the answers I am able," Ursula said, smiling indulgently at Cindy and looking her over once again.

I wondered what Ursula was thinking. Her eyes were intense, but not easy to read.

"Well, I'm sure you're tired from your journey," I said. "Food is being prepared, and we have two cabins ready for you and your comrades. So please accept our hospitality and relax for a while."

"Thank you, Mr. Beck. Show us where you want us."

"Call me Charles, please. This way."

I led the four of them to their cabins, with a crowd of chatty Hobbeseans following in our wake.

"You'll find a dish of dried berries and fresh water in your cabins. Refresh yourself, and we'll fetch you when dinner is served. But do be prepared for questions, if you don't mind."

"And, perchance, a tour of your village later?" Ursula asked.

"We'd be delighted," I said.

Cindy and I left them to their rest and headed to the outdoor tables to help prepare them for the feast.

"She seemed somewhat unusual," I said as we walked along.

"I thought she was striking," said Cindy. "There was something about her face. She seemed... noble."

"Hmm. Well, it'll be interesting getting to know her better over dinner."

Chapter 30

Our guests had completed a ten-mile hike through pathless woods to reach our community. Not an extreme hike, but tiring enough, so I urged the others to not ask questions until after they had finished their meal.

As we all sat down at the banquet tables and turned our attention to Eileen's feast, everyone did a good job holding back. During our repast, it was Ursula and her companions who had all the questions. They seemed eager to know about how we did things in Hobbes, and why we had merged our three communities. Our clan answered their questions freely and completely.

Then, as Eileen served out the apple pie, the dam broke and everyone besieged our guests with their own questions about Acceptance. I let the others sate their curiosity while listening to every word.

Ursula did most of the talking, with the other three piping up now and then. They told us that Acceptance contained nearly three hundred souls. They received a lot of their protein from fish, since their community was on the juncture of the lake and river. They hunted nearby bogs not only for deer, but elk and moose that sometimes made an appearance. Their use of plants was much more extensive than our own, thanks to Ursula's comprehensive knowledge.

"Natural herbs were a hobby of mine in the days before," Ursula explained. "I studied them in my leisure, and so had a solid background. Fortunately, the plant life in this area is similar to what I knew, and since we've been here, I've refined my knowledge. You'd be surprised what the local plant life offers."

"I've been trying to learn about plants myself," said Cindy, her eyes bright with interest. "I understand a few things, but most of it was from trial and error."

Ursula looked at Cindy. "That's pleasing to hear," she said. "I'd be delighted to teach you what I know, if you would share your discoveries with me."

Cindy smiled. "I would like that," she said in an almost bashful tone.

"Have you found other communities?" asked Eileen.

"No, we haven't," said Ursula. "And we have systematically explored a sizeable area."

I considered what she said. Hobbes was only ten miles away, so it puzzled me that with so many people in their village, they hadn't come across us earlier in their systematic explorations.

I noticed Ursula looking at me.

"And you, Charles Beck. Don't you have questions?"

"Ah, I do. Plenty. But I didn't want to overwhelm you."

"Well, it was a wonderful meal. My compliments to the chef, or chefs."

"Indeed," said Jason, young man in his twenties with a tanned faced and dimpled chin. "Even without the herbs Ursula provides, the food was quite flavorful."

"Well, you have Eileen to thank for that," I said. "She's one of our greatest assets."

"Ah, it was nothing," Eileen replied, placing a new pie on the table. "I always loved cooking for company."

Ursula leaned back and crossed her arms across her chest. "But now I have finished my delicious meal. So please, Mr. Beck, ask your questions."

"Okay," I said. "What do you know about why we're here?"

Ursula smiled. "When you come out to play, you don't waste time, do you?"

"It's the most pressing question in everyone's mind."

"Well, I'm afraid I can't offer much you don't already know. We woke up in our village, just like you."

"But your community is so much bigger. And, from what I understand, more developed."

"We try to do what we can, and we've been established for longer," said Ursula. "But are we that different from you?"

I wondered how she knew their community had been established longer than ours. I supposed someone told her when we had all awoken.

"I assume you are aware of the distortions," I said.

"The distortions?"

"Yes, those weird phenomena just over our heads that divert arrows."

"Ah, those. Yes, we are aware."

"What can you tell us about them?" I asked. "Are they observation chambers? Are there beings inside them?"

Ursula frowned. "Beings?"

"Yeah. The ones that put us here."

"Oh, you mean the Benefactors!" said Jason, his face aglow.

"The what?"

"We call the ones that placed us here the Benefactors," said Ursula. "It reflects our appreciation for our new life."

"Appreciation? But our life is miserable!" exclaimed Rebecca, who was sitting next to Jason. She grabbed a lock of her hair. "Look how groddy I am."

"Those you call Benefactors, we consider the bane of our existence," I said, using air quotes when I uttered the word 'Benefactors'. "We call them Little Perverts because of the way they watch us. We have more choice labels whenever we get irritated enough."

"Are your lives in Acceptance different from ours?" asked Phil. I noticed he had donned a new raccoon hat for the occasion.

Ursula looked around at the faces all turned to her, her expression radiating noble kindness.

"We are better off," she said. "But not in the way you think. Not because we've figured more things out." She stood up and placed her hands on the edge of the table. "I want to tell all of you about our community. About how we do things and why. And I would like you to consider joining us if you wish. It is open to anyone willing to accept our creed."

"This is unexpected," I said. *Was she really giving a recruitment pitch?*

"What creed do you mean?" asked Cindy.

Ursula looked at Cindy and smiled. "To accept what has been given us. We believe that the lives we live now are better than those we lived when the world was filled with the trappings of modern society. The Benefactors have freed us from the yoke of our previous culture, laden as it was with unhealthy technologies. They have purged our world of these elements. Those of us who live in Acceptance are thankful for it. We live each day in gratitude to them for taking the effort to purify our world and to give us a better life."

"This is crazy!" I said, standing up. "Why should we be grateful? We teeter on the brink of destruction. We have no medicine, so any of us may get sick and die in horrible pain any day. Every little thing we do, whether it's preparation of food, or curing buckskins, or keeping the damn bugs away—" I punctuated the comment with a slap on my arm, "—saps our strength. Life is damn hard, and that is an undeniable fact."

I was just getting started. "And I haven't even mentioned the awful things these beings did. Not only did they 'purge' us of society, as you say, not only did they obliterate centuries of industrious effort without regard to our wishes, they committed an act of genocide on a scale never encountered in history. As far as we know, there are fewer than four hundred humans left, out of several billion. Maybe there are more around in little communities like ours, but nothing like what was here. Your 'Benefactors' murdered humanity! There is no other way to say it."

"You express yourself eloquently, Mr. Beck," said Ursula. "But let me point out a few things. First off, yes, many who were part of our former civilization are no longer in our world. That is true. I'm not suggesting that specific human beings have benefited from our Benefactors' designs, but humanity itself. Can you imagine any way our previous culture would have stepped back from our technology-laden lifestyle? It would have been impossible. The Benefactors have done this for us. The new world order that emerges over time will comprise healthy, happy, hardworking primitive humans without destructive technology in their lives."

"Are you for real?" asked Cook. "Pardon me for saying so, but you sound like an evangelist."

Chelsea stood up, her eyes ablaze with passion. "She's not

239

an evangelist! We share a vision of a better world, and the Benefactors have given us the path." She had hardly spoken a word during her visit, but her high, squeaky voice rang out as her long, braided hair swayed with her emotional outburst. "Our choice to walk down the path is a free one."

"The steps the Benefactors took were necessary," added Jason. "Or else we would have been stuck living like we were."

"Which you think is bad," I replied. "Let's, for the sake of our discussion, set aside the question of mass murder, and let me ask you why our world was so bad and why this—whatever you want to call it—this existence is better."

"Humans are a proud race," said Ursula. "Over the centuries, we have used our energies and minds to create many things we were proud of. We built machines to make things we previously had to make by hand, or to accomplish tasks that were performed manually. We created advanced technologies, far removed from nature, to entertain ourselves, while our imaginative input was kept to a minimum. We mass-produced consumer products that anyone could afford and few people had to be involved in the making. We figured out how to alter the genetic make-up of the food we eat, to make it easier to produce and distribute. We supplemented our diet with nutrients because processing our food diluted their nutritional components. We propped up our aging bodies with surgeries and medicines, having spent years with little exercise.

"Yes, we were proud of all these accomplishments. But it does not mean we were better off. We humans seem to be naturally disinclined to exert ourselves, but that does not mean that disinclination should be encouraged. Consider how we feel when we start an exercise regimen. We don't want to do it, but we are better off when we do. The same goes for effort in living our lives. Spending all day working in the field for our daily bread or in a shop crafting an item or tool not only takes effort, but serves another need. Surely you have felt it, Mr. Beck. The gratification of having carved out a decent life here. Figuring out how to use the tools and produce your own food. You do all this yourselves, you and your compatriots. No one does it for you. That is meaningful.

"But it doesn't stop there. Your cooperation with others, and your reliance upon them, has helped you, I would wager, establish connections with the others here unlike any you ever had in your previous life. No need for video games when you can entertain yourself with the company of the members of your society. Recall the trends that were prevalent in our former world—our world before the Benefactors came. There was a growing awareness of the importance of natural foods, with whole components. A growing rejection of modified foods that didn't taste like they were supposed to and didn't nourish our bodies like the original versions. And do you really think the people of our society were better off depending on mood-enhancing medications?"

"Many times we weren't," I said. "But it cannot be denied that modern medicine improved our health and lifespan. That's an empirical fact."

"Mr. Beck, suppose I told you I could double your lifespan, and that I could ensure that you never got sick during that life. All you had to do was live out your existence in a protected bubble twenty feet in diameter. Would you do it? Of course not. More years of life or greater health are valuable only if we can live a good life. If our life is miserable or deprived, keeping on keeping on is not preferable."

"That sounds like bullshit," said Trey.

"I don't think it is bullshit," replied Samuel. "We work much harder in this environment. And our lives, no doubt, will be shorter. But why is hard work bad? Why is discomfort bad? It's not, if we get something out of it. I am happier now than I have ever been in my life. And healthier."

"It's true," said Christie. "I get a lot of satisfaction figuring out how to work with animals."

"Y'all are crazy," said Amber. "What I wouldn't give for a cigarette and a few hours of tube time. Fuck all this hard work."

"Not everyone will agree," Ursula said. "But if you believe that your life, as we live it now, is a good life, if you believe you can be content living this way, and confronting all the challenges it entails, then we want you to join us at Acceptance. There you will find like-minded individuals who express their appreciation for what we have and feel joy when they awaken in the morning. Those of you who harbor resentment toward the Benefactors and discontentment for our new reality are toxic to our spirit and are not welcome. Carry on here or wherever, and try to make the world more to your liking, if you can."

I shook my head, then glanced up at a nearby distortion. "Ursula, members of your community are welcome to visit Hobbes and even benefit from our innovations if you wish. But I feel certain that those in our community are committed to moving forward. No one here that has worked on our palisade wall or tilled our fields wants to give up what we are accomplishing here. And, eventually, our communities will start to resemble those we once had. It may take a long time, but we are determined. This isn't "Acceptance". We don't accept the way things are. And I must say I'm not pleased that you have used this opportunity, provided by our generosity, to recruit members of our community to yours."

"I regret that you see it that way," Ursula replied. "I don't wish there to be any hostility between our communities. But many here have asked what we are about, and I wanted to give them an answer. And now I have. It's up to each individual to decide what they want to do with that information."

"Well," I said, "it's getting late and I am sure you and your compatriots are exhausted."

"I am pretty tired," admitted Chelsea.

"So let's call it a night. Tomorrow morning, if you're still interested, we will take the four of you on a little tour of our community."

"I look forward to it," said Ursula. "And then, Cindy, perhaps you and I can spend time together walking these woods. I'm interested to see what grows around here."

"I would be delighted," replied Cindy.

Chapter 31

The next morning, Ursula and her comrades enjoyed a breakfast of eggs and bacon, and then I led our guests on a tour of our community. I was proud of what we had accomplished, but, after Ursula's comments from the previous evening, I wondered if she would hold our progress against us. More importantly, whether she would hold against us our view of the future. Our eagerness to change our situation may not sit well with her so-called benefactors.

For our first stop, I led the group through the gap between the springhouse and the trough we had dug for the palisade. We approached a small structure, the function of which was clear before we reached it.

"As you can tell by the smell, this is our latrine. It's important for health reasons to keep our bodily wastes in one location, although everyone pretty much urinates wherever the urge strikes them. It will be the first structure we rebuild once we have bricks and mortar developed. But even this version, designed by Howard, is clever."

We stepped inside to see a log plank, laboriously planed by hand-held blades, forming a bench with three openings.

"Fortunately, we rarely have to share the bench, but sometimes we do."

We walked around to the back of the structure and I gestured toward a smelly pit full of waste. "You see that the contents of the latrine are discharged into this pit. We also dump our food leftovers in it. We plan on using the mixture for fertilizer in our fields and garden as soon as we figure out a way to distribute it. It's a noxious mixture."

I pointed up toward the sky, chuckling softly. "And directly above it is one of the viewing chambers. Probably not one of their favorite observation points."

"I see," replied Ursula. "A coincidental arrangement, no doubt."

Moving on from there, I showed Ursula and her companions our expanded garden and grain fields, our new irrigation ditches, and took them to the completed section of our palisade wall, which now reached about halfway across the peninsula. A stack of freshly cut trunks were piled nearby, ready to be added to the wall.

"When it's finished," I began, "it will stretch to the other river. Then we can sleep more peacefully. It will prevent animals from sniffing around the cabins at night, unless, of course, they can swim a river."

"Well, then it won't keep out bears or wolves, as both can swim," chirped Chelsea.

"Yes, they can swim," I said. "But would they? If the wall is erected, I don't think a bear would swim across a river so he can come into our camp and sniff around. The same would be said for wolves and other wild canines."

"If they're hungry enough, and they smell food, they will swim, I assure you," said Ursula. "But if you re-route the wall in such a way that it includes your garden, at least it would keep deer out of your carrots." The mocking tone of her comment was hard to miss.

"Sorry you're not impressed," I said.

"Well, I see you and your community have been active. In no time, the place will be barely recognizable."

"That's the plan," I said.

I led the tour to our freshly completed brick kiln. Stacked alongside it were bricks of different colors. They were the result of Howard's experiments with various combinations of clay, straw, and other ingredients to make the best quality bricks.

"As soon as we refine our brick recipe, we'll construct brick buildings. Howard says he can build brick fireplaces that will provide more warmth and draw away the smoke. We'll probably have to use some kind of mud mixture for mortar in the beginning, but if we figure out where to find lime, maybe we can create a longer-lasting version."

Ursula and her entourage picked up a few of the bricks and looked them over, but set them back down without much interest.

"I'm not sure I see their advantage," said Jason.

"Well, structures with bricks keep out the moisture and cold better, and there are fewer insects and fires."

"My cabin is snug and dry and free of bugs and vermin," said Ursula. "Are you sure you're not taking this step just because you can? Or because it brings you closer to the life you had before?"

"It's an improvement," I said, annoyed that she was missing the obvious. "Brick structures are better than log structures. Why do you think we switched to brick buildings to begin with?"

"There're a lot of reasons we did things in the past, and many of those reasons had nothing to do with actual improvements. Just the opposite, in fact."

"Steps like these improve our lives," I said, not hiding the irritation in my tone.

Without further discussion, we continued the tour. At lunchtime, we sat down on the small beach on the South River, joined by several Hobbeseans.

"Did you enjoy the tour?" I asked, gnawing on a carrot stick. It was clear Ursula didn't approve of what we were doing, but I wondered how she would choose her words.

"I'm impressed with much of what your people have accomplished," she said. "But some of it concerns me. I don't believe it's wise to distort nature to whatever extent one desires just to serve man."

"What does that mean?" asked Cindy, who was sitting next to Ursula.

"Well, take your waste disposal system. We have our own latrine system for collecting waste to use as fertilizer, for example. That's a direct use of nature. But some of your efforts, especially the brick kiln, are different. They take us one step further removed from the system in which we evolved."

"Who cares, if it improves things?" I asked.

"The reason much of our former technology was toxic to humanity was that it pushed us away from nature, away from the womb from whence we came. Using manure to fertilize fields or branches to build a sieve for trapping fish are examples of using nature directly. Such actions do little to harm our ecosystem or disrupt its balance. But you and some of your colleagues wish to take it beyond. It's not so much the bricks themselves as what they represent. I view them as the first steps toward the previous unwholesome arrangement. The farther our technology is removed from nature, the more damaging it is to both us and our world. I don't just mean measurable things like pollution and premature extinction of species. It damages nature's spirit.

"In our former society, artificial machines created even more artificial machines. Think about the computerized robotics needed to build computer processors. We must strive to ignore the urge to change the world to make it more our own. We must avoid the temptation to put the stamp of humanity on our world."

I looked at her, shaking my head. "Have you always hated humans so?" I asked.

"I don't hate humanity," she replied. "I want to protect it from its destructive tendencies." She studied her tomato for a moment and stood up, quietly looking in silence at the others seated on the beach.

"The spirit of this place is in clear contrast to that of Acceptance. There is a trend evident. Your actions express a desire to change things into something more akin to where we came from. You want to control your environment and alter it. We want to accept it, and use it to thrive.

"All of you have a choice to make. Decide whether you want to continue down this path of change or focus on something that is more meaningful. If you want to join us at Acceptance, and I am convinced your intent is genuine, then you are welcome."

I was annoyed with her for revisiting her recruitment pitch. But I wasn't too worried. I assumed everyone at Hobbes was as excited as I was about our progress. If I had realized that many of those around her were listening, then I would have thrown her out. Instead, I shook my head and politely bit my tongue.

Chapter 32

After lunch, Ursula took an eager Cindy walking through the woods to discuss the local plant life. I stood with Ramiro and others on a cluster of rocks on the river bank, spearing fresh fish for dinner. I found the concentration required—steady gazing into the shallows, watching for moving shadows—a diverting activity. It kept my thoughts away from Ursula's annoying rhetoric.

That evening, I awaited Cindy impatiently, pacing back and forth in my cabin. She came through the door, carrying bundles of freshly-cut plants in a basket made of woven cattails.

"Oh my God!" she said, her smile beaming. "I've never had such an eye-opening experience! You wouldn't believe what treasures the woods around us contain."

She spread the plants out on the cabin table.

"Looks like you have quite a haul," I said. Her enthusiasm was contagious.

"I do. Let me tell you about them. And let me tell you about Ursula!"

"You two hit it off pretty well, I presume."

"Oh, God, yes. We connected on so many levels. And she's so beautiful. Don't you agree she's beautiful?"

I shrugged. "She *is* physically striking."

"She's so knowledgeable. And I like her style of leadership. She doesn't force anybody to do anything. They feel compelled by her because they sense her goodness and confidence in what is right."

"Hmm," I said. "Sort of the opposite of me."

She looked at me with obvious surprise. "The two of you are different," she said. "But there are good things about you, too."

"Like what?"

"Well, you're smart. And just. You're very just. You want to do what's right. But your style differs from hers. She's a unique individual."

"Well, she and I disagree on many things, especially how we should look to the future. And I bet she wouldn't like all my rules."

She smiled at me. "No, she wouldn't. But that doesn't mean we shouldn't have them. I like your rules." I kissed her on the forehead.

"Aren't they wonderful?" she asked, standing back from the table and looking over the plants. "Some are herbs for seasoning food. Some are medicinal. See these blackberry leaves? They can help those stomach aches of yours." She held up a bundle of leaves. "And these are willow leaves. Would you believe they contain aspirin? And see these strawberry roots? They're good for cleaning teeth."

"Are those violets? And that looks like clover."

"Yep. You can boil their leaves and eat them."

"And pine cones! Don't tell me you can eat pine cones."

"No, silly. But you can heat them up to release the seeds inside and eat them."

"And acorns, too? You remember we tried those. Too bitter."

"Yeah, but Ursula says just to soak them in water for several days and the bitterness will leach out. This is wild angelica. Eat it all. This is calla lily. You cook and eat the roots. Ostrich fern fiddleheads make a nice salad—they're everywhere this time of year. This is called galingale. You can boil the roots and roast them to make a kind of coffee."

"Hmm. Is that... cannabis?"

"It is! It grows wild in these woods, although it's not plentiful. Nor is it particularly potent, according to Ursula. But it would still be fun. Wanna try it?"

"I guess. Sure. But what with? Did you find rolling papers out in the woods?"

"Nope, but I have this." She handed me a small pipe made of whitish-orange clay. "Jason made it."

I inspected the instrument. "Well, let's get high."

We passed the pipe around and soon found ourselves in each other's embrace. Our love-making was passionate and satisfying, and afterward we lay there in silence.

I didn't want to ask, but I had to. "Cindy, I get that you admire Ursula. But what do you think about her views?"

Cindy sat up and studied my face. "Why? Are you worried that people are listening to her message?"

"A little. Do you think anyone would take her up on her offer? I would hate to lose anybody."

"You don't like what she has to say, do you?"

I looked down and let out a slow breath. "I don't get it. Settling for our current life does not sit well with me."

"But why is it so important that we spend so much energy changing the way we live? You've heard me say this many times. We work hard, yes. But life is good. We make love all the time, we live in the fresh air, and everything we have, we make ourselves. What's wrong with that?"

I shook my head emphatically. "It's not just about how we live now. It's about how our choices are constrained by others. We were put here without our consent. We are *forced* to live this life."

"Charles, listen to what I am saying. I fear you're confusing the quality of life issue with the feelings of resentment you harbor toward these beings."

"Don't you fucking resent them?" I said, the words exploding from my mouth. "Sorry. I didn't mean to sound so aggressive. But look at what they've done, what they've taken. And we're forced to survive without medical care, without the necessities of life. My body aches from all the work I do. What kind of life is that?"

"Don't you see? Sure, all that technology and medicine made our lives easier. But easier does not translate into better. Like Samuel said the other day, why is hard work bad?"

"What about Sylvia and Jace?" I wanted to snap her back into reality, and make her remember her family and life.

Cindy shrugged. "What about them?"

"Your children were taken from you. Would Benefactors do that?"

Cindy didn't respond. She looked down at her feet.

"I do miss them so," she said, tears welling up. I felt a twinge of guilt for trying to manipulate her, but I had to make her understand and stay on my side.

"We owe them hell for what they did to us, not reverence. And certainly not *acceptance*." I practically spat out that word.

"It's possible they're alive. Perhaps they'll show up in a community somewhere. Maybe I'll see them again one day."

A tear slipped down her cheek and I felt awful. I put my arms around her.

"Sorry if this sounds harsh, but the chances of that happening are slim."

She pushed herself away from me. "I've thought a lot about this, Charles," she said, her voice cracking. "Phil, Carmine, Samuel and I have had a lot of talks. You don't understand or agree, but there is a lot to like about living this way. I stink and itch, but I am so much more alive than I ever have been before. And that's the way Ursula feels. In the old days before all this, she would go out into the woods collecting plants and wonder if we had lost our connection to where we came from. And now, she lives in the woods. Sometimes, Charles…" Cindy took a breath and looked in my eyes, her lips pressed together, "…sometimes I'm actually glad for the alien Watchers. I sometimes considered them benefactors, of sorts, even before Ursula came."

I felt like my world had just crashed around my ears. *Did those words just come from her mouth? Was she serious?* I threw my hands up into the air. "You gotta be kidding me! You've got to be fucking kidding me. How long have you felt this way? Or is it just Ursula putting these ideas and words in your head?"

"I've tried to explain it to you, but we just see things really differently, Charles, on this one thing. But this one thing is really important. I'm ready and able to accept this new life. You are not. It's clear." Now tears streamed from Cindy's eyes.

My own eyes prickled and there was a lump in my throat. I searched her face, her eyes, but I could not understand her view. And she was right—as much as we may love each other, this one thing was huge. It fundamentally impacted the way one viewed life. To ignore the difference would be as difficult as an atheist trying to ignore the beliefs of their Christian lover.

My head was reeling. Cindy got dressed slowly, in silence. "I need to walk." I said and left her without another word. I needed the seclusion of the trees.

Chapter 33

The next morning, a large contingent of our community met Ursula, Jason, Tom, and Chelsea at the bridge over the North River to see them off.

Ursula looked at me with a cool smile. "I hope that touting our values has not strained our relationship, Mr. Beck. We are neighbors in a land with so few of us, so we must be friendly to one another. Don't you agree?"

"I agree. No worries. We're all friends." Despite my words, I stood back from the group with my arms crossed. Everyone else shook Ursula's hand. I did not.

"Perhaps your community will join us at one of our upcoming ceremonial festivals," Ursula offered.

"Perhaps. We'll see," I said. Then, looked around at everyone. "We're free to do as we please with our free time."

Ursula looked over those gathered around her. "Think it over. Should any of you want to come, you have an open invitation to visit Acceptance and see it for yourself."

She couldn't resist. I couldn't believe the nerve of this woman!

"Don't expect too much," I said. "We've got a lot of exciting things going on. It is our goal to make our world better."

"Well, you and I quibble over the definition of 'better'. But we will further that discussion on another day. We must be off."

With a last wave, she and her comrades crossed the bridge and stepped into the thick woods. I breathed a sigh of relief.

I had to consider seriously whether anyone would take her offer. There was sympathy for her beliefs within our community, and there would be benefits being a part of a larger community. But surely her wacky views, like referring to the beings who'd put us here as "Benefactors", would ultimately deter those in sympathy. In any case, I had no control over who decided to join Ursula at Acceptance. What I had control over were our efforts at Hobbes to develop our community, to make it more comfortable and convenient, not to mention more secure and healthy. That, I had realized, was the only way to strike back at the alien Watchers for what they had done to humanity. We had to show them we would not be put down. We couldn't do this by burning or dousing their chambers, but by showing them we would rise once again.

As I walked back to the cabin to fetch my bow, I pondered the fanaticism of Ursula and her followers. What if one day we encountered cities? Would the people in Acceptance still prefer to remain as they were? It seemed hard to understand, but I could envision Ursula, Chelsea, and the others refusing to leave their village, even if a hot shower and air conditioning awaited them.

What nutcases.

But then there was another view, one that whispered from the recesses of my brain. What if the people of Hobbes, by not following Ursula's creed, would be judged by the Watchers? Maybe they *wanted* us to accept our lives and to think of them as benefactors, and if we didn't think of them that way, then they wouldn't keep us around. The thought was a chilling one. Would they just put us back to sleep?

It was something to worry about, but if they put us all to sleep and forced us to start over again, well... there wasn't a lot we could do about it. And I had no intention of changing my mind about living freely and improving our lives as we saw fit. That is what humans do. We grow, learn, expand, and advance. I couldn't deny or change that.

And there was plenty to do around Hobbes. Brick dwellings. Running water. Enclosed living areas. Improved crop yields. Trapping beaver for their fur. We had to grow. To innovate. To change the land and make it suitable for us humans and to make it our own. To build on our first primitive efforts and to reach for something more like what we had. The Benefactors be damned.

To keep our group focused and together, and to keep their minds off the wacky views of our neighbors in Acceptance, I decided it was smart to redouble our efforts on our improvement projects. If everyone was working hard and saw significant progress, then they would see the sense of keeping our community together and moving forward. We could ill afford to lose anybody.

Therefore, in the days that followed Ursula's visit, I became more of a taskmaster than before. I spent all my time at the work sites, urging Howard on with the brick kiln, or the work crews felling trees and erecting them in the palisade ditch we had dug.

Almost immediately, I noticed it.

It was hard to pin it down at first, but it became clear before long—there was a new kind of resistance to my urging. Everyone did their share, but I sensed resentment when I would urge them onward. Sour looks, shaking of heads, and even unfriendly expletives. Breaks became more frequent, often in larger and larger groups. And usually involving the same individuals.

Conversations would often cease as I approached. There was a lack of warmth and companionship from many whom I had considered my friends. I wondered if some kind of mutiny was afoot.

Instead of picking up, the pace of our progress slowed. But I plowed ahead, pushing our projects along. Then the other shoe dropped.

Cindy and I were sitting in my cabin one early evening, relaxing after a hard day's work. She seemed quiet, distracted. I figured she was just tired.

There was a knock on the door. I opened it, and there stood Phil, Samuel, Carmine, and around twenty others.

"Charles, we need to talk," said Phil.

"What is it, Phil? You wanna come inside?"

"Nah. There're too many of us," he replied. "Look, this is simple. We've all discussed it long and hard, and we have decided we want to go visit Ursula at Acceptance. To see what it's all about."

"All of you?" I said, looking over the faces. Christie was there, and Dillon.

"Well," said Phil. "All of us are going, but like I said, this is provisional. We just want to check it out."

"Some of us," said Samuel. "The rest of us know we want to leave this community for good. And you'd better not try to stop us."

"I wouldn't do that," I replied. "Everyone here is free to do what they want."

"You wouldn't know that by the way you slave-drive us."

This was Wally. He had never breathed a discontented word to me before.

"I'm just trying to carve out a good life for us."

"We don't all agree with your view of a good life," spat Samuel. "We don't agree that we should hate those beings that put us here. There is wisdom in the path they chose."

"Samuel's right," said Phil. "You have a vision of the future that seems to ignore all we have learned. You want the old world back one day. We want to learn to live in the new."

I stepped down from the door and walked out among them. "You are free to do what you want. But realize that every one of you is valuable to our community. We've been thriving and growing. If all of you leave, we lose a lot of steam."

"We understand," said Dillon. "And we regret it. But there are still more than half who will stay, plus whoever returns. You have Howard, Eileen, Cook, and many others. You'll manage."

"I'll be sorry to lose you, Dillon. We made a great hunting team. I'll be sorry to lose all of you."

"We leave tomorrow, early," said Samuel. "You've been alerted."

Phil shook my hand. "Best of luck to you," he said, and wandered off.

I bade farewell to the others who were leaving and wondered why, during all this, Cindy had stayed inside the cabin. After the group dispersed, I walked back inside with a sense of foreboding. Cindy was sitting on the bed, a pained expression on her face.

"I know it's tough losing our friends," I said, desperately hoping that was the cause of her distress. "But they'll only be ten miles away, and no doubt some will return."

Cindy said nothing, but kept staring at the floor. I sat beside her and rubbed her back.

"I'm going to Acceptance," she said finally. I had already known it. Her voice was quiet and even.

"Why?" I asked.

"I have to. I'm joining the others in the morning. I'm one of the provisional ones. I want to see how they live there, see how it feels under Ursula's leadership, and then decide if I want to stay. I may come back. I don't know." She was still looking down.

Somehow, I knew she wouldn't. I believed she knew she wouldn't either. To lose the one that was so important to me in this hard life was a rejection the likes of which I had never felt before. It was deep, visceral. Without Cindy, there would be little left for me in this brutal struggle.

"But I love you," I said, not knowing what else to say.

"I know you do," she said. "And I have strong feelings for you, too. But dammit, Charles, I like this life. I don't want to press and press to go back to where we were. And you are, frankly, obsessed. So I want to see what the alternative is. It's the way I feel."

"You say you have strong feelings for me. But you didn't say 'love'."

"I loved you, without question. But now, since Ursula came, I've questioned a lot of things. I'm not sure what I think or feel."

"God," I said, and lay down on the bed, looking up at the log rafters. I was overwhelmed. Without Cindy, I wasn't sure I could go on. I needed her in my corner. What else was there?

Cindy remained standing quietly for several minutes.

"I'm going to my cabin," she said finally. "I'm sorry."

261

I didn't respond. She closed the door behind her and left a cold emptiness in the room. I did not sleep all night.

Chapter 34

Without almost half its occupants—we now had twenty-four people—Hobbes was a shell of its former self. Like a beachfront amusement park closed for the summer, the bustle and sense of community were gone. Our groups were smaller. Our meals quieter.

The following days crept by without joy. We adjusted to our revised workloads, but it took time. There were fewer mouths to feed. But with fewer people, everything seemed harder. Felling and moving medium-sized trees, for example, now required just about everybody in the camp, especially the task of moving the log to the palisade foundation and mounting it in position. Progress on all our projects slowed considerably.

The reduction of our numbers had one positive effect—none of those remaining displayed the lack of enthusiasm so evident before. All of us now seemed of one mind. We were a little afraid of what would happen to us. But we were a determined group. We wanted our old world back and we were willing to do what was necessary to make that happen.

We still had Howard's engineering skills, Cook's competence, and Trey's athleticism and energy, so I still had high hopes for our future. But without Cindy in my life, it felt one-dimensional, and that one dimension was work. I felt lost and lonely. There weren't any bright spots in my days, and not a lot to look forward to.

For the sake of the others, I tried to project a sense of indifference over the loss of so many of our community members. I often suggested that many would return after they got a taste of Ursula's world. But as the weeks went by, we saw no sign of our former comrades.

Frequently, I dwelled on the things I had said to Cindy that might have driven her away. I convinced myself it was inevitable she should leave. She was the exact opposite of me. She was a ray of sunshine. She was always looking for the positive. She was witty and fun, easy-going. She had endured my discontent, but I saw now it had degraded our connection. She felt no animosity toward the alien Watchers, if, in fact, that was what were in those distortions. That was an attitude I had refused to tolerate, much less accept. Really, how could she be happy with a controlling, pessimistic, malcontent like me? Always complaining, always reminded of how things had once been better. Not letting things go. I wished at times I had been more open about things, but I just didn't understand this concept of accepting our predicament. Should slaves accept their station in life and not try to escape? It didn't make sense.

She didn't understand my resentment over having so much stolen from us. And that was so hard, because I still wanted her—her vibrancy, excitement, and curiosity—in my life. The love of my life was gone. My personal future looked even bleaker than ever before. But I couldn't let it show to the others, so I spent a lot of time alone, pondering these many questions. And moping.

Was I being obsessive about our predicament and the ones who put us here? The immediate intellectual answer was always "no". We were forced to live our harsh life. Our loved ones were taken from us. Our culture, filled with the technological accomplishments of mankind, was obliterated. How could I forget all that? It was unreasonable to expect me to do so. And it was bizarre that others viewed the alien Watchers as benefactors because we were learning to appreciate a simple, rustic life. I would agree there were many good things we never noticed before. But there was no way it made up for everything we had lost.

But that was Cindy's way. That was what she believed, and her convictions were part of the woman she was. I came to realize she was probably never returning to our community—at least not in the sense of being a part of it again. I did hope she would visit at least. I missed her desperately.

In my mind, I ran through the unattached women in the camp—Louise, Veronica, Rebecca, and a few others. I couldn't imagine a relationship with any one of them.

I faced the fact that I would probably remain alone forever.

One late afternoon, we had just finished adding three logs to the palisade wall and were resting from the effort, when we heard loud bellowing and calling out from the north. I recognized Dillon's unique way of approaching the settlement. Maybe he had come back. My hopes soared.

We all gathered at the North River bridge as Dillon and Wally came out of the woods, beaming.

"Howdy, Hobbeseans!" said Wally. "May we visit your fine community?" We shook hands warmly.

"Of course," I said, slapping Dillon on the shoulder. "This is your home. Welcome back."

We followed them to the banquet tables, where we each took a seat, happy to see our old friends. They looked around the community with eager eyes.

"I see the wall has grown," said Dillon. "You guys have been busy."

"We have," I said. "But the pace will pick up now you two are back."

The two of them were quiet for a moment, and then Dillon looked at me with an embarrassed expression. "We're not here because we're coming back," he said. "We were hunting in this area and wanted to drop by to visit. Sorry to give the wrong impression."

"Oh," I said, my voice sinking along with my hope.

"Are any of the others coming back?" asked Eileen. "I miss everyone so much."

"I don't think so," said Wally. "Everyone likes it there."

"And Cindy?" I knew the answer but couldn't help asking.

"Yeah," said Dillon, his voice quiet. "She's staying, too."

"But why?" asked Cook. "Why are you guys all staying?"

"It is difficult to put into words what's special about Acceptance," said Wally. "But it has to do with letting go and, well, accepting, like the name says. That reduces the stress, man. You are okay with things." He shook his head in confusion, eyes wide. "It's just easier on your soul."

"You have to experience it for yourself," said Dillon. "All of you."

"In fact, one reason we stopped by is to invite everyone to come to Acceptance for our big summer solstice celebration," said Wally. "It's one week from today."

When I heard the word "our", I realized we had truly lost

them. But these guys appeared to be happy and talked a good line about Acceptance. So maybe I shouldn't be so stubborn. Maybe we should go check it out. The prospect of seeing Cindy gave me a spark of something positive.

"The whole community is invited," added Dillon. "There will be a big fat feast and games, and I'm told it's a lot of fun. And nobody wants any hard feelings between us. What do you say, Charles? When's the last time you had fun?"

I didn't recall. Although I was certain Cindy had been with me.

Dillon and Wally stayed overnight. I gave them as much extra food as they could carry—our orchard was now producing more fruit than we could consume. They stashed it in bags of woven grass. I told them I would mull the invitation over, but knew I would go. I feared that further exposure to Ursula and her wacky views might induce more of our group to convert, but if they left, then that was probably inevitable anyway. More importantly, I cherished the chance to see Cindy again.

Chapter 35

The next week, everyone in camp loaded up with all the food they could carry and started out on the ten-mile hike to Acceptance. Everyone was excited about the prospect of seeing our friends and making new ones. It would be nice to take a few days off from our strenuous workload and just socialize. It put into sharp relief why our ancestors so enjoyed their square dances and ceremonies. The pleasure of social gatherings seemed intensified because of the life we led.

So as we left Hobbes, Cook in the lead, we all had a little pep in our step. The first five sweaty miles were through dry, thick woods, with an occasional creek to keep us company. After the fifth mile, the forest opened up. Sphagnum moss became plentiful and we were assaulted by gnats and mosquitoes.

Cook pointed to the left. "A quarter mile that way is a huge bog that connects with the western edge of the lake. I understand that moose and elk can be found within its confines. Lots of wolves, too."

"Are we in any danger?" asked Rebecca.

"Not with this many people," replied Cook. "We'd scare them away."

A few easy miles later, our group reached a small river and followed it upstream, which took us toward the north, where a range of mountains loomed. And then, as we exited a dense copse of trees, we beheld the lake, its large surface a glittering turquoise color. It abutted the foot of the mountain range, the fuzzy outlines of the nearby peaks reflected in its surface.

Near the lake, the village of Acceptance came into view as the river turned to the left and merged into the lake itself. Its buildings were clustered on either side of the river bank and along the lake shore. Woods were cut back several hundred yards from the outlying buildings, and the land was clear around the lake. Most of the area looked like grass or bogland. It was a green and pleasing setting. I felt the cooling effect of the lake and the nearby mountains. Compared to compact and claustrophobic Hobbes, Acceptance seemed like a land of legend.

Workers tending the fields saw us approaching and called out to alert the others of our presence. By the time we reached the outskirts of the little town, a group of over a hundred people had gathered, watching us expectantly.

It had been a long time since I had seen so many people at once. I found myself self-conscious and brushed the dried mud off of my buckskins. As we came nearer, I saw Ursula in the middle of the throng, her striking appearance causing her to stand out. At her side stood Cindy. I so wanted to look into her face, hoping there would still be an obvious and undeniable connection when our eyes met, but she wouldn't look my way. I swallowed a lump in my throat. Something was definitely different.

"Greetings, citizens of Hobbes," said Ursula in a loud voice. "Welcome to Acceptance. Welcome to the Feast of Summer Solstice."

Everyone walked up to us and put their hands on our

shoulders as we walked by. It was a friendly gesture, but exacerbated my uneasiness among so many new people. My responses to their greetings were short and reserved. Some of the other Hobbeseans were more receptive.

We moved beyond the big cluster of people and walked into the village down a hard-packed dirt pathway, Ursula leading the way. For the first time, I relaxed enough to take in my surroundings.

Though the cluster of cabins was larger and arranged in a grid pattern, the buildings were much the same as in our other communities. These seemed more orderly, and most of the cabins had artistic displays decorating their exteriors, something no one had bothered to do in Hobbes. Many cabins had bundles of dried plants on wicker racks mounted on the walls outside their doorways.

The other buildings were also similar—the meeting house with a large outdoor kitchen, the utility buildings, the fields; they all seemed much the same. But it was the people that were different. Their buckskins were clean. And though their hair seemed longer than ours, it didn't look as matted and greasy. They all had a slight herbal smell, rather than the sweaty stink of humanity. Many of the women wore jewelry fashioned from stones or shells. And they supplemented their buckskin outfits with pieces of fabric. *Where did they get fabric?*

There was another difference I didn't quite apprehend at first, but it soon came to me. The citizens of Acceptance were not swatting away bugs, which were active in the fading twilight. Nor were they scratching at their scalps. They had obviously figured out how to keep the lice and flying insects away!

Ursula led us to a row of cabins facing the lake, then turned to us. "We vacated these ten cabins for your group. I'm afraid that some of you will have to double up."

"No problem," I said. "And thank you for you hospitality."

"That journey can tire, so this evening please just relax. Visit with old friends or make new ones. We will bring food to your cabins, so you can retire at your pleasure. Tomorrow, the celebration begins early, with our feast celebrating summer solstice at high noon. Make yourself at home.

"But before you disperse, everyone please take this ointment, made from delphinium seeds. You will be glad you did." She showed us how to rub the ointment into our hair. It had an interesting smell, and she assured us that by morning time, most of the lice would have departed our scalps.

"And this oil is distilled from birch bark," she said, holding up another container. "Spread it over your skin to help fend off mosquitoes."

Now very fragrant, but free of flying annoyances, I was eager to see how Christie, Phil, and the others were doing after their weeks in Acceptance, but it was Cindy I was most curious about. Many of us gathered in the open work area, lit by a ring of torches. I looked around for Cindy, but didn't see her milling about with the others.

I walked up to Jackie and gave her a big hug.

"How's it going, kiddo?" I asked. "Have you found your Nirvana here?"

"It ain't Nirvana, but there is a lot to like about this place."

"Its location is impressive."

I glanced around the group.

"I saw her heading to the main meeting house," said Jackie, in a confidential tone. "She spends a lot of time there."

"Thanks." I gave a quick wave to the others and headed

toward the large building on the other side of the community's central courtyard. The door was cracked open and light shone out.

I poked my head inside and saw Cindy standing by herself at a big table. Two torches were burning, casting plenty of light. I was struck by the walls, which were covered with racks made of branches and twigs. Every available space on every rack was filled with drying plants. There must have been thousands of dried plants of all varieties lining the walls.

"Hi, Cindy," I said.

She looked over at me and smiled. She didn't act surprised. "Come in," she said. "Welcome to my botanical wonderland."

I stepped inside the door and was overwhelmed with an amazing array of scents, most pleasant, some uncertain.

"Wow," I said. "You and Ursula have been busy."

"Yes, we have," she said, beaming with pride. "It's not just us two, of course. Others helped. But it is mainly Ursula and me that categorize the plants according to their purpose." She nodded toward the opposite wall. "All the plants on this wall have medicinal value. This group is for flavorings in food. Those up top are mixed into ointments to repel bugs or burned so that their smoke repels mosquitoes. And this one? You crush its leaves and toss it into slow-moving water. It stuns the fish and they float to the surface."

"Interesting. And where's the cannabis?" I said, jokingly.

"Oh, we have some, but we don't store it here. It gets used too quickly. Ursula keeps it in her cabin. Do you want some?"

"No," I said. "Not really." I took a step closer to her. "You seem happy here."

"I'm happy. But I miss you. I miss all the others. And I'm glad you came to celebrate with us."

"You surprised me by not coming up to me when we said our hellos. Why retreat here?"

Cindy lowered her head and studied the floor, a gesture I had seen hundreds of times before. "It felt strange," she said finally. "I wasn't sure what to say."

"Well, I miss you, too. I think of you incessantly, night and day."

Cindy gave me a weak smile which wasn't encouraging. I decided to test the waters. May as well know right away where we stand.

"Maybe we can spend the night together?" I moved next to her, and tilted her chin up toward my face, but saw tears forming.

"Charles, I'm not sure how to say this, but Ursula and I… well, we have a special bond."

"I know you do," I said. "You have much in common, and she does have a presence about her."

Cindy nodded in agreement and then shook her head. "Yes and no. We have become good friends. But there's more."

"What more?"

"We've become lovers," she said and moved away from me, feigning curiosity in some drying plants.

It was a blow that was totally unexpected. I felt like slumping to the floor, but forced myself to stand up straight.

"What? Really? Are you serious?" I asked incredulously. The image of Cindy's naked voluptuous body entwined with Ursula's popped into my mind, and I felt the burn of envy in my chest. I never knew Cindy was bisexual. We had never talked about it.

"Look, it's obvious that you're infatuated with her. And being out here in nature fires the libido. But Cindy, she's a woman. A woman who's a good bit older than you, I might mention."

"It's hard to explain, Charles. Yes, she's a woman, and yes, she's older than me. But we connect on a level at which I've never connected with anyone before."

"Even me?"

Cindy didn't answer my question. "Well, now you know, I should leave. There's no reason to stress Ursula. As special a person as she is, she is human and gets jealous. And she knows about our history."

I threw my hands in the air. "Yes! Let's not stress Ursula. Fuck ol' Charles and the fact that he's lost the love of his life, but let's not get Ursula upset."

"I'm sorry, Charles. I'm glad you and the others came, but let's not make this more difficult than it has to be."

With that, she left the building. I sat down and watched the torches cast dancing shadows on the plant-covered walls.

Chapter 36

Early the next morning, I awoke before sunset and lay in bed, letting my mind race. The cabin was built according to the same pattern as my own, yet there were differences. The chairs in the room had seats made with wicker backrests. Herbal scents sweetened the air. And the remnants of winter fires had a different odor to them, suggesting that different wood had burnt in the fireplace. The air, coming from the mountains to the north and cooled by its transit across the lake, whistled through the cracks. It was refreshing and stimulating.

My thoughts soon wandered to that painful subject—Cindy. Somewhere among this village of three hundred souls, she lay. Probably with Ursula beside her. I turned over on my side and pulled my legs up to my chest.

I heard a quiet knock on my door. *Could that be her?*

I jumped up and answered it. Cook stood in the dim light of early dawn.

"I've been up and looking around," he said. He glanced around him, but no one was yet stirring. "There's something you should see. Come with me."

Without questioning him, I threw on my buckskins and followed him out into the misty morning air. It wasn't dark,

275

but it was far from daylight. The community was still quiet.

He led me down a faint path through the woods, and as he approached a large boulder, he stooped down and put his finger to his mouth. I stepped quietly and looked around the edge of the boulder.

About twenty yards away stood Ursula, stark naked and standing in front of a stone and wood structure which had the look of an altar. I watched her kneel before the structure as she reached toward it, holding a small metal sphere. The mists were still hanging in the air, so I couldn't see clearly, but it appeared perfectly smooth and about the size of a grapefruit. It was an object none of us could fabricate in our primitive conditions.

She began nodding her head, whispering words, but her voice was too low to make them out.

"What is that she has in her hand?" I whispered to Cook.

"I don't know," he whispered back.

"And who's she talking to?"

Cook shrugged and shook his head.

We stayed hidden behind the boulder and, after about twenty more minutes of holding the sphere and nodding, she stood up and slipped on her buckskins. We watched her put the sphere into a bag and depart. Cook and I approached the altar.

"Was she worshipping those beings?" asked Cook. "Her Benefactors?"

"I wouldn't be surprised," I said. "But it almost sounded like she was communicating with them. And that sphere she held. I could tell that it was made out of metal. No one here could make that. Where did it come from?"

"You think... it came from them?"

"Maybe." I picked up a palm-sized rock and threw it hard into the space directly above the altar. I followed its trajectory as it arched through the air and then, abruptly, changed its path, moving in a perpendicular direction.

"A distortion!" said Cook. "Was she talking to it?"

I shrugged. "Or praying to it. Who knows?"

"God. Do you think she worships these things?"

"Yep," I said, nodding my head. "It sure looks like it."

We heard a door shut in the distance and faraway voices.

"Sounds like the village is stirring," said Cook. "We'd better get back."

We snuck back to my cabin without being seen. We stepped inside and sat pondering what we had witnessed.

"If she's communicating with these beings, we need to know about it," I said.

"What should we do?"

I bit my lip. "We should confront her, in front of the others."

"But what if she was just worshipping them and not actually communicating?" asked Cook.

"Then the Hobbeseans need to know that, too. It might alter their opinion of her. They need to understand that this is a cult."

"But today? During the feast?"

"Why put it off?"

* * *

During the hours leading up to feast time, there were organized games and competitions. Despite my questions about Ursula's relationship with the alien Watchers, I enjoyed myself. There were many new faces, young and old, and everyone was laughing, their eyes wide with pleasure. I watched several athletic contests, such as footraces and wrestling, and became engrossed in a giant chess game played with sections of cut logs and squares traced out on the sandy lake beach. In another area were displayed artistic sculptures. Several of them were by the same artist—creations made of shells and pine cones by a man named Adolfo—but other artists had pieces on display, too. It had been so long since I had seen art, I found myself fascinated.

All the revelers were in prime festive form, no doubt helped in part by a beverage I noticed being passed around. We Hobbeseans gleefully joined all the merrymaking. My eyes scanned the surrounding faces constantly, looking for Cindy. I caught a few fleeting glimpses of her, but she kept a low profile.

Finally we sat down for the big meal itself. The food was a treat. Despite Eileen's skills, the meals we had in Hobbes had become boring and repetitive. But this food was accented with bright, herbal flavors that were new and delightful.

Cindy sat next to Ursula, almost opposite me. I watched her from time to time, and never once caught her looking in my direction. I wondered what she knew about Ursula's dealings with the alien Watchers. It was possible she knew nothing. But dammit, if Ursula was communicating with those responsible for us being here, she and everyone else deserved to know.

After the meal, I stood around with other Hobbeseans, trying to find something useful to do during the cleanup. The citizens of Acceptance were reluctant to let us do much. I interpreted that as a gesture of goodwill.

"Hey, copier salesman," someone behind me said. I felt a large hand on my shoulder. "Try some of this."

I turned around to see Samuel holding out a flask. His face

was flushed and he was smiling. Not a common sight on his normally sulking visage.

I took the flask and sniffed at its contents. "It smells... alcoholic."

"It's mead!" said Samuel, chortling. "Made from honey! Damn good. Take a swig."

I sipped some down and enjoyed the sweet burn. "Not bad," I said, nodding. But I handed the flask back. I didn't want to get tipsy if I was to call Ursula out.

At that moment, someone jumped on my back and clung there, piggyback style. I heard Rebecca's giggle and gently dislodged her.

"Hi, Chuckie," she said, her stance unsteady. "Isn't this place great?"

She was well on her way to being more than tipsy.

"You don't mind if I have another swig, do you, Sammy?" she said. She reached for the flask and gulped down a hefty swallow. "It's so good."

I left the two of them to their own devices and found Christie standing with several others. They were looking over small squares of material. As I walked up, she handed me one.

"Feel this," she said. "It's made from bamboo."

I felt the cloth. It was a tad coarse, but wasn't too bad. "I wouldn't mind a whole outfit made of this. It beats buckskins, especially in the summer."

"Here, this one is made from stinging nettles, but it doesn't sting! And this one is from hemp."

"Hemp?" I said. "I know they made rope out of it, but clothes?"

I touched the other samples. They all were coarse, but still, they were cloth.

"The problem is weaving it," said Chelsea, whom I recognized from her visit to Hobbes. "Since we don't have looms, all the threads have to be put into place by hand. Time consuming. To make an entire suit of clothes would take many hours of work. But look at this." She handed me a brownish, floppy piece of material. It wasn't fabric. I took it in my hand and held it up to the light.

"What is it for?" I asked.

"It's paper, silly," Christie said. "Compliments of Ursula. You mash up cattail fibers to make it."

"And this is the ink we make from pokeberries," added Chelsea, handing me a small clay vial filled with a pinkish-purple liquid. "Use goose feathers to write with."

I nodded in appreciation. "This could be useful."

"Ursula is amazing, isn't she?" replied Chelsea.

"Yep," I said. "Amazing."

I left the group and wandered down to the beach. Cook was watching a wrestling match. The contestants had disrobed. No one wanted to tear their precious buckskins.

"Just like the ancient Olympians," I said as I stood beside him.

Cook looked at me. "Hey, Charles. When do we act? Ursula is over there with those people."

I spotted Ursula just a little ways along the shoreline, chatting with a group that included a few Hobbesian's, and gesturing out toward the water.

"I'm having second thoughts," I said. "Everyone is having such a good time. I hate to spoil the mood."

"I know, but shouldn't we find out the truth?"

"I suppose," I said, letting out a sigh.

I walked up to Ursula and stood there. She was pointing out an island in the middle of the lake, where moose sometimes swam to dine on the watercress and other aquatic vegetation. She sensed I was there and turned toward me.

"Well, hello, Mr. Beck. You look like you have something on your mind."

I looked at the others. Samuel was there. And Rebecca and Carmine.

"I do have something on my mind," I said. "Cook and I saw you at your altar this morning. It looked like you were worshipping the beings who put us here."

"Were you spying on me, Mr. Beck?"

"I wouldn't call it that. No. We happened to see you…"

"Yes, that is correct," she said, cutting me off. "I give thanks to the Benefactors every morning. It is part of my daily ritual."

"Does everyone know that?"

Ursula smiled and looked around. "I think so."

"But it looked like you were communicating with them. Do you talk to them? We have the right to know."

"Damn you, copier salesman!" cried Samuel, who happened to be standing next to Ursula. "You rudely interrupt our celebration, after we were generous enough to invite you?"

"We have a right to know," said Cook, who had just walked up. "Does she talk to the alien Watchers?"

"Why is it any of your business what we do in this community?" said Samuel. "You're not one of us, so just shut your trap."

"We're not part of this village, but we are part of this world," I replied. "And those beings set this up. We have a right to know."

Samuel was about to respond, but Ursula held up a hand

and shook her head. "Please, Samuel, don't be that way. Mr. Beck wants to know and he should know." She turned to look at me. "Everyone should know. Follow me to the courtyard. I'll address all of the Hobbeseans."

Chapter 37

Ursula stood before one table and looked over the crowd in front of her. The word had gone out and everyone gathered around. I was amazed at how quiet the crowd had become.

"Members of Hobbes and of Acceptance," she said, her voice loud enough to reach everyone. "I have something to say that most of you know, but many of the newcomers do not."

Ursula lowered her head and considered for a moment.

"To begin with, yes, the Benefactors have contacted me. Although I've never beheld one in person, they spoke to me, in the beginning. So I know a few things."

She looked at me and held out her hand. "Do you mind?" she asked. I grasped her hand and, using me as support, she stepped nimbly up onto the table.

"Our world," she said, sweeping her arms around her, "is now a vast wilderness. It's natural to ask why. And what our role is within this unblemished world. This is what I know. Thirteen years ago, I woke up in one of these cabins, just like the rest of you."

"Thirteen years!" I exclaimed. Chatter erupted among the current and former Hobbeseans.

"Are you saying we had been asleep for thirteen years before we woke up?" asked Cook.

"At least," replied Ursula. "When I awoke, I lay naked in that cabin there." She pointed to a nearby structure. "I was afraid at first, but I began to hear them. It wasn't like a voice as we would normally experience, but thoughts entered my mind. They said I was chosen, because of my beliefs, to lead humanity to a new world order. I wasn't able to ask questions or respond in any way. I could only hear their wishes."

"They contacted you?" I asked, although it was clear that was what she was saying. "Only you?"

Ursula nodded. "As far as I know. These beings—they call themselves the Hormvisi—turned our planet into a stable ecosystem where no species has an unnatural advantage over the others. They eradicated all of our cities, factories, roads, and all the trappings of our advanced civilization."

"Everywhere?" I asked. "Are there no cities left anywhere?"

"I'm afraid the answer is no. Our world is now a vast, pristine nature preserve. There is nothing left of our former world. But the Hormvisi had no desire to eliminate humanity. We are a legitimate part of Earth's natural ecosystem. However, if we are to be allowed to exist, we must exist in a manner that is not disruptive to the system they created."

"So these distortions, are they chambers of some kind?" I asked, gesturing to the air above me. "Do they contain members of these... Horvisi?"

"Hormvisi. I don't know. I wasn't able to ask questions. I could only receive their instructions. They made no mention ofthe distortions."

"Okay," I said. "Let me see if I have this right. We can be a part of this nature preserve. Just another species among many. But only if we remain in a primitive state and don't muck up the balance of things."

"That's right."

"So what happens when we do what comes naturally? What happens when we develop beyond our initial primitive state? Will they put us to sleep?"

"Hmm. The answer to that question is connected to another one you probably have. Why is it we've been here thirteen seasons, and you, only one?"

"That *is* a good question," said Howard.

"Because," began Ursula, her eyes intense, "the Hormvisi set up Hobbes, Salty, and Shady as feeder communities. They wish to seed their nature preserve with humans, but they have to protect it, so they must ensure that the humans in this world will accept their conditions. That the members of human communities will be happy living in our natural state, closely connected to nature. So I, and those who work by my side, were tasked with the mission to recruit individuals that are content with our plight. Those not content are refused admittance. They are filtered out."

"Filtered out?"

"Yes. They were asked to go their own way. The Hormvisi set up this preserve with a specific purpose—to establish the Earth's ecosystem in a stable balance. When you awoke, you were given implements and a way of life they ordained as acceptable. By being forced to live in those conditions, everyone developed a good idea as to whether or not they liked it. It is the responsibility of the leadership of Acceptance to recruit those individuals content in this new world. I have now done so for thirteen years."

"I can't believe this crap!" cried Trey.

"So these Hormvisi shits want mindless sheep who will acquiesce to their meddling with our autonomous civilization?"

I asked. "A society of fucking sheep."

"If you want to view it that way."

"And what if we change our minds? Or what if we join but our children grow up to be different?"

"There will be no children," replied Ursula. "We are all infertile."

My mouth dropped. All the other Hobbeseans stared at Ursula, dumbfounded. We quietly wrapped our minds around this disturbing bit of news.

"What do you mean?" asked Christie, breaking the silence. "We can't have children?"

"Sorry, Christie," said Ursula. "No children. Ever."

"But why?" Christie persisted. "Why prohibit children?"

"It's their means of control," I said, understanding their intent. "Newly born humans, once they grow up, may or may not follow the Hormvisi's creed. They don't want to risk that."

"Very good, Mr. Beck." said Ursula. "That is correct."

"Okay, then what happens when the members of your privileged community die off?" asked Cook.

"The Hormvisi want to build the population up to a certain level and then keep it there. But they can't do that by allowing us to breed. Instead, they keep the population of Earth in sleep stasis, and awaken those they need. The ones awakened give their new life a test run, and either are or are not filtered out. Acceptance and, later, similar communities will continue to grow. As some die off, new recruits replace them."

I scowled at her. She made no mention of what happened to those that were "filtered out."

"So are you saying that everyone is still alive somewhere?" asked Veronica. "Our families and friends?"

"Yes. Every year, a new batch of them are awakened."

"Why didn't you tell us this to begin with?" asked Trey. "Instead of going through all this shit?"

"Because," said Ursula. "I had to find out which of you had a natural inclination to join our community. The acceptance of our way of life had to be genuine and not based on fear of the Hormvisi."

I recognized the implications of the fact that she was revealing this to us. It was too late for those of us that hadn't already joined to change our minds. But I really didn't give a fuck. I climbed up on the table and stood next to Ursula.

"Let me get this straight," I said, speaking to the crowd. "Every year, a new group of us wake up and are forced to live in the woods. After they've been at it a while, they encounter Acceptance and you recruit the ones you deem acceptable. So one question remains… what happens to those you reject?"

"I don't know," said Ursula.

"What the fuck does that mean?" asked Trey. His tone was angry, belligerent.

I shook my head in puzzlement. "For thirteen years, a percentage of the people who wake up in these communities are told to take a hike. And you don't know what happens to them?"

"They don't come around anymore, that's all I know. They may have migrated to some other area. We just don't encounter them."

Her words gave me a chill. I turned to her. "You don't encounter them anymore?"

Ursula shrugged. "They're not here. That's all that I can tell you."

I shook my head and glanced over the Hobbeseans standing in the group. They all seemed perplexed, lost. I turned back to Ursula.

"This is a lot to take in. Do you mind if our group gathers to discuss this? Privately?"

"Of course," she replied. "I'd recommend the beach."

Chapter 38

All Hobbeseans walked down to the lake and stood in a cluster on the wide, sandy beach while the festival, now centered on Acceptance's central courtyard, continued unabated. My head was spinning with all this new information, and from their expressions, I gathered the same was the case with the others.

To begin with, it rattled us to have our fears confirmed—that alien beings were responsible for our plight. Little else made sense, really. But to now know, for a fact, that we were being manipulated by beings from some other world was deeply unsettling. It meant that we were dealing with a multitude of unknowns. What did all this mean for our future? What if we kept on with our improvements? Would something happen to us? What if we played along and created our own little model community, at least according to the Hormvisi's ideals? Would it matter?

If these Hormvisi beings were, in fact, inside the distortions watching us, it seemed unlikely we could hide. They were invisible and, as far as I could tell, everywhere. And how could we fight them? Even with better weapons than bows and arrows, if they put us to sleep, we would be defeated.

We discussed our situation for a long time, trying to make sense of it and cover all bases. About the injustice of it all.

About our options. About our future. And as our impassioned discussions ebbed and flowed, I found myself increasingly comfortable with the position of defiance, to continue to move forward with what we had started. The Hormvisi be damned!

I was pleased that many of the others felt the same way. We weren't willing to give up our essential human nature—innovators striving to improve our lot, even though it meant taking our chances with whatever the Hormvisi would do to us for not playing along. Cook and Trey, in particular, strongly agreed.

"If we do this," I began, looking at them both, "we may hear a weird clacking sound in the sky one day, fall asleep, and never wake up again. In fact, maybe that's what we should expect."

"Yeah," said Trey. "But if that's what happens, then that's what happens. Besides, even if we play along, what do we get in return? A hard life on the edge of survival until all the energy of our bodies is spent? I'd rather risk the wrath of those beings for the chance to live a better life."

"I feel the same way," said Cook. "I don't want to give in. We shouldn't have to give up what we are. Who knows, Ursula might be mistaken, or lying. We might even be rewarded for our innovative tendencies."

I shrugged. "It's possible."

Much to my chagrin, Daryl, Rebecca, and Howard were inclined to submit to the wishes of the Hormvisi. They wanted to join Acceptance. But if that wasn't an option, they wanted to set up Hobbes in accord with principles followed in Acceptance.

I noticed several people looking behind me over my shoulder and turned to see Cindy standing there.

"Can we talk?" she asked. "Somewhere alone?"

"Sure," I said. I excused myself from the group and strolled with Cindy along the lakeshore. The heavy sun cast long shadows across the surface of the lake as it dipped below the tree line.

"I hope you realize I knew nothing of all that," she said. "I would've told you."

"I believe you. And Ursula knows you would have. That's why she kept you in the dark."

"But it doesn't matter. I'm trying to convince her to bring all of you into our fold. I told her you would live according to the Hormvisi's wishes. To stick to the creed and be happy. Then we can all live here and carry on with our lives."

Her concern touched me, and I stopped to look into her eyes. "Thank you for your efforts. I really appreciate them. But I doubt she'll change her mind. And even if she did, most of us would prefer to carry on with what we started. We are determined to continue developing Hobbes."

"How can you say that?" asked Cindy, her forehead wrinkled with concern. "You realize they'll eliminate you! These Hormvisi won't let you carry on with your projects. It worries them, because it shows you're not content with your plight, and they'll react by removing you from their preserve. Is that what you want?"

"I refuse to live this way. Now we know that alien beings are behind everything. They stuck us here and forced us to live this way. I can't call them our benefactors, and I can't just accept things as they are. I want to improve. Don't you see? It's a part of what we are to make our world a better place."

Cindy put her hand on my shoulder. "Okay, I think you

don't realize some things. I discussed all this with Ursula while you and the others were out here. The Hormvisi don't care if we improve our lives as long as we don't develop disruptive technologies. We have paper now, so we can write literature and philosophy. We can pursue art and music. We can become socially enlightened and intellectually accomplished. We can grow as humans as much as we want. Because none of these things threatens the balance of their nature preserve. We just can't aspire to develop technologies that alter the system."

"Besides bricks, what have we done that is so bad?"

"It's not so much what you've done, it's what you and others of your mindset strive for. To develop in such a way that pushes mankind further from nature. That's what Ursula means by toxic technologies. But writing literature on natural paper, and creating sculpture out of objects found in nature, such as clay, or playing music with, say, bone flutes. None of these things goes against the Hormvisi's plan." She took my hand and clasped it between both of hers. "So, you see, we can grow and innovate. We can continue to be full-blooded humans."

"That's something, I guess," I said, mulling it over. "I'll consider it. And I appreciate you caring enough to come tell me."

"Of course I care for you, Charles. I never stopped."

I smiled at her. "But don't expect too much. Living in a society where the desire to improve is suppressed…"

"Only those improvements requiring problematic technologies."

"Yeah, only those. But still, those are the ones that improve our health and make our lives easier and longer."

"But," said Cindy, leaning closer and looking me in the eye, "they are not the ones that really improve our lives." I knew she was referring to all the positive realizations she'd made since winding up here.

"That's the question, isn't it?"

Cindy squeezed my hand and made to leave. I stopped her and brought my face close to hers. Her familiar scent electrified me. She didn't pull away so I breathed her in. After a few tense seconds, I leaned forward to kiss her, but at the last moment she pushed me away.

"I can't, Charles," she said, looking down at the ground and shaking her head. "I want to on some level, but I can't. I'm with Ursula now."

I nodded. "Okay," I said, and stepped back.

She left, leaving me to my thoughts.

Chapter 39

I made my way back to the cluster of Hobbeseans still engaged in conversation on the lake shore. There wasn't much left to say, so, subdued and thoughtful, we headed back to the revelers in Acceptance. The mead was handed around, and I took a long, grateful swig.

Amber, Rebecca, and a few others wanted to explore the possibility of still being allowed to join Acceptance, and they asked me to approach Ursula with them. We found her attending a plant display with Cindy.

"We have a few questions, if you don't mind," I said.

"By all means," replied Ursula, who had a striking splay of flowers draped around her neck.

"We are now fearful of our fate. Many of us are not willing to give up our belief that real improvement means evolving back to where we were before these aliens took it all away. But some, now knowing the circumstances, wonder if it is still possible to be a part of your community."

Ursula looked at Cindy and then me. "Cindy has argued that we should take in whosoever wishes to join us. But I'm afraid that I cannot. I don't know what fate is in store for the members of your community, but it doesn't lie with Acceptance."

"So none of us can join you now?" asked Amber.

"That is correct, my dear. Those of you still at Hobbes have revealed your true colors. We must keep our numbers pure. We hope you visit from time to time and remain friends. But when the purpose of our gathering is over, we will ask you to leave, to return to Hobbes or wherever you chose to live. But let's not worry about that now—it's time to celebrate the Solstice." She gestured at the festivities around her.

I thought her reaction was a bit cavalier. We were all doomed to an uncertain fate, and her suggestion was to party. But the three of us returned to the celebrations. I wondered how they would enforce excluding us from their community. Would they repel us with threats? I kept an eye on sulking Samuel. His visage was dark with a drunken leer. I was certain that he would be happy to use whatever means necessary to keep me away.

None of us were pleased with being excluded, even those who had no interest in joining what was to all intents and purposes a religious cult. Standing naked before altars and worshiping the Benefactors—the whole thing smacked of idolatry, elitism, and brainwashing. But we were here to enjoy ourselves and such occasions were rare, so when the mead flask was handed my way, I drank heartily.

Despite the revelry around us, most of the Hobbeseans were subdued. We often huddled together as nighttime descended. Physically, we were a part of the community at this moment, but it was temporary, and we all knew it. We would be shunned tomorrow. I felt protective of my small band, and stayed close to them, trying to buoy everyone's spirits.

A few of the former Hobbeseans, now converted and perhaps feeling guilty about their situation, came by to offer encouragement. But I noticed they didn't stay with us long, as if we were blighted by some disease. Only Christie, who had been Cook's lover from time to time, and Dillon, spent much time in our company.

I enjoyed the burn of the mead again and again.

Later that evening, many of us milled around the banquet tables snacking on leftovers from the day's great feast. Ursula and Samuel were there, nibbling on a venison roast and engaged in companionable conversation. They seemed to be good buddies.

I felt compelled to approach Ursula one more time. She wiped her blood-red fingers on her cloth tunic and looked up at me. There was no friendly smile this time. That was okay. I wasn't in a friendly mood.

"I have a question," I said. "Why did they choose you? Why are you, personally, tasked with the responsibility of selecting the ones you deem worthy?"

"She was chosen by God!" said Samuel, his voice slurring. "Our civilization has paid the price for our wasteful, sinful lifestyles and these beings are His angels.

"You're drunk," I said.

"Perhaps the Hormvisi are angels," Ursula said. "I've never seen them."

"That's bullshit!" I said, throwing my hands into the air. "It's all bullshit! It makes no sense."

"It makes sense," replied Ursula. "Mankind's technology was toxic to the world, not only directly through pollution and the extinction of organisms, but also spiritually, by taking humanity so far away from nature. The Hormvisi, our Benefactors, have saved us from our plight and redirected our path."

"No," I said. "It *doesn't* make sense."

"Can you be more specific, Mr. Beck?"

I paced back and forth, running my hands through my hair.

"Geological forces cause environments to change. And changing environments mean changing species. It's the way of nature that species go extinct, just as they come into being. Sometimes the extinction is abrupt, like when some cataclysmic event occurs or when humans eradicate the special environment of a particular species. Other times it's much more gradual. But there is no preferred state of nature, and whole civilizations just don't disappear or go to sleep, just so some other life form can recreate what they think is pure." I used air quotes around the final word. "It should remain in constant natural flux."

"Maybe, but I still don't see your point," replied Ursula. Samuel moved closer to her, as if he needed to protect his queen.

"The point is, why did they choose this eco-state?" I waved my hand through the air in a sweeping gesture. "Why artificially make humans non-disruptive? In a natural setting, one species often muscles out its competitors because of some advantage. A bigger claw or a sharper sense of smell helps them win out. Development of technology is humanity's advantage. Why is a bigger claw okay, but advanced technology not? It seems arbitrary to prefer one over the other."

"Hey, copier salesman," said Samuel. "You flap your lips a lot."

"No!" I cried. "This is a valid point. There is no preferred natural state of things. Species go extinct and come into being all the time. A virus could evolve through natural channels and destroy all animal life. There would be nothing less natural about such a scenario. Life is a constant war of survival, and anything can happen. So to say that humans are to be limited, forced to live a certain way, is to impose artificial restraints on our world system. How could these beings possibly value their object of study if it's tainted like that?"

"You're full of bullshit," said Samuel.

"I agree," said Jason, who had walked up to stand next to Ursula. His face was stern, unfriendly.

"No, no," said Ursula. "He's actually right. You're a deep thinker, Mr. Beck. And I take your point. But no one said the Hormvisi created this preserve as an object of study. I believe it expresses their nature. A kind of artwork, if you will?"

This was new. "We are part of an artwork?"

"Are you serious?" blurted Trey.

"Yeah, I think so. In a way. So the answer to your question—why set up the limitations of our society the way they have—is that the choice was based on aesthetic considerations."

I scowled at her. Was she really suggesting our world had been undone because of aliens' art project?

"Look at it this way," she continued. "Our society not only wants to use the resources of our planet. They want to clear forests, and build factories and cities. Mankind wants to convert the planet into man's image. But this conflicts with the Hormvisi's preferences. They reject the aesthetic qualities of man's image stamped on their nature preserve."

How can you argue with that? They don't like the looks of humanity's technological footprint.

"So, you're saying the Hormvisi don't care for the way humans adapt the world to their advantage, in the same way

I don't care for pointillist paintings?"

"Yes, you could say that. They prefer this vast nature preserve to be a certain way, as do we. And they don't want us to muck up their vision."

I recalled our earlier speculation that we might be part of an interstellar zoo, or even a reality TV show, as Amber had proposed. Those possibilities were degrading enough. But this—that we were part of an artistic creation—seemed even worse because it was so subjective.

"What can you say to that?" asked Cook. "It's so bizarre."

"Do you know this for a fact?" I asked.

"I don't," said Ursula. "But I suspect it is true. Otherwise, little makes sense."

"That's fucked up," said Trey.

"You know, you have an extensive vocabulary," said Ursula, looking at Trey.

"And you're fucked up," he added.

"Hey! Watch it!" said Samuel, stepping between Trey and Ursula.

"It's okay, Samuel," said Ursula dismissively. "It's easy to see why they aren't part of humanity's plan for the future."

"Humanity's plan?" I asked, my voice rising. "Did you call it *humanity's* plan? Yet you support a race of beings who aren't human and who wish to reject humanity's nature because it is aesthetically displeasing. It's not humanity's plan. We're dolls in a doll house. It's the Hormvisi's plan."

"All I know," said Samuel, walking up and poking his finger into my chest, "is that before long, you will be outta here, and the rest of us will live our lives and not have to listen to your mouth."

I pushed his hand aside. "Get away from me, you drunken

lout!"

Quickly, Ursula stepped in between us. "Stand down, Samuel."

It was a brave gesture. Noble, really. She was trying to defuse the situation. But I had a belly full of warm mead, and I wasn't ready to play nice.

Chapter 40

"So, Goddess Ursula, do you have any remorse for deciding who lives and who dies?" I asked, emphasizing the term "goddess", but it occurred to me how accurately it fit.

"I never said you would die," she said, her voice monotone.

"You come into our community, like a snake in the grass, and take our people away. You're a recruiter for another race of beings. That's gotta make you feel a little weird, you crazy bitch."

"I believe you're drunk, Mr. Beck."

"I don't give a damn if I am. You need to hear this. You come across as a caring, noble person, but you aren't. You are the executioner. And you justify your actions by your pseudo-religious rituals. Don't you? You tell yourself you're doing good for humanity, although you're not. But how else can you get to sleep at night?"

"Whew," said Cook. "I wouldn't want to be you."

"I sleep just fine, Mr. Beck. I genuinely believe the Hormvisi *are* Benefactors. That they have shown us a better path. True, that better path aligns itself with the designs of the Hormvisi, but why should that matter, as long as it's good?"

"You're grasping at straws, aren't you? We're dolls in a doll house."

"You said that already," said Samuel.

I looked at Cindy, who had been quiet the whole time.

"You take our citizens and you take my girl. And you leave the rest of us out to dry. That's not good. You're not good. That's the bottom line. Do you understand me? You're not good!"

"Okay, Mr. Beck, that's enough." Ursula said with finality.

"You've crossed the line, copier salesman," said Samuel, poking his finger in my chest again. "You walk away, or you get what's coming to you."

"And what the fuck's up with you?!" I cried, pushing his hand away again. "You were one of us. Now you're a sheep."

"I was never one of you," spat back Samuel.

"And Cindy, how can you stand there and say nothing? You left me for this woman. What does that say about you?"

"Can you blame her?" said Samuel, leering at me. "Such a fucking loser."

"Fuck you." I took a wild swing at Samuel's jaw, all my resentment and fear balled up inside my fist. Samuel instinctively ducked to dodge my swing. But my drunken punch was so badly aimed that he moved directly into its path. So to my surprise, my haymaker connected with a solid, satisfying crunch, pain exploding through my knuckles. Samuel fell backwards onto the ground, winding up on his ass. Ursula backed away.

"There's no place for violence here!" she cried. It sounded odd hearing her voice raised.

Jason and several other men from Acceptance were upon me immediately, and I started swinging at anyone who came near.

"You're serving aliens!" I cried. "Don't you see that? Alien servers!" Out of the corner of my eye, I saw Samuel had recovered from my punch and was launching himself through the air toward me. I spun around to avoid him, and he landed on my back. I couldn't hold his heavy weight, and went down where he pinned me to the ground. He pummeled the sides of my head with his fists, and I covered my face with my hands, wishing I wasn't so drunk.

I heard Cook and Trey yelling for them to let me up, and there was more scuffling. I wanted desperately to get up and vent my anger, but Samuel had me in a vice grip. His blows to my head continued.

Somewhere in a fuzzy mist I heard Cindy yell, "Stop it!" Shortly after that, I blacked out, no doubt due as much to my heavy intoxication as Samuel's battering fists.

* * *

I came to slowly in my borrowed cabin. Despite my throbbing head, events from the previous evening started coming back to me.

Ursula's proclamation that we couldn't join Acceptance... the mead...my fight with Samuel...getting thrown to the ground.

Everything hurt. I sat up and touched my face gingerly. There were a few tender areas, but my skull bore the brunt of the blows. The lumps were numerous and sore.

"That ape could've given me a concussion," I said out loud, wincing with pain as I did so. My mead hangover just added to the discomfort.

I had to pee, so I stood up carefully and made my way to the door. But the thing wouldn't budge. I pushed harder, but to no avail. It was barricaded from the outside. I tried the window, but the shutters were closed and secured, again from the outside.

"Hey! Anybody out there?"

"Yeah, whaddaya want?" came an unfamiliar and unfriendly voice from outside.

"Let me outta here. I can't open the door."

"Maybe later."

"What? Let me the hell out of here! I gotta pee."

"There's a pot in the corner," the voice returned.

Confused and offended, I found the clay pot and relieved myself, then sat back down on the bed to think this through. Why was I locked inside the cabin? Where were the others? Through the wisps of my hazy memory, I pieced together that most likely Ursula deemed me a threat and had, essentially, put me in jail.

But I didn't have to wait long. There was a knock, and the barricade was removed. The door swung open. Standing outside were all the other Hobbeseans, including Trey and Cook. Cook's eye was black and Trey's upper lip was swollen and blood-encrusted.

Standing around our group were about one hundred people, mostly men, many holding clubs or farm implements. Ursula came forward.

"Thanks to your behavior last night, you and all members of your community are banned from Acceptance. Violence is not part of our creed. You are no longer welcome here and must leave Acceptance at once."

I looked at Ursula with contempt. Behind her stood Samuel, the impact of last night's haymaker still clear on his jaw. I resisted the temptation to make a snide comment. I was sore and hungover and wasn't up for another confrontation. I wanted to get home.

Cindy, once again, was nowhere to be seen.

"Have fun fucking my girlfriend," I replied. I looked at the other Hobbeseans. "Let's clear this joint. The party's over."

We were a quiet and unhappy group as we hiked the ten miles back to Hobbes. After a few miles, I became nauseated and vomited several times. And I wasn't the only one in our group to do so. But we kept moving forward and, after a few hours, the exertion cleared our systems of the previous evening's excesses and we felt better. Trey and Cook talked about their role in the evening's scuffle. They had both taken a few swings at the nearest member of Acceptance even as they were overwhelmed. They had been battered, held down, bound, and barricaded in their own cabins.

"Basically, we got our asses kicked," said Trey. "But we were badly outnumbered."

"Was it just you two?" I asked. "Did anyone else take part?"

"I wanted to," said Amber.

I gave her a weak smile and kept on trudging. Home was still a long trek away.

A mile or two later, Amber came up to me. "Hey, Charles, what will happen to us?" she asked.

"I really don't know," I said. It was a question I had to spend more time thinking about.

"I don't think we can ever go to Acceptance now," said Amber.

"You mean, because of my behavior last night?"

"Yeah, that, and the fact that Ursula is a bitch."

"Can't argue with that."

Chapter 41

The next day, as I woke fully recovered from my hangover, the full impact of our situation sank in. As I ran through my morning chores—bathing, collecting wood, scrubbing dirty buckskins, fletching new arrows—I pondered the drudgery of it all. There would be no Cindy in my life now. And with our numbers reduced, our prospects for significantly altering our lives were poor, at least in our lifetimes. We couldn't even fall back on the hope that our children would continue our work, since there would be no children. We would carry on with our projects, and some of these might make a difference, such as our planned irrigation systems and brick buildings, but our lives would continue to be a pale imitation of what we had before the Hormvisi came. Just like the namesake of our town had said, our lives in nature would remain solitary, poor, nasty, brutish, and short.

And there was more. I had showed my ass at Acceptance. I had demonstrated that I was not in control of my passions, not only in front of Ursula and the others at Acceptance, but especially Cindy. I had reinforced for her the reasons she had left—that I wouldn't let go of my resentment toward the Hormvisi and get on with my life. That I wouldn't enjoy what we had. And I had showed that I couldn't get over my resentment toward Ursula for taking Cindy away from me. Anyone could see I was not a master of my passions.

Yet, as the days wore on, the members of our little community continued to view me as their leader. We got up every day and attended to not only to our day-to-day duties—hunting, trapping, tending the fields, tanning hides—but also our community projects. We made slow but steady progress. There was little else we could do except, perhaps, fall into hapless despair.

The concerns of the others in our little group were often voiced. They wondered what was in store for us. Ursula had not been specific, but I figured something would happen. It wasn't feasible that the rejects from the thirteen previous seasons would have just wandered off somewhere. Would we be destroyed? Or would we be put back to sleep—to be used for what? Experiments? Torture? Or to lie in stasis for centuries until the Hormvisi tossed our inert bodies out with the trash?

I cringed at the thought of Cindy lying in Ursula's bed, but I took solace in knowing her fate was not aligned with ours. And I didn't give up all hope for our future together, despite how shaky the situation had become. Maybe she would come back somehow, and we could return to the life we led before.

As I recalled our days together, only a month earlier, I now saw with great clarity her point that our life had been good, and that we should move on and just be happy. I asked myself if I would give up the opportunity to return to our former world if I could have Cindy back in the current one. *Hell yes, I would!*

Had I been a fool not to appreciate what I had? I now thought so. Could I change my view after all this time?

And would these Hormvisi leave us alone if we showed an allegiance to their creed, even without the blessing of Acceptance? It was worth considering.

One late afternoon, an hour before sunset, we got a glimpse of the yellow wolf near the fringe of our camp. Everyone retreated to the security of their cabins while Trey, Cook, and I grabbed our bows and arrows and attempted pursuit. But the light was fading and, somehow, my burning need to wreak vengeance on the yellow wolf was not what it had been. We returned to Hobbes shortly after we left—empty-handed.

As I sat quietly at our dinner table, chewing on chunks of roasted venison and carrots, Amber came over and sat beside me, placing her hand on my shoulder.

"Just wondering how you were doing," she said in a sweet, soft voice.

"Me? I'm good. We weren't attacked or anything."

"No, I didn't mean the wolves. I meant Cindy. I know how much you cared for her. How're you holding up?"

"Oh, that. Yeah, I miss her terribly. But we've got to keep moving on. What other choice do we have?"

"Well, you have other choices," she said.

"What do you mean?" I asked, though I knew her meaning. But Amber didn't respond. She smiled and rubbed my shoulder.

"You know, Amber," I began, "I've noticed that you've changed over these last few months. I'm proud of you."

"What do you mean?" she asked.

I looked around the table. Trey and Cook were engaged in their own conversation, and, besides Eileen attending to the cooking fire, everyone else had left the dining area.

"Oh, just your tendency to, um, jump around from guy to

308

guy."

"You mean I'm not fucking around anymore."

"Yeah, you seem like you're growing up a little."

Amber smiled. She grabbed a strand of her hair and pulled it along her face as she tilted her head sideways. It was a gesture I had seen Rebecca do many times, who pulled it off adorably. Amber didn't have her grace. Still, it was cute.

"Well, I gotta hit the sack," I said, and got up from the table.

Back in my cabin, I undressed and was about to douse the torch when there was a knock. I cracked the door and looked out. It was Amber. She was holding a bundle of buckskins.

"What is it, Amber?" I asked. "I'm about to go to bed."

"Sorry to bother you, Charles," she said. "But I was going to wash my buckskins in the creek, and I thought about the wolves around the camp and got scared. Do you mind if I wash them in your basin?"

A few of us had large clay wash basins in our cabins, which we kept full of water for occasional indoor washing chores, especially on nights when mosquitoes were unbearable.

I sighed. I wasn't all that tired, and having the lamp burning another thirty minutes wouldn't matter.

"Okay, Amber. But please be quick about it. It's hard to sleep with the torch burning."

"Thank you, Charles." Her voice seemed raspy. She waited until I was under my buckskin cover before coming into the cabin.

I watched her plop down her armful of buckskins and the carved scrubbing board we used for washing our clothes. She had a bar of Rebecca's lye soap in her hand. Then, without a pause or apology, she stripped off the set of buckskins she was wearing and knelt down next to the wash basin, her back toward me, and scrubbed.

Nudity was not an uncommon sight in our rustic community. Many times, those washing their buckskins in the creek would also wash the ones they were wearing, allowing both sets to dry in the sun as the owner bathed in the river. So the fact that Amber disrobed in front of me was not entirely in contrast to common practice. The fact she did it within the confines of my cabin, was, however, less common.

As she leaned further into her work, the torch, which was mounted near my bunk, cast its soft light upon her, giving me a detailed view of her bare posterior. Now riveted, I watched as her movements scrubbing the buckskins caused her to rock back and forth. She set one piece of buckskin to the side, now clean, and picked up a new piece, leaned forward, this time with even more tilt, and scrubbed with vigor.

As I stared without reserve, I noticed her scent filling the small confines of the cabin. It was the musky, distinct aroma of human sex. All certainly part of Amber's design. She knew exactly what she was doing and I believed she was becoming aroused by her coy game. I was also responding. It had been a month since Cindy and I had made love.

After another ten minutes, during which I watched lustfully, she twisted the set of freshly scrubbed buckskins, squeezing out the excess water, and set them aside. She then stood up and faced me.

"Sorry, Charles," she said. "They have to drip for a while. Do you mind if I wait?"

I looked over her nude body. Her breasts were smallish but well-shaped. And the months of hard work had toned her body, which had formerly been full-bodied. Her waist was still thick, but there was no excess fat. Lean muscles showed clearly in her abdomen and thighs. I ached to draw her to me.

"I could climb in there with you while I wait," she added with a sly, demure smile.

I swallowed to remove the lump in my throat. "No, Amber. It's not a good idea."

I had a full-mast erection and Amber noticed the bulge under my buckskin blanket. I shifted the cover to hide my arousal.

"I know you want to," she said, sitting on the edge of the bed and gesturing toward my crotch with her chin. "I saw the proof."

As she sat, I caught a strong whiff of her sexuality and wavered for a minute. She sat there looking at me, quietly confident she would have her way. There was no mistaking that I wanted her. But I knew that for Amber, whose mind confused lust with love, crossing that line would create expectations and misunderstandings. I didn't feel what she wanted me to feel. As leader of the community, I preferred the resentment of rejection, a cleaner, nobler problem to deal with.

I let out a sigh and steeled myself. "I want to, Amber. You are an attractive young woman with much to offer. But I can't make love to you. I still have hope one day Cindy will come back."

"Cindy!" cried Amber. She stood up, scowling. "You reject me while she's fucking Ursula?"

"Amber, don't you understand? It's not about who's fucking who. It's about my heart. It's about love."

"Well, fuck you!" she said, shaking her head in obvious exasperation. "You're one strange dude." She grabbed her buckskins and stomped, buck naked, out the cabin door.

* * *

The next morning, I saw Amber sitting next to the grain storage bins, grinding corn into cornmeal. I sat down beside her. She glanced at me but said nothing. She kept grinding away.

I was about to tell her I was sorry for the previous evening, but she spoke first.

"I was such a jerk, wasn't I?" she asked. "I thought about it all last night and all this morning. You wanted to, but you didn't. Even though no one would know, you didn't. And you didn't because you love Cindy."

Surprised, I exhaled with relief. I had no desire for animosity between Amber and me. I considered her a friend.

"Yes," I said, "and I still hope to get her back."

"I was so pissed at first. But now, I feel different. You're a good man, Charles, and you want to do the right thing, even if it's hard. I admire you for that."

"Well, thank you."

"You're welcome. And now, I want to tell you something. The only way you will ever get Cindy back is to get over it."

"Huh? What do you mean?"

"You've got to let her go and be okay with it. 'Cause then it means you'll do what she prefers. And you've got to let the Little Perverts go and live life for what it is. And let the yellow wolf go, although you loved Missy. You've got to accept life for what it is."

"By God, Amber, I had never pegged you for a philosopher."

"Whatever," she said. "If you do all that, then she may come back to you. 'Cause she loved you once, and there was a reason."

"Yeah," I replied. "You're right. I kinda had that figured out already."

"Then do it!" said Amber.

I scratched at the dirt with the toe of my moccasin. "What if I do all that? It will only bring Cindy back if she knows. But we're banished from Acceptance."

"She'll find out sooner or later, trust me. Besides, we haven't banished *them* from visiting here."

"True," I said, thoughtfully.

"So do it. Let it all go."

"I'll try," I said, and gave her a hug. "And thanks for being a buddy."

"Thanks," she said, blushing. It was a side of her I'd never seen before, and I was impressed.

Chapter 42

The next day, I took down a doe, and engaged myself in stripping off the skin. But I had trouble with the crude iron knife I was using. Since it was made of low-grade iron, the only kind we had available, it wouldn't hold its edge well, and the forceful action meant blood sprayed everywhere. I was near the end of the task, covered in red from head to toe, when I heard her voice.

"Hi, Charles."

I looked up from my gory chore and saw Cindy standing there, along with Christie and Dillon. I was stunned and just stood there looking Cindy dead in the eyes. I couldn't believe it!

"Cindy! What are you doing here?" I asked, then reluctantly moved my eyes to the others. "Hey. Dillon. Christie. God! It's good to see you!"

"Good to see you, too," Christie said, smiling as she looked me over. I looked down at my buckskins.

"Let me clean up so I can give you a proper welcome. My other set of buckskins are drying by the creek."

"Take your time," said Cindy.

I ran to the creek and grabbed my clean buckskins, then headed for the river bank, where I took a cleansing plunge.

My mind was racing. *What could they want? Are they just visiting or are they coming back? Are they planning a coup or mutiny and want support? Did they get kicked out of Acceptance and need asylum? God, could I be so lucky?*

Hurriedly, I donned my fresh buckskins and, with my heart racing, I ran back to find Cindy, Christie, and Dillon in the middle of most of the Hobbeseans.

Without hesitation, I walked into their midst and up to Cindy and gave her a big hug. I also hugged Christie and Dillon. "God, I've missed all of you so much." My gaze settled on Cindy. Just in case she wasn't here to stay, I wanted to take all of her in to remember later.

"We've missed you, too," said Christie.

"Why have you blessed us with your visit? Heading to old Salty for apples, perhaps?"

"No, Charles," said Cindy. She looked into my face and hesitated before speaking. "We've come back," she said finally, "to Hobbes. If you will accept us."

I gaped at her, uncomprehending. "You've come…"

"Will you have us?"

I said nothing as my eyes brimmed with tears. I couldn't believe what she was saying. "You're coming back to Hobbes?"

"Yes, Charles. All three of us." She looked at Christie and Dillon and then back at me. "Something has happened, and things have changed," she said slowly, as if choosing her words carefully.

"What's happened?" I asked.

She pursed her lips and reached into a shoulder bag she carried. She pulled out a small metal sphere about the size of a grapefruit.

"Ursula had that!" I exclaimed. "The morning Cook and I

315

saw her at her altar."

Cindy brought the sphere to her chest and tears began to flow. Christie put her hand on her shoulder.

"Better get everybody here," said Christie. "We have something to tell you. Something important."

I stood up and looked around. Louise and a couple of others were weeding the garden. We retrieved everyone and stood around Cindy, Christie, and Dillon.

Cindy composed herself and climbed onto the big dinner table, sitting on its edge and placing her feet on the bench. "Two nights ago, I woke up in the middle of the night and was alone in my bed. Ursula was nowhere around." She still held the sphere in her hand and gazed at it, her mind elsewhere.

After a moment, she regathered herself. "I was worried. Perhaps she was sick, or sleepwalking. The moon was in full light, so I went out looking for her. I didn't see her around the village, so I tried her altar. She was there, but she wasn't alone. Samuel was there. And Carmine and Phil and a few others.

"I was puzzled. Why this secret meeting? I stayed hidden and listened to them talk for some time."

"They were going put all of you to sleep," blurted Dillon. "Or at least try to."

"They were, but they can't now. We've got the sphere," added Christie.

We all looked at the sphere.

"What does the sphere have to do with it?" asked Cook.

"Yeah, what—" I began.

"Just let me explain," said Cindy, cutting me off. "They said that ten days after the summer solstice, which is today, the Hormvisi will send out a signal that will put everybody into sleep stasis."

"Except for those protected by the sphere!" added Christie.

"Two hours before sundown," said Dillon, excited and concerned. "And look, the sun is edging toward the horizon."

We all looked up at the sun.

I was getting confused. "Back up a bit. Ursula uses the sphere to put us to sleep?"

"No, no," said Christie. "The sphere protects us from being put to sleep. Anybody near it when the sounds begin isn't affected."

"That's what I understand," said Cindy. "Those who do not join Acceptance are put back to sleep. The people of Acceptance are spared that fate because Ursula has the sphere and it somehow cancels out the effect of the sound. After overhearing her explaining all that to the others, I went back to the cabin, not sure what to do. I acted like I was asleep when she returned and I saw where she hid the sphere."

She looked at me and the others—people she had known for months and with whom she had come together to survive many hardships. "I accepted much of what Ursula said. I loved her so much. But this... it's wrong. Before, I could believe that those refused admittance to Acceptance wandered off somewhere. But to kick everyone out and have them put to sleep—you may never wake up again."

She began sobbing. I put my hand on hers.

"I'm glad you came to us," I said.

"I had to, Charles. I couldn't let that happen. So the next day, I told Dillon and Christie about what I'd learned. We stole the sphere and came here."

"We didn't want to be a part of it," said Dillon. "Now, all of Acceptance will be put to sleep. And we will do our best to take care of them. But I'm not sure they would have done the same for you guys."

"And besides," said Christie, looking at Cook, "we like you better."

I looked up at the sky again. "Let me get this straight. In a few minutes, that awful clacking sound will begin, putting to sleep everyone not near the sphere, including, now, everyone at Acceptance?"

All three of them nodded.

"Better them than us," said Trey.

"But what happens after—" started Eileen. But a series of loud clacks cut her off. It was awful and piercing. And nauseatingly familiar. There was a brief silence before more clacks sounded. I felt my body pulse with every one.

"Oh my God!" cried Eileen.

"Is the sphere working?" asked Rebecca, her voice laced with anxiety.

We all looked at the sphere. Flashing red lights now peppered its surface, previously an uninterrupted metallic silver. After about twenty seconds of silence, the clacking sound began again, but this time, in sequence with it, the sphere emanated its own annoying sound, just a little out of sync, and vibrating when it did so. By the next round of clacks, the sound from the sphere perfectly synced with the sound of the clacking, and both sounds became muted, even though the red lights surged in intensity with the rhythm of the clacking.

"It seems to be working," said Howard. "It's using some kind of superposition to cancel out the clacking noise."

"It's a lot less piercing," observed Cook.

"And that's what matters," said Cindy. "At least, that's what

I gathered."

I considered what the people at Acceptance would do about now. I thought of Ursula's angry face when she discovered her sphere was gone, along with Cindy.

"By now, Ursula will know the sphere is gone, and since you are gone too, she will likely figure out you took it here," I said.

"That's right," added Trey. "Won't they come after it? There are more of them than us."

"Maybe not," I said, thoughtfully. "At this hour, darkness would catch up to them soon after they started. They would have to camp and then continue in the morning. They wouldn't make it."

"That's right," said Dillon. "They risk falling asleep in the middle of the wilderness, where they would be eaten by wolves or coyotes."

"It's our opinion they will all stay in Acceptance," said Christie. "They'll probably shut themselves inside their cabins, hoping to keep predators away."

It made sense. Being put into sleep stasis was not desirable. But at least it allowed the possibility of being awakened one day. Getting eaten in the woods meant the end of the story. I wouldn't risk it if I were in their situation. I would stay put and hope to eventually see the light of day.

I watched the red lights on the sphere rhythmically surge in intensity as its sound cancelled out the clacking noise.

"What do we do when it's all over?" asked Eileen. "We can't just leave them there."

"No," I said. "We can't."

"We must go see," said Cook. "We'll have to make sure no one went to sleep out in the open."

"How can we be sure that this thing works?" asked Rebecca, watching the sphere anxiously. "If all of us fall asleep right here, we might get eaten by wolves, too."

She had a point. It seemed like the sphere was doing what Cindy said it would do, but better safe than sorry.

"Okay, I recommend that we all go to bed soon and make sure your doors and windows are securely closed. Assume you'll be asleep for many years. Keep yourself protected."

"It should work," said Cindy, watching the pulsing red lights on the sphere. "That's what they said."

"We want to be sure," I replied.

"Wait a minute," said Rebecca. "I'm not going anywhere except right next to that sphere."

"Hell no! I'm not, either," said Trey. "We don't know how far its range extends."

I looked over the worried faces. "You are probably being overly concerned. But everyone is afraid, so let's all bed down in the meeting house tonight, with Cindy in the middle. Okay, Cindy?"

Cindy nodded. "That's fine, but I've got more to say."

Her quiet tone grabbed everybody's attention.

"I didn't hear the details, but once we're put to sleep our bodies are removed—carried away. To where, I don't know. Then, just like they did for us and others before us, the citizens of Acceptance come out to Salty, Hobbes, and Shady. They fix up the communities, clear out any progress we made, and make them ready for the next batch of folks that awaken."

"You're fucking kidding me!" said Amber.

"Well, we already planted the fields," mulled Cook. "It wouldn't be that hard to do."

"I'll be damned," I said. "So Ursula, Jason, and the others set us up at the beginning and left us there to live or die according to our luck and determination."

"And sat back to wait until we contacted them," added Trey.

"I see the logic of it all," said Cook. "That way, all the newbies get a good taste of this kind of life, and by the time Ursula offers admission into Acceptance, they know whether they want to or not."

"Logical, perhaps," said Cindy. "But it's wrong. Which is why I couldn't allow it."

We all sat and watched the surging red lights on the sphere as we talked. Though the clacking sound itself was dulled, I felt it vibrating in my bones.

"Well, you guys, I'm sure I speak for all of us at Hobbes when I say thank you. Thanks for saving us from whatever fate Ursula and the Hormvisi had in store for us."

"Amen to that!" said Amber.

"I suppose we'll get to meet the Hormvisi finally," said Cook. "They'll have to bring a fresh supply of bodies and get rid of the sleepers."

"I wonder what happens to the sleeping bodies," said Trey. "Do these Hormvisi fucks just take them away? Or dump them in a hole?"

"I don't know," I said, shrugging. "But they can't delay. Many would have lain down out in the open."

"Assuming that they care if we get eaten by wolves or not," said Eileen.

"Well, we can't assume anything," I said. "If we wake up tomorrow, we'll head to Acceptance and do what we can to protect those who are vulnerable to attack. If the Hormvisi are there, well, we will ask them what the fuck do they think they're doing."

"I suspect they won't be too happy we mucked up their system," offered Christie.

"Wait," said Amber. "If we go to Acceptance and the Hormvisi are there and pissed off at what we did, won't they do something bad to us?"

"They might," I said, "although there's no point in hiding. They know where we are. But no one has to go. You can stay here if you want."

"Will the sphere stay here?" Trey asked.

"No. It goes with Cindy," I said. "It's hers now."

"Then I go where the sphere goes," said Trey. "Just in case."

"Okay," I said. "Everyone to bed and prepare for the worst. If we awaken, we'll have a busy day ahead of us."

Everyone ran to the cabins to retrieve buckskin blankets for the night, leaving Cindy and me alone for a few moments as we walked to the meeting house.

Cindy took my hand and looked into my eyes.

"Charles, so much has happened. Ursula is not who I thought she was, so I've come back to Hobbes. To my friends. But I'm not clear what that means for you and me. My emotions are in a whirl and I need to sort through them. Please don't expect anything. Okay?"

"I understand," I said. "But I'm glad you're back, even if it is as a friend."

"I expect the sphere will protect us, but just in case it doesn't, I want you to know I never stopped loving you. I just have to figure out what kind of love it is."

An hour later, we were all lying on our pallets and looking up at the ceiling of the meeting hall, Cindy lying in the middle.

"In case the sphere doesn't do its duty, this might be the last time we see each other," said Veronica. "Better say your farewells."

We all looked at the strange woman. As usual, she was right. We took our time saying goodnight.

Chapter 43

The next morning the sun rose, the birds sang, and everyone in Hobbes awoke without incident. The clacking noises were still there and we were aware of them. We felt their vibrations. And the red lights continued to surge on the sphere. So we decided to hang out in the meeting house with Cindy, just in case. And then, a few hours later, the red lights on the sphere blinked off and there was no more clacking sound.

No one fell into sleep stasis. The sphere had worked.

We wanted to get to Acceptance as soon as possible, so we gathered a few things and headed out. Despite the fear of confronting the Hormvisi, no one was interested in staying behind. Everyone wanted to follow the sphere, which Cindy kept in her possession at all times. There was no guarantee that that God-awful racket wouldn't start up again.

We weren't sure what we would find when we got to Acceptance, but we were concerned there would be bodies lying outside cabins. We would have to move them somewhere safe. As we hiked along, we discussed just moving everybody to the big meeting hall to free up the cabins, and then we could move into them. It wasn't so much that we liked Acceptance's site better than Hobbes's location, although that was a consideration. Rather, if the Hormvisi found us at

Acceptance, they might mistake us for Ursula's bunch. It didn't seem such an advanced civilization would make such a mistake, but there was always hope. Maybe we all looked alike to them.

As we walked along, Cindy was often by my side. But she remained unusually quiet, and it was easy to imagine why. She had saved me and the others at Hobbes from sleep stasis, but not those at Acceptance. She had shunned her new lover and her new friends, in favor of us. It was a tough position to be in.

"What do you think these fuckers will look like?" asked Amber. "Little and green?"

"If I were them, I would stay away," offered Trey. "They just might get their asses kicked."

"I would be surprised if they are there," said Cindy. "They seem to somehow handle everything from afar."

I walked up to Cindy and spoke to her softly. "You doing okay?"

"I'm not looking forward to this," she said.

"But you don't think we will confront the Hormvisi."

"No. I'm not worried about them. It's the others. I'm responsible…"

She looked down at her feet for a few minutes, walking straight ahead.

"I would have gotten more of our friends out of Acceptance," she blurted out. "But I had to keep my actions secret. I knew I could trust Christie and Dillon. I wasn't sure about the others. I couldn't risk it."

"I understand."

"Oh, Charles," she said. I saw her eyes watering. "Ursula was so special, and I had so much affection for her. But you.

The others. You're my family."

I reached over and took her hand. "Thank you. We all thank you."

"And you and I, Charles... I don't know. You can't let go of things, and that means you stay unhappy."

"But I'm learning," I said. "Really, I am. You'll see."

"I hope so. I really do."

* * *

A few hours later, we reached the river that flowed out of the lake, and followed its bank until Acceptance came into view. As we approached the outskirts of the community, everything was still and quiet. We saw no one. No people and no strange aliens. We spread out and looked about carefully as we got closer, in case anyone had been in the surrounding fields when they lay down to sleep. But it appeared that everyone had had the good sense to get inside the town before that happened.

We walked down the main lane between the cabins and saw no one. But when we opened the door to a nearby cabin, we found, as we had expected, someone asleep inside. He was a thick-bearded man lying naked on the bed. A set of buckskins were hanging on the bed frame.

"That's Vernon," said Christie.

"I didn't know him," said Cindy. "But I recognize him."

I walked up and shook him by the shoulder. He didn't stir.

"Mister. Vernon. Wake up. Wake up!"

Still no reaction.

"Trey, you and Dillon grab that washing basin. Dump it over his head."

They picked up the heavy clay pot, still half full of water, and poured it over the sleeping man's head. His breathing continued to be slow, deep, and steady.

"He's out cold," said Trey.

We went into other cabins and found their occupants lying comfortably in their beds and irretrievably asleep. Ursula was the only exception. She was in her cabin, but sitting at her table, with her head slumped over on the tabletop. She had been writing on a piece of cattail paper with a goose feather quill. I picked up the brownish sheets and read aloud.

Cindy, Charles, and other members of Hobbes. I have been betrayed, and by the time you read this, I, along with the other members of our beautiful community, will be in sleep stasis.

As painful as this is to accept, I must accept it. For it is imperative I convince all of you to carry on with what we have started. If you do not, the Hormvisi will come and my fear is that they will remove humans from their preserve.

I am not clear what you know, so I will tell you all. It was me and my companions at Acceptance who placed all of you in your cabins last summer. We set you up„ giving you what you needed to survive without undesirable technologies in the three feeder communities the Hormvisi had established. It was our mission to select from among you those who would be willing to live under our principles. The others are put back into sleep stasis. Again, it was our mission to return those who were deemed unacceptable to their sleeping chambers, where they would be kept safe until their fates were determined by the Hormvisi.

It should have been those at Hobbes who were put to sleep, but without the protection of the sphere, our entire town will meet that fate. I beseech you. In fifty days after summer solstice, a new Hormvisi signal will ring out through the land. It will awaken every sleeping person not in a sleeping chamber.

You and your small crew must use the sphere to lower the

chambers—just press the orange light—and lay out new people in all three communities. Weed the gardens, repair the tools, and replenish the livestock of Shady, Salty, and Hobbes, so that when the newcomers awaken, they will have a functional community at their disposal. They will survive, or not, but if they do, they will know whether or not they are content with their lives.

Keep us safe, and we will awaken with all the others. We can help you carry on with our mission—to create communities of humans content to live as we must, according to the principles the Hormvisi have laid down.

If the others and I are awakened, be assured there will be no animosity. We will accept you among us, and we will work together to build our future. I give you my word.

Gently, Cindy took the note from my hands. Tears were flowing from her eyes.

"She was enlightened in so many ways," she said. "But she let her convictions cloud her judgment. It could happen to any of us."

"I guess she had little a choice," I suggested. "I'm sorry, Cindy."

Cindy nodded.

"Well, we had better lay her down in her bed," I added. "And I guess remove her buckskins, if she is to remain asleep for a long time."

"Please, just move her to the bed and leave the room. I'll prepare her for her long sleep. She deserves dignity."

We left the cabin and waited outside for Cindy to say her farewells. I wondered if she regretted her choices. It was too late now to change things.

"What now?" Trey asked while we waited.

"If we move here, we must move the bodies out of the

cabins," I said.

"But we'll need the meeting hall," said Howard.

"We can build another one," I suggested.

"If we erect a building, what we should do is build a specific place for the bodies," said Trey. "A place where they can be tended to."

"Please don't call them bodies," said Cindy, coming out of the cabin, her eyes red. "They are living, breathing people. They're just in stasis."

"Sorry," replied Trey. "I just want them somewhere where they can be taken care of effectively."

"May I borrow your sphere?" I asked, extending my hand to Cindy. To my surprise, she seemed distrustful. Suspicious.

"Why?" she asked.

"The note said something about pressing an orange light to lower the sleeping chambers. I wonder if she meant the distortions. I want to try to lower one. I promise I'll give it back."

She looked at me for a moment and nodded her head. "Of course, Charles."

I took the sphere and looked over its surface carefully. There were no lights to be seen. "Hmm," I said and walked toward a distortion hovering near the dining area. As I stood underneath it, the sphere's surface displayed a small orange light. I pressed on the light.

A humming sound came from above. We backed up to look at the distortion. It was no longer invisible, but could be seen as an elliptical shape with a smooth metallic surface, much like the sphere I was holding. Whatever caused it to be invisible had been turned off.

Then the ellipsoidal chamber, about the size of a small

house, lowered to the ground.

"What do we do?" asked Cook. "There may be Hormvisi in there." He was nervous as a cat. He and most of the others looked on the verge of dashing away.

"Maybe we can talk to them," I said. "This might be our chance."

"Or our end," said Cook.

"We'd better go!" cried Amber. "We've gotta hide."

"Okay," I replied. I looked around. "Behind the meeting hall." I pointed to the nearby structure. All twenty-five of us dashed to the security of its solid walls. Several of us peered around the corner of the building and watched as the large, egg-shaped metal object continued to slowly move toward the ground. Three feet above it, the chamber stopped, and we froze as a portal opened on the side of the thing and a ramp extended.

"Oh my God," said Rebecca.

"Better run!" said Howard, his voice urgent. "To the tree line."

"Wait," I said. "We gotta wait. We can't run away."

"Shit," was Howard's only response.

We all stood firm and watched. Through the opening, I saw dim lights on the inside and waited for whatever alien form the Hormvisi took to emerge. I was prepared for the worst—horrible insect-like beings with tentacles and pincers, dripping organic goo from their orifices. Our bodies remained tensed, ready to scatter among the trees at the slightest sign of hostility. But we waited in vain. Nothing happened.

After a few minutes, my muscles started cramping from being tensed so long. "If there're any Hormvisi in there, they sure are taking their sweet time."

"I guess they realize we're bad-asses," suggested Trey.

"Yeah, right," responded Cook.

"This is ridiculous," said Cindy. She stood up and walked toward the open door of the structure.

"Cindy! What the fuck are you doing?" cried Cook.

"Cindy. Cindy!" I called at the same time. She waved us off and kept walking.

"I can't let her go it alone," I said, and ran after her.

"Freakin' crazy people," said Cook, but he, too, followed us.

"The rest of you stay put," I called back over my shoulder.

"No problem," replied Trey.

As we neared the portal, we crept as quietly as possible. From the bottom of the ramp, the interior of the thing looked like it was filled with rows of stacked shelving, but I could make nothing out with clarity. A thick and not unfamiliar odor wafted out of the chamber.

Cindy stared hard at the portal and then turned to me. "Okay, let's see what's in there."

She placed a foot on the ramp. I was amazed at her courage.

I grabbed her hand and followed her up the ramp. Side by side, we walked through the portal entrance.

There was no movement inside. The air was thick but breathable, drenched with a musky scent. What I had identified as shelving units filled the chamber. We moved toward them in the dim light. Looking closer, we saw human forms lying on the shelves. The shelving structures were tiered bunk beds, most of which had naked bodies on them. Some children and elderly were among them. I walked up and looked at a few faces. They were slowly breathing.

"They're in sleep stasis," I said. "Should we try to wake

them?"

Cindy shrugged.

"Mister. Mister," I called, shaking a man's shoulder. "Wake up. Can you hear me? Wake up."

There was no response.

"They're like the people in the cabins," said Cook, who was now standing behind us. "Out cold."

"Let's spread out," I said. "Shake a few more bodies."

We went around the interior of the chamber, but had no luck waking anyone. Aside from the tightly grouped bunk beds and a few inert panels displaying flashing lights, there was nothing else inside.

We walked back down the ramp.

"What's going on?" called Trey, peeking around the corner of the meeting hall. "Did you see the Hormvisi?"

"Nope. These things are just full of people."

Chapter 44

The others came forward cautiously. Some went up the ramp to look inside. A few were content to take our word for what the chamber contained.

"So the distortions didn't contain the Little Perverts after all," Rebecca said, reemerging from the chamber after looking around inside. "They were us."

"And we wanted to harm them," said Howard. "We tried to burn them. Our own kind."

"Do all the distortions have sleeping humans in them?" asked Trey.

My mind was racing. We had come across so many of these chambers. They seemed to be everywhere. Some were even in the middle of the wilderness. There may be thousands of them spread across the globe.

"Somebody, count the bodies in there. And the empty beds."

Cook came back in two minutes.

"Two hundred and twelve people. Seventy-two empty beds."

"So there's room for nearly three hundred people in one of these chambers. And they are everywhere. Maybe around the whole world. Maybe enough..." I took a breath, "...to hold the entire population of the world."

"The numbers work out," said Howard. "We had over seven billion people on the planet. There would have to be a handful of chambers per square mile, assuming they're all the same size and spread evenly throughout the planet."

"Our loved ones!" cried Eileen. "They're still alive!"

"Perhaps," I said, "But don't get your hopes up. Even if they're alive they are in stasis so we can't wake them up."

"Somebody, please explain what is going on," said Rebecca.

"This is where Ursula puts the undesirables," I said. "Those folks that don't accept her creed. And it's also where she gets the new people to set up in Salty and the other feeder sites."

"On the appointed day, the Hormvisi broadcast a different signal that awakens the new people put into the settlements," added Cindy.

"Every year, the process begins all over again," I said. "A new batch of folks at Salty, Hobbes, and Shady. They learn how to survive. Some are okay with the life, some hate it. Ursula recruits the ones who like it, and the others are put to sleep and placed back into the chambers. It's their way of growing the human population in their Earth preserve."

"I suppose these beings never intended to allow the population to grow to anything like it was," pondered Trey.

I shrugged. "I'm not sure, but I don't see how."

"The question is," began Cook, "where are the Hormvisi now? Are they up there somewhere looking down on these developments and maybe getting pissed, or has everything been set to autopilot with Ursula in charge, and maybe they check back in from time to time?"

"In other words," began Trey, "are we about to have a shit storm of alien vengeance rain down on us any minute?"

"We can't worry about that," I replied. "There's nothing we

can do about it if that happens. We've got to figure out what to do now."

"So, everyone will wake up in fifty days?" asked Eileen.

"Except those closed up in the sleeping chambers, according to Ursula's note," I said.

"Well, we should start searching the chambers," said Eileen. "Our families are probably in one of them."

"Perhaps we should put the sleeping Acceptance people back in these chambers." It was Veronica speaking.

We all looked at the large metallic chamber.

"I suppose it's safer than the meeting hall," I suggested.

"That's right," said Howard. "As we discovered, nothing can harm it."

"That's a great idea!" said Trey. "Then we get to decide which of these assholes gets to wake up in fifty days."

I looked at Cindy. "They'll be safer in there. Then we can all move to Acceptance. And then we hope that the Hormvisi assumes we are carrying on with their program."

Cindy nodded. "It makes sense. Let's do it."

We all agreed. We would move the sleeping members of Acceptance to the empty beds in the floating chambers. It gave us something to focus our minds on as we tried to process what we had learned. There were now twenty-seven of us, and we had nearly three hundred sleeping bodies to move. We began by building stretchers out of saplings and spare buckskins—of which there were plenty.

We began carrying the sleeping bodies up the ramp and into the chamber, sliding them into the narrow space allotted each bunk.

"Pretty claustrophobic," I observed. "I'm sure glad it's not us."

"Well, we may end up here yet," said Cook, who had the other end of the stretcher. "The Hormvisi won't be too happy we put their friends to sleep."

"Maybe they aren't aware of it," I suggested.

Cook shrugged.

After several hours of carrying the members of Acceptance into the descended chamber, we completely filled up the empty beds.

"Okay, see if you can close this sucker up," I said to Cindy, who was keeping the sphere. She pulled it from her bag and pressed a purple light, the only one showing while she was near the descended chamber. The ramp retracted and the portal closed without a visible seam. Solemnly, we all watched the chamber rise up and then, in an instant, it was invisible again.

There were still over two hundred bodies to move to other chambers, but the day had been a long one, with the hike and the excitement of discovering the first chamber and filling the empty beds. We decided to rest and wait until the next day to move rest of the sleepers.

We settled into the now unoccupied cabins. Everything was still an unknown, and we weren't certain what the next day would bring. Would we awake and find the Hormvisi standing around the village courtyard?

I bade Cindy goodnight and watched her enter her cabin, clutching the metal sphere close to her bosom. I was exhausted, but my mind was racing too much for a peaceful night's sleep. I finally drifted off with dreams of naked zombies running amok.

Chapter 45

The morning broke bright and clear, and to everyone's relief, no Hormvisi were to be seen. After a quick breakfast, we lowered another chamber and continued our task. It took the whole day, but we placed every sleeping body into the chambers, some of our friends among them. We left Phil's raccoon hat on his head as we laid him in his bunk. And Cindy's eyes watered profusely as she and I transported Ursula's body. I understood her feelings. She had strong affection for Ursula and many of the others in the community. But I reminded her they were not dead, and that we could awaken them later.

We had to lower three other chambers to have enough room to fit everyone. None of us could help looking over the faces of those inside, hoping to see our families and friends from our old lives, but no one saw any familiar faces. As we raised the last chamber full of sleeping bodies, we stood around and looked at each other.

"Okay, boss. Now what?" asked Trey. He was looking at Cindy.

"Well," began Cindy, "we have to decide whether we will continue Ursula's mission."

I looked up at the sun near the horizon. "That's a big

question, and I'm starving. Let's sit down and discuss it over dinner."

Christie shook her head. "The fate of the world is in our hands, and you want to eat."

"It's best to decide the fate of the world on a full stomach, I always say," offered Cook.

"All right, smartass," quipped Christie. "Fine. We'll eat."

Our whole group fit around one of Acceptance's dining tables. Plenty of food was stored close at hand. With Cindy and Christie's help, we were soon all munching on watercress, apples, and smoked fish. We found ourselves quite hungry and were silent as we plowed into our food. I mulled things over while I ate.

There was grain already growing in the fields at all three feeder sites, and the orchards were fine. Even the gardens were in good shape. There were extra animals, tools, and iron in Acceptance, since we had put the occupants to sleep.

Dillon broke out the mead and handed it around in clay cups.

"Better loosen up our heads if we're to decide the fate of the world," he said.

I smiled, gulped my portion, and stood up.

"Here are my thoughts," I said. "If we keep Ursula's mission going, there would be lots of hard work ahead of us, especially since our number is so small. We would have to make sure all three sites are prepared—food growing, animals healthy, metal implements repaired. And we would have to break down the extra cabins at Hobbes and rebuild them at their original sites."

"A lot to do in fifty days," said Cook.

"We can do it. But we would have to get to work right away."

"Why don't we just pull *everybody* out of those chambers and let everyone wake up in fifty days?" asked Eileen. "Let's repopulate the world."

"I afraid most would starve," replied Howard. "Our communities can only support a handful of people."

"And what happens if we didn't continue this cockamamie mission?" asked Trey.

"I would be concerned that Ursula's prediction was correct. That sooner or later, the Hormvisi would figure out something was wrong with their preserve, if they don't know already. And that they would come and fix it."

"By 'fix it', you mean…" said Trey.

I shrugged. "Start over? Whatever it is, I don't think it would be good for us."

"So you're saying we would have to clear out of Hobbes?" asked Amber. "Leave it behind and move to Acceptance? And just hope that they don't notice there are a lot fewer of us?"

"That's right," I said. "Or if they do notice, maybe they would assume that an illness wiped a lot of us out."

"Then what?" asked Howard. "Do we open the chambers in fifty days and put new people in the cabins and let them wake up, just like what happened to us a year ago?"

"That's if we follow Ursula's path," Cindy said.

"The path of the Hormvisi," I added.

"But then what do we do?" asked Howard. "Do we head back to Acceptance and let these new people figure out how to survive on their own?"

"It may not be a bad idea," offered Trey. "It keeps appearances in place. You gotta believe the Hormvisi somehow monitor the progress of their seeding process, even if they're not here in person."

"Then one day the new members of the communities stumble upon us at Acceptance and then what? We put some of them to sleep and recruit the others into our cult?" asked Veronica, cutting to the chase.

"No!" said Cindy, standing up. "I didn't put three hundred people to sleep just to keep doing what I found unacceptable to begin with! We can't do that. It's wrong."

"We may have to," said Howard. "If we don't keep the seeding process going, the Hormvisi might interfere."

"There is always an alternative," returned Cindy.

"What happens if we set up the feeder communities like the Hormvisi want, but we help them out?" asked Cook.

"But if they know what's afoot, they may lie about joining us," complained Howard. "We were kept in the dark so that Ursula could determine which of us would be content living our lives in accordance with the Hormvisi's principles. If we just let everyone join us, some of them will want to implement new technologies down the road. The kind the Hormvisi would be pissed about."

I stood up and paced. "It may not matter," I said.

I began to work through the scenario in my head. What if we set up people in Salty, Shady, and Hobbes and do help them survive? Help them learn what we learned the hard way? If we then accepted everyone into our growing community, then yes, we would have people who would want to violate the rules. They would want to make their lives easier by developing new technologies and not care how far removed they were from nature. That could trigger the Hormvisi's anger, who may then decide to remove humans from their nature preserve.

Yet, maybe not. As Cindy had pointed out earlier, we could

continue to develop in other ways, even under the limitations imposed by the Hormvisi—literature, music, art, philosophy. Our growing community would have the advantage of becoming increasingly socially enlightened before problematic technologies had the chance to rear their ugly heads. We would be in a better position to make the right decisions about how to use the technology we developed. It wouldn't be a return to the world we had before, but at least we would, to some degree, step outside of the Hormvisi's plan.

I thought it would work. It was a risk, sure. But it allowed us to make our own decisions about our development. It coincided with what the Hormvisi wanted, but that didn't make it bad. We would develop a society of socially enlightened individuals who would only gradually and selectively introduce new technologies, thus avoiding toxic and disruptive ones.

I recalled Ursula's words, and thought about the irony of the current situation. Wasn't that what she wanted all along? Was my limited defiance—to simply disrupt the system of the feeder colonies—sufficient to allow myself to live contently? As long as I had Cindy by my side, I could do it.

I stopped pacing and looked around at the faces of my new family. "We can do this," I said. "We help out the new people and accept everyone. We just count on our community developing in the right way and not allow discontented individuals to tip the cart."

"So, you want to keep Ursula's program in place," began Cindy, "but without the unsavory elitism?"

"Yeah," I replied.

Cindy rubbed her chin and nodded. "Imagine that we succeed. Wouldn't that be cool?"

I put my arm around her shoulder and squeezed. "Yes, very cool."

"Hey," said Trey. "We get to choose who we want to wake up in fifty days? So we can wake up some of our friends we just put in these chambers."

"I would suggest we wake up those from Acceptance," Cindy said. "So next year our work load would be less."

"Maybe," I said. "But we must consider that carefully. I'm not sure everyone would be okay with our plan."

"And if we found family members in one of these chambers, we could wake them up," suggested Eileen, her eyes aglow with excitement.

"If we find them, sure."

"Okay," said Cook. "I say let's do it. Let's keep it going and reseed the Earth with humanity."

"A new breed of humanity," said Veronica.

"Here's to a new world order." I raised my clay mug of mead and took a hefty gulp.

"Maybe the Hormvisi *are* benefactors," said Cindy.

"Maybe, maybe not. Regardless, it will take a lot of work."

"But let's rename this place," said Rebecca. "Let's not call it 'Acceptance' anymore."

"I got it!" said Amber. "Let's call it 'Reinvention', since we are reinventing society."

We looked at each other and frowned.

"Nah. Too awkward," I said.

"All right, Mr. Critical. What's your suggestion?"

I looked up in the direction of the chamber that hovered near our tables. "How about 'Newday'?"

Everyone nodded and raised their clay mugs. "To Newday," Cook said. "May it prosper."

Chapter 46

Before setting up in Newday, we needed to return to Hobbes to collect our supplies and belongings. On the way, I took Cindy's hand, and she didn't seem to mind. For miles, we walked hand in hand behind the rest of the group, slowly dropping further behind.

"This is so exciting," said Cindy.

"Yes, it is," I said, glancing at her. "Are you sure you did the right thing?"

"I like our plan better than Ursula's," she said.

"We can always awaken Ursula," I said. "If you want to bring her back."

"Yeah, we can. And we will eventually. But we need to be in charge for a while to establish our system. Plus, I don't want to complicate things with us. I miss you, and am glad I'm back with you."

"You are?" I said.

I stopped walking and brought her closer. She wrapped her arms around me and we kissed passionately. "We can make this happen," I said between breaths. "Now that we are together."

"That's not all we can make happen," said Cindy, breathing heavily. She began loosening the leather thong that held up my buckskin trousers. I looked ahead. The rest of the group was out of sight.

"We think alike," I said, giving her another lingering kiss while my hands found her breasts under her tunic. I was about to lift her tunic over her head when we heard branches breaking nearby. We froze and looked up to see a young buck thrashing through the forest not twenty yards away. He sensed our presence and stopped, disoriented. It was our normal procedure to carry our bows with us whenever we travelled through the woods, so I pulled my bow off my shoulder and slowly pulled out an arrow from my quiver, but before I could take a shot, there was more thrashing in the woods and the buck took off. Then from the thick brush emerged the yellow wolf. Having been in hot pursuit of the deer, it hadn't noticed us until it, too, stopped and stared at us, a mere twenty yards away.

The woods between us and the wolf were open and I had a clear shot. I drew back the bowstring and looked my nemesis in the eye, and it looked back at me, growling menacingly. But then, in an instant, my nemesis changed. It became nothing more than a wolf. A wild animal in the woods, trying to survive. I had no fear and I had no hatred. I lowered the bow.

Cook called out for us from down the trail, wondering what we were doing back there. The wolf flinched at the sound of Cook's voice, looked at me one more time, and bounded off into the woods.

Also by Emmett Swan

Cadaver Swords
In the island nation of Dalmeer, magic is channeled through three mountains of solid crystal, a magic that only the Mediums of the Crystal Mountains can harness. Having learned their lessons the hard way, the people of Dalmeer established a sacred covenant to keep the Mediums in check and ensure peace.

Perhaps all covenants are destined to be broken.

When the Medium of the Gray Mountain contrives to murder the entire population of the island of Bewel and then animate their corpses to form a great army of cadavers, it is up to a rustic grave digger, proud of his profession, and a female warrior, cast from her army, to travel to the great northern wastes and locate the reclusive Medium of the Blue Mountain. If they can recruit her aid and make it back to the capital in time, they just may save the citizens of the land from the bite of Cadaver Swords.

Forest of Lost Secrets

Jessica never knew magical elixirs existed. At least not until her parents sent her to Ireland to spend the summer. Having lost her boyfriend in a tragic accident, she was unable to shake the suspicion it was her fault. She didn't think a new country would change anything.

But as she explores the lands around her Aunt and Uncle's manor house, she discovers a beautiful forest which seems the perfect retreat. Filled with old, gnarly trees, the forest slowly reveals its secrets. Then, one moonlit night, Jessica hears a quiet, troubled voice among the sound of wind. Three brothers, from a noble estate two hundred years past, have been cursed and need her help.

Jessica finds herself in a race to save the lives of the brothers while preventing a war between two realms she never knew existed. Her only hope is to use the red elixir to travel to the land of Derfaria and confront the evil Keeva. But unless she can put her personal loss behind her and open her heart to a new love, she doesn't stand a chance.